DEC 3 1 2002

NAPA CITY - C...

3 1128 00851 1505

P9-DDC-837

The Seeker

The Seeker

Margaret Buffie

Kids Can Press

NAPA CITY-COUNTY LIBRARY
580 COOMBS STREET
NAPA CA 94559-3396

Text © 2002 Margaret Buffie
Cover illustration © 2002 Chris Albert

All rights reserved. No part of this publication may be reproduced, stored
in a retrieval system or transmitted, in any form or by any means, without
the prior written permission of Kids Can Press Ltd. or, in case of photocopying
or other reprographic copying, a license from CANCOPY (Canadian Copyright
Licensing Agency), 1 Yonge Street, Suite 1900, Toronto, ON, M5E 1E5.

This is a work of fiction and any resemblance of characters to persons living
or dead is purely coincidental.

Many of the designations used by manufacturers and sellers to distinguish their
products are claimed as trademarks. Where those designations appear in this
book and Kids Can Press Ltd. was aware of a trademark claim, the designations
have been printed in initial capital letters.

Kids Can Press acknowledges the financial support of the Ontario Arts Council,
the Canada Council for the Arts and the Government of Canada, through the
BPIDP, for our publishing activity.

Published in Canada by
Kids Can Press Ltd.
29 Birch Avenue
Toronto, ON M4V 1E2

Published in the U.S. by
Kids Can Press Ltd.
2250 Military Road
Tonawanda, NY 14150

www.kidscanpress.com

Edited by Charis Wahl
Cover designed by Marie Bartholomew
Dedication page art by Jim Macfarlane
Interior designed by Stacie Bowes
Printed and bound in Canada

CM 02 0 9 8 7 6 5 4 3 2 1
CM PA 02 0 9 8 7 6 5 4 3 2 1

National Library of Canada Cataloguing in Publication Data

Buffie, Margaret
     The seeker

(The watcher's quest)

ISBN 1-55337-358-8 (bound).   ISBN 1-55337-359-6 (pbk.)
     I. Title. II. Series: Buffie, Margaret. Watcher's quest.

PS8553.U453S43 2002   jC813'.54   C2001-903739-2
PZ7.B895Se 2002

Kids Can Press is a /orus™ Entertainment company

For Christine and Douglas, whose adventures
together have just begun, and

For my sister Erna, whose many adventures
I've enjoyed sharing!

Who had power had all but his soul
Who thirsted for power drank only dust
Who feared power found it in others
Who hid in power's shadow viper be
Who turned from power gave his soul to yee

Written by Cill of Barroch after the Battle of Moling

1

I'm standing outside Mom's bedroom on the third floor of Argadnel Castel. I'm invisible and intend to stay this way for a while. I don't want anyone to know I'm back until I know what's going on. I could try to *ooze* right through the door, but I'm not very good at that yet. More than once I've gotten caught smack in the middle of a wall or wooden entrance and had to be hauled out by a disgusted Master. Instead I push the heavy ebony door open a crack and slide in that way.

Mom's large chamber is dark except for a streamlight from the arched ceiling that drops over a hammock bed floating above the black marble floor. I can hear the soft hush of water from the fountain. Her room is usually full of light, fresh air and Branwen's flowers. Now it smells musty, with a curious smoky edge.

I tiptoe to the side of her bed. She's asleep. The angle of light shadows the deep sockets below the fine arches of her brows. A wild flush of alarm races through me. I barely recognize her. She's bone thin. The skin stretched tightly over the sharp bones of her face is yellow and waxy. For some time before I left for my Watcher training, Mom was growing thinner and grayer. I knew she would probably never fully acclimatize to the light air of Argadnel, but this is bad, very bad.

I'm glad I didn't speak or call her name, for a tall shadow slides out from behind the filmy curtains at the head of her bed and turns into a man in an orange tunic, fitted leggings and a flat red hat of bloodsnake skin. That and the yellow and red tattoos are the symbols of a healer. He murmurs softly while he passes a dish of smoldering blue smoke over the slender figure in the bed.

Lately, I've had a strong urge to come back to Argadnel, and I'd just about made up my mind to ask Master Histal for permission to visit, when I found a scrap of paper on my bed that said "Belldam Leto is dying. Come back." I'd shown it to Histal, and he'd allowed me to transport to the island. Now I stand like a ghost, trying to remember that my own feelings of panic, of worry, don't matter — that, as a Watcher, I must assess what's going on so I can find a solution.

Another tall figure moves out of the shadows, followed by a slender gray hound wearing a collar of moonstones, the gem of Argadnel royalty. I feel a leap of joy at the sight of my sister, Summer, followed by a wave of dread. I concentrate on regaining control. I'll be no use to her otherwise.

"Allopath Bachod. Tell me. Can you help her?" Summer's voice is choked and tight.

The healer bows to his new queen and in a cold distant tone says, "She will not help herself, my Suzarain. Something is tearing away at the Belldam's spirit, but she will not tell anyone what it is."

Summer grabs his arm. "But you're a healer! Give her something to make her stronger — just until we can find out what's wrong. Please."

The healer pats her hand briskly. "It is much more difficult than that, Suzarain. Come, child, let your servant escort you from here, so I can continue my work. You cannot keep interrupting me."

A young woman, with the winged crest of stiffened hair and long fluttering black chiton of a high-order servant, appears at Summer's side. Gormala, my sister's new primary servant. Her broad cheekbones and narrow black eyes are typical of a native Argadnelian. But not the smirking mouth and fawning manner she adopts around Summer. She lays a hand on Summer's arm in a possessive, motherly manner that makes me grit my teeth and gently pulls her to one side. I can't stand Gormala, but I'm also afraid of her, of the control she has over my sister. I've tried to get Summer to replace her, but no luck so far.

Summer, sobbing, allows herself to be taken from the bedchamber. I want to go to her, comfort her. But I can't. No one on this island trusts me. Both Allopath Bachod and Gormala would ban me from Mom's side, given half a chance. I have to stay invisible and in control. I have to act like a Watcher. Assess. Absorb. Learn. Then, and only then, *act*.

As soon as Summer leaves, Bachod stops his ministrations and stares down at the figure on the bed. Then he lowers himself onto a heavy black chair, looking like a gaunt orange vulture perched on a branch, waiting for its victim to take her last breath, his yellow eyes never leaving her face.

I slip to the side of her bed and gently lift her hand. I feel for her pulse — when I finally find it, it's ragged and slow. I swallow hard. Keep the panic down. No tears allowed. I glance over at Allopath Bachod. He's seen Mom's hand move. He sits forward, his eyes riveted on it. I lower her hand. It lies still on the white bedcover. He slides back in his chair but stays alert.

If Mom dies, what will become of my sister — of me? Of Dad? Mom *can't* die. I won't let it happen. I run my fingertips along her arm, trying to send some of my healthy life source into it. But her skin is lifeless, sliding loose and dry under my touch, like crumpled silk. I bite my bottom lip hard to keep silent.

I was brought up as a human and now I must learn to suppress all my learned human emotions in order to become a good Watcher. If I'm to help

Mom, I have to follow my Watcher instincts, which are telling me to stay cool and rational. As my trainer Histal says, "Emotions never solve a problem."

I try to dissolve the heavy dread in my chest, wondering why it's so hard to rid myself of everything my human parents taught me. It means nothing that we aren't related by blood, whatever Histal and my other teachers say about my being a Watcher, not a human. *Mom, Dad and Summer are my family.* I won't let go of that.

Histal, a High Master at the Watchers Campan, has been teaching me to study life auras. I narrow my eyes and fix my gaze just above Mom's head. A thin flutter of gray with patches of sulfur green and small spots of sickly white emanate unevenly around her head and shoulders like dull gauzy fabric. Gray indicates a spirit sick with dark thoughts, and the sulfury mustard green indicates pain and discomfort. But it's the white spots that jolt me. Histal says when a spirit gets close to death, the aura turns completely white and increases in intensity. Have I been right all along? Can she actually be dying of loneliness and grief? Mom's been fighting homesickness and worry about Dad ever since she's been here. She's fought hard to keep her spirits up for our sakes. Is she losing the battle?

I look around the darkened room, blinking back tears. How did Mom, Summer and I end up so far away from home? One minute we were an ordinary family living on a bee farm in Manitoba and the next we were transported to a place as mad and out of control as Alice's wonderland.

In order to save Summer's life, we had to leave Dad behind on the farm. Ever since we came to this island of Argadnel, all I've wanted is to go home again, to put my family back together: to fill jars of golden clover honey with Mom and help Dad with his crazy environmental art projects and play with Summer in the warm sunny fields of Sweeney Bee Farm. I'd never complain about the hard work or loneliness again. I just want to be a regular girl. I want everything to go back to the way it was.

But I'm not a regular girl. And the life we once had can never be again. My only hope is to get Dad here with us, to make a *new* life together in Argadnel.

I have to fix this. I have to. But how?

It was eight and a half months ago that I discovered I wasn't just plain old Emma Sweeney who lived in the country on a bee farm with her family; that my sister wasn't my sister and my mom and dad weren't my mom and dad. In just a few days, I was shaken out of my small protected life and thrown topsy-turvy into worlds that I had no idea existed.

When it was all over, I wasn't Emma Sweeney anymore.

I was a *Watcher*.

I'm still finding out what that means. It's hard to

explain, even to myself. For one thing, Watchers have some pretty astonishing abilities. They can appear and disappear at will, change shapes, even transport from one world to another in the blink of an eye. I still have to learn many of these things. Watchers live in a secret place and rarely allow anyone from outside to go there. Yet they do things I find hard to understand — like send new Watchers to protect important "youngers" from different realms, to make sure no one hurts them — kind of like guardian angels. That's what they did with me. And many fully trained Watchers take part in War Games between empires, as guides and observers. The thing I have trouble understanding is that they will work for *anyone* — even the most greedy rulers of some pretty scary worlds. Most Watchers don't seem troubled by this. They appear, fulfill a particular job called an Obligation and then vanish again. On Earth we'd call them mercenaries. But the Watchers have one rule that can't be broken. No violence is allowed except to protect the one you've been sent to watch.

As a tiny younger, I was spirited to the town of Bruide in Manitoba. Leto and Dennis Sweeney, who were staying at her father's, Ewan MacFey's, bee farm had just lost their first baby at birth. That same night, Ewan brought me to the farm and gave me to his daughter and her husband. He told them that I was a local child whose young mother wasn't able to look after her properly. Leto and Dennis, desperate for a child, believed him. Mom, Dad and I left the bee farm. We moved around the country for a long time after that.

Seven years went by. I grew up as any Earth child in a loving family would. Then Mom — Leto — got pregnant again, and we all came back to the farm a few weeks before her due date. *This* time, Mom's new baby was stolen without her knowledge, taken no one knows where, and another dark-haired baby was put in its place.

That changeling child, the daughter of the murdered king and queen of Argadnel, became my sister, Summer. She'd been sent to my Earth family by Fergus, Supreme Player of Cleave, until the time was right for her to take back her island kingdom.

I was almost sixteen when Grandpa MacFey died. We hadn't seen him since Summer was "born." Mom brought us back to the country once more, this time so she could run the bee farm. It was bad timing for us, because the man who'd killed Summer's parents and taken over their kingdom had also just died — and the throne was now free for the little princess. Almost immediately, Fergus decided to go to Earth and retrieve her. His plan was to control my sister's kingdom — she would be queen in name only.

During Summer's young life, I'd watched over her, as she'd always been rather sickly. But as she grew older, she developed longer bouts of a debilitating illness that no doctor was able to diagnose. That final spring we spent on Earth, she grew much worse, and I became obsessed with her welfare and safety. As she got sicker, I kept an even closer watch, making sure she didn't get overtired, demanding more doctors see her, losing sleep with worry and knowing in my heart that her young body was losing the battle against this unknown sickness. Little did I know a more immediate threat was looming.

Bear with me, because it gets complicated. In late May, our dad, Dennis Sweeney, an environmental artist, began to build a modern stone henge — a big circle of Plexiglas stones, really — in Grandpa MacFey's deserted cow field. He hadn't a clue, but he was building it right over a circle gate that opened on two different worlds — Fergus's land of Cleave and an equally dangerous place, the sea realm of Fomorii. Even worse, Dad's configuration of "stones" was so well placed, they actually heightened and sped up the circle's power.

Where are these worlds of Cleave and Fomorii? I don't know. Are they parallel universes? Maybe. There are hundreds of such places, according to Master Histal. I only know that they aren't part of Earth, at least as humans know it.

It turned out that Fergus of Cleave wasn't the only one who wanted to control Summer's island world.

His enemy, Rhona of Fomorii, found out where Fergus had hidden the young princess, and she and her Druvid Huw planned to grab Summer first.

At various times in June, the two groups emerged through the circle gate in our farm field, intent on stealing Summer. But it wasn't just a race to see who could become controller of Summer's island world. No, it was all part of the Game.

You see, Fergus and Rhona are competitors in the Game, which seems to be a never-ending plunder of weaker kingdoms by stronger ones. Two or more powerful clanns will set up a Game — competing for a prized kingdom, rich land, hidden treasure or a strategically placed world. If it means fighting one another, the Players drop all allegiances and go head to head. For Fergus and Rhona, Summer was the latest target.

Fergus and his sister, Branwen, in the human form of father and son, took over the farm next to ours as market gardeners. They wanted to make sure they got the right child, and as they didn't know Rhona was on the move, they weren't in much of a hurry. I think Fergus saw a visit to Earth ("Eorthe," they call it) as a break from the intensity of the Game. Two of Fergus's people also came to town in human form, as mother and son — his Druvid Mathus, who'd shape-changed everyone, including himself — and a Watcher named Tamhas, who attended our school as Tom Krift. It was his job to keep watch over all of us until Fergus decided it was time to take Summer.

When Watchers are ordered to give up a changeling child, they obey immediately. When Fergus decided to remove the tiny princess from our farm, he certainly didn't expect to have to fight me for her. You see, unlike most Watchers, I'd bonded strongly with my family, especially with Summer. My Watcher instincts were always to watch over her and keep her safe — but my *feelings* went much deeper than that. There was no way anyone was going to take her away from me or my family. I guess in Watcher terms, I'm a freak.

Tom started to work for Dad. He puzzled and worried me. I had strange dreams and a growing certainty that my family was in terrible danger, and I couldn't help feeling that somehow Tom was involved. But for some reason I still don't understand, Tom left Fergus's Players to become my friend and Summer's protector. And thanks to him, the Game ended in a draw, with Rhona and Fergus agreeing to control Summer and her kingdom together.

Mom and I, with Tom's help, stopped Rhona and Fergus from taking Summer away without us, but only by agreeing that we would come to live in the strange misty world of Argadnel with her. We begged them to let Dad come with us. But they refused. Instead they wiped out all his memories of us. We'd had no choice. We were forced to leave him behind.

Branwen admitted to me once that Dad is still on the farm. Knowing he's there and doesn't remember us, is painful, spirit-destroying, especially for Mom.

My family is alive, but torn apart. I look down at Mom and pledge to put us all together again — whole and complete. Starting now.

2

I sit for what seems like hours, my hand over Mom's. Now and again I see a flutter behind her eyelids and once her finger moves and curls over mine. She knows I'm here.

When I think she's going to open her eyes, I lean close and whisper, "It's Emma. Don't look at me. They don't know I'm here."

Her mouth smoothes into the faintest smile. Allopath Bachod senses the change and glides out of his chair to hover over her. He lays long bony fingers across her forehead and shrugs. Then he walks away and, a moment later, I hear the swish of the door closing.

I become visible as Emma. Mom is still a bit frightened by the way I look as a Watcher. I don't blame her. I always jump when I catch myself in a mirror — small, white, strange-eyed — like an ancient creature from a folktale. I wrap my fingers around her hand and I'm holding a thin pouch of delicate bones.

"Mom?" I whisper. "It's okay. He's gone."

Her eyes open slowly, and she gives me a smile of such sweetness it's suddenly hard to breathe. Then she frowns, pulls me close. "Oh, Emma. I'm so glad you're here. I've missed you." Every word is breathless and labored.

"I didn't know you were this sick, Mom. I would've come back sooner. Why didn't you send for me?"

"I was worried that you'd —"

I finish for her. "— get myself into trouble charging around trying to find out why no one was making you better?"

She smiles again, but it dissolves into a kind of wide-eyed bewilderment. "What's happening to me, Emma?"

"Mom, I think you're sick from sadness."

A tear rolls down her temple into her hair.

"Would you like to go home, Mom?"

A slight cough nearly makes me jump. "Now, now, Watcher, this is not helping the Belldam Leto, is it?"

A small man moves from the shadows of an arched doorway near the head of Mom's bed. When he drops the hood of his silver-gray chiton to his shoulders, the long pale face of Emissary Bedeven moves into the streamlight. Bedeven is of the Fomorii tribe. He has eerily blue skin that, to my sensitive nose, always smells faintly of rotting sea mollusks. Over his left eyebrow is a tattoo of a shark's eye, a darker blue than his own and so perfectly rendered that I keep expecting the painted eye to blink when he does. Bedeven is Rhona of Fomorii's representative in the Argadnel court. Read that as *spy*.

The Fomorii tribe lives under a vast purple sea. They are humanlike in shape, and yet each is missing an eye, hand or foot. Their queen, Rhona, appears to be missing all three, for she walks with a limp and one eye is dull and cloudy. Her right hand is clearly not of her own flesh, but dark gray and rigid, covered in thick scaly skin. Bedeven's arms and his right hand are smothered in swirling blue tattoos. His left hand looks as if it's been dipped in iridescent fish scales, like Rhona's. He should be head to toe fish scales, because he slithers around the castle like an eel, keeping track of everyone's goings-on.

Rhona is someone I wouldn't trust as far as I could throw her. But I wouldn't trust Bedeven even *that* far. His long pale hair, usually encased in an elaborate net of pearls, is unadorned today, fashioned into a short tail with a plain gray cord — his usual "sneak around corners" outfit.

"Bedeven," I say firmly, "I want to be alone with my mother."

He smiles such a fawning, syrupy smile it's a wonder he doesn't stick to himself. He half bows his head, and his hooded gaze slides over us. "A reminder, my dear Watcher," he says, in his soft, lilting tone. "You are not allowed to roam around invisible in the castel. I will have to report this. Also, as Rhona's emissary, I have the right to know anything of importance that may be said."

Mom lifts one hand and speaks in an amazingly strong voice. "Leave us, Emissary. *You* have no right to be in my quarters."

Bedeven bows to Mom. "It is my *lawful* right, Belldam, under the rules of the Game to —"

I push my face into his. "Get. Lost."

He continues to smile, but his eyes are icy, and I'm sure I hear a sea snake hiss. My knees are jelly, but I stare him down defiantly. He bows low to Mom before sauntering out of the room. I bet he has listeners and toadies in every nook and cranny of this building. Maybe even hidden in this room — spies like Gormala, who think that joining with him against Mom and me will protect their new Suzarain ... or give them power over her. It's that last possibility that worries me.

Mom grips my hand tightly, pulls me close and whispers, "You know I can't go back to the farm."

"Yes, Mom," I whisper. "I'm sorry I suggested it. But *I* can go."

"No. Forbidden ... Bedeven heard you ... they'll be watching like hawks." Her voice grows feeble, her breathing tight and hard. "Emma, sweetheart ... please ..."

"Don't worry, Mom. Tom and I can figure out a way there and back without anyone knowing."

We're whispering in our own language, not Argadnelian. Any spies and listeners might catch a few words, but they won't understand everything.

"If I could just *talk* to Dad, I'm sure he'd remember me and I'd convince him to come here."

"Even if you did," Mom gasps, "he'd need Fergus's and Rhona's permission. *Impossible*."

I nod. "I'll just check on Dad. Make sure he's okay. Without anyone knowing. Won't that help a bit?"

She sighs raggedly. "Yes ... but *you'd* be in danger."

"We'll be careful and quick," I lie through my teeth. "I've done scarier and tougher things in training. Please trust me, Mom?"

"You'll do this ... even if I forbid it ... won't you?" she says, holding my hand tightly.

"Yes, Mom. *Yes.* Because it will help you —"

"Please ... *please* ... go carefully, Emma." Even with this bit of hope I've offered, the sadness in her eyes doesn't recede.

"What else is wrong, Mom?"

She shakes her head. "Nothing ... nothing."

"Mom, please, can't you tell me?"

She looks around as if searching for something she can't find. "... even more dangerous for you ..."

"What is?"

She whispers again, "*Impossible*."

That's when I think I know. I lean close to her ear. "It's your real daughter, isn't it? The little girl Fergus stole from you and Dad when they left you Summer."

She shakes her head again, but her eyes have the fixed intensity of a deep inner pain. I've hit the mark.

"Mom — I *can* find her for you," I whisper urgently.

"Leave it, Emma," she sighs. "Wish ... hadn't said anything."

"I can do it, Mom. I'm learning new skills all the time, and Tom will help me. He was a Master Watcher for a long time before —"

Mom holds up her hand. "Emma, we're living in a medieval court. Intrigue and secrets ... danger." Her voice cracks. "I worry all the time ... about Summer ... about you and your dad. And I started dreaming about my baby girl ... many nights in a row. They *stole* her, Emma. She may not even be ... alive, but ... now ... I'll never know ..." She puts her fingers to her lips to smother a sob.

"Mom, I'll find her."

She moves her fingertips to my lips. "I've tried ... to be strong, Emma. For Summer's sake ... needs me here. Tried ... to stay well." Her voice catches deep in her throat. I wait while she collects her strength again. "But I ... can't ..."

Her smile is so sweet I could blubber right here, but I draw on all my Watcher disciplines. "I'll fix it, Mom. I'll make sure Dad's okay. I'll bring him

here, *somehow*. And I'll find your … real daughter."
I would give anything to be her *real* daughter.

"Emma … my sweet girl … *you* are my daughter.
Don't risk your life. My strength … it would leave
me completely then."

That's all the permission I need. I hold her hand
until the rhythm of her breathing tells me she's
asleep. As I get up from the bed to go in search of
Tom, the big door swings open and three people
enter. Allopath Bachod, Summer and, right behind
them, Gormala, a look of haughty anger on her
face.

3

"Emma!" Summer cries. "Bedeven told me you were here."

She rushes at me and hugs me hard. I whisper in her ear, "We need to talk. Just you and me. Get rid of them."

Gormala is already fussing around Mom, pulling at her covers.

"Leave her," I snap. "She's sleeping."

Gormala gives me a curl of the lip, then lifts Mom's head and pats down her pillow. Mom jerks awake with a soft cry. Blood flushes my face, but I say nothing. Gormala knows she can ignore me. I call Argadnel home only because Summer insists on my doing so. I have no power. No authority. And Gormala takes full advantage of it.

Allopath Bachod is also suddenly very busy, passing his smoking plate over Mom and chanting. Putting on a good act for his little Suzarain.

Summer holds me tightly, trembling from head to foot. "He — he says that Mom is — that she's probably going to —" She chokes on the last word.

I look into my little sister's frightened eyes. When we lived on the farm and she suffered more and more from that strange illness, I was terrified that she'd die. Now, we know that she *was* dying from Earth's atmosphere. As an Argadnelian, she was like a freshwater fish dropped in the ocean. She's completely healthy here and has grown at least an inch for each of the eight and a half months we've been on the island. She's still slim as a reed, but her face is older — angular and sharply planed, like her fellow Argadnelians. Still, her warm black eyes, narrow nose and thick dark hair are the same. She looks as old as me now, but I still have that same fierce need to keep her safe.

She's become a funny mix of the old Summer and the new young queen known as Suzarain Elen. Suzarain means "queen" in Argadnel, but to Mom and me, she'll always be Summer.

When we lived on the farm, Summer loved to dress in bright colors, paint her fingernails with vivid nail polish and decorate herself with Mom's cheap jewelry. She's no different here, except she gets to wear real jewels and handwoven fabrics banded or shot with gold and silver. Today she's a streak of sunlight in a yellow and gold chiton, with a red hood crusted in small rubies. Her neck band is eight strands of perfect yellow pearls, pink moonstones and sapphires. Her hair sparkles with slivers of aquamarine. She's as unlike her black-attired Argadnelians as she can be, but they smile and tolerate her strange ways because she is the child of their beloved murdered Suzar and Suzarain. Now that she's been restored to the throne, the island people guard her like hawks. They've never really trusted Mom and they *certainly* don't trust me — or my influence over their new ruler.

Becoming the Suzarain of an entire, though small, world overnight can be pretty heady stuff. Mom and I have tried hard to keep Summer's size nines firmly on the ground — reminding her where she grew up and what kind of people raised her. Her new clann thinks my job as her Watcher is over and I should go away and watch over someone else. They don't understand that Mom, Summer and I are a *family*.

Soon Summer'll start taking lessons in Game Playing — her Council, manipulated by Fergus and Rhona, has ordered it. They want to make sure the young Suzarain will be able to handle herself if Argadnel is suddenly thrust into a deadly Game started by some other greedy world leader. And there's not a thing I can do to stop this training or the possibility of Argadnel becoming involved in a Game.

I've noticed subtle changes in my sister's attitude toward me since Gormala became her favored servant. There's a new arrogance and a distant coolness in her manner now, and I'm worried these will only increase once she begins her Game training.

I can only hope that our years together as sisters and the love we share for each other and our parents will keep us from a serious falling out in the future.

"Don't be afraid, kiddo," I say, hugging her tightly. "Mom'll be okay. I'll do everything to make sure she recovers. I promise. But, I *have* to talk to you."

She turns and calls out. "Gormala. Allopath Bachod. You may go. My sister and I wish to visit with our mother."

The Allopath glances over but continues his low chanting.

"Allopath," Summer warns.

"I heard you, my Suzarain." The man speaks in a high singsong voice. "But *that* Watcher has no station, no right to be here. I cannot allow it."

"Quite right, Allopath Bachod," Gormala says with a curt nod.

Summer sucks in a deep breath and, in a voice I don't recognize, snaps, "Gormala. Allopath. Leave us. Now!"

Hands clenched tightly, shoulders hunched, Gormala looks like a crow who's eaten a poisoned mouse. The Allopath's smoking dish stops in midair. Then, very slowly, he puts it down and bows over my mother. He slides past, a malevolent scowl on his tattooed face. That look should frizzle me in my boots, but I smile sweetly. Gormala, after more fussing over Mom, bows to Summer, sneers at me and stalks out.

Will I ever get used to it — the hatred and fear I see in so many who surround my sister? Everything in this place seems to vibrate with danger.

I look at Summer and whisper in English, "Why didn't you send someone to get me?"

She flushes uncomfortably. "I wanted to. But Mom said she'd let me know when it was time. She said that you would only try to help, and there is *no* help. She was afraid you'd get yourself into trouble." She hugs me again. "But I was sure you'd *know* we needed you."

I ask, "Could someone be doing this to Mom?"

Summer shakes her head. "No. I make sure that any food brought to her is tested by both me and the servants. And I watch Allopath Bachod every second he's in here. I breathe the stuff he burns. I take tiny amounts of the herbs he gives her."

"Jeez, Summer. You have to be careful."

She smiles. "I trust my own people."

"It's not just *them* I'm worried about," I whisper fiercely.

"It's not poison, Emma. It's something else … something deep inside Mom. The Allopath says her body is healthy but her spirit is dark and sick — her aura is thin and a terrible muddy color."

I nod. "Yes, I've seen it. Listen, Summer. Mom and I talked and —" I hesitate. Can I trust her to keep her mouth shut or will she tell Gormala my plans?

"What?" she asks.

I shake my head. "It's best you don't know. I'm sorry."

Her eyes widen and in her new *Suzarain* voice she says, "I *order* you to tell me."

"No. You'll blab to Gormala and she'll tell Bedeven, who will tell Rhona and Fergus. It's too dangerous."

Summer clutches both my arms, her fingers digging into me. "If it's going to help Mom, you know I'd cut my tongue out before I said a word to anyone."

"Even Gormala?"

"Yes. Of course. Emma ... you're my sister. I would never blab a secret you gave me. *Never.*"

I take a deep breath. "Okay. But I'm going to telepath it to you. Ready?"

She nods, looking at me eagerly. When I telepath what I'm going to do, her open expression of anticipation freezes, then melts into astonishment.

She can't telepath back, so she whispers fiercely, "You can't. Don't even think it. The terms of Fergus and Rhona's Game settlement forbid it."

Just as fiercely, I telepath back. *Who cares? Mom needs to see Dad. To make sure he's okay. This is why she's so sick.*

"But Emma, Dad's been made to forget us. What's the point?"

Does that mean you've forgotten him? I ask, as gently as I can. What I really want to do is shake her, hard.

"Of course I haven't," she says, but at least she looks ashamed — and guilty.

"Well, he wouldn't forget us, Summer. Not *Dad*," I say out loud. "Not Dennis Sweeney."

Mom struggles to lift her head off the pillow. Her eyes, like Summer's, are wide with alarm. "Emma, please ... don't speak so loudly ... dangerous."

Summer pushes me to one side. "Now look what you've done." She eases Mom back onto the pillow. A faint smell of lavender floats up from the bedclothes, along with the clouded smell of sickness. I march Summer into the shadows.

"How dare you touch the Suzarain," she snarls.

"Oh, give it up, Summer," I growl back.

She wails, "But you *can't* do this. They'll kill you. I couldn't stand it if —"

I hug her tightly and say in her ear, "I'll work it out, kiddo. I give you my solemn promise as your Watcher."

"Oh, Emma," she moans. "Why do you have to do this stuff? Why can't we just put up with things as they are?"

I glance over at Mom.

In a thin whisper, Summer says, "Yes. Okay. We'll do it for Mom. But you can't fail."

I smile. "I won't." She doesn't look convinced. "Can I have a few minutes alone with her?" I ask.

She gives Mom a kiss and leaves the room, wearing her regal air as tight as a second skin. But I know that inside she's just a scared kid.

Like me.

4

Before I turn to Mom, I try to get my shaking under control. If I'm going to find Dad and help Mom recover, I have to be a Watcher, not a human. Many times in my life, I felt more like an observer than a participant in my family's lives, but I always knew they loved me. And I loved them. I was a nonstop worrier, too — filled with irrational fears like what if Leto and Dennis suddenly stopped loving each other and got divorced? What if one of them got hit by a car and died? Or what if one of them just went away and never came back? And my later fear, which *wasn't* irrational and was therefore more painful — what if Summer died of her illness? That fear kept me alert, guarded, anxious. I was a Watcher even before I knew what one was.

Normally, a young Watcher doesn't stay very long with what they call a "being" — a catchall word for any member of a world. And once the Obligation is over, they usually don't see the family or the younger they've been guarding ever again.

But for some reason, Histal has agreed to let me return to Mom and Summer whenever I like, "within reason." I suspect he knows I'd never be able to concentrate on my training if I couldn't check on them now and then. He thinks that, with enough training, I'll eventually let them go.

Never.

I don't know who I really *am*. I'm definitely not human, but I'm not much of a Watcher, either. Most of the time I can fake being cool and calculating, but on intensive missions, it's hard. Histal says my human-behavior training, and the weaknesses that go with it, always end up ruling my Watcher instincts, and if I don't learn to control these weaknesses, I won't make a good Watcher. Well, this mission of saving Mom could be the test. Maybe I can be a good daughter *and* a good Watcher.

I go to Mom's bedside. She smiles bravely. I try not to cry — after all, Watchers never cry.

"I'll see you soon. I'll tell Dad you miss him."

She nods, her eyes full of sorrow and worry. As I walk across the smooth black floor, she calls out faintly, "I love you, Emma."

I close the door behind me and lean my back against it. The hallway is empty, but every shadow seems to pulse with a nameless threat. I slide onto my backside and let the tears pour down my face. When they stop, I don't feel any better. My eyes ache and my chest is tight. As I get shakily to my feet, the door at the end of the passageway creaks open. I sigh. Just what I need. Branwen, Fergus's sister.

Branwen uses glow spheres as decorative accessories; three of these orbs highlight a chiton of grayish green that floats like wings behind her. Her hair is coiled around her head and polished to a high, hard gloss. Two long, thin pins topped with bobbles of jade stick up like antennae from the elaborate spiral of hair, giving the final touch to this human moth. Did I say *human*? Not likely. But she *is* a showoff.

Her lips purse as she eyes me up and down.

"Where have you been?" she says imperiously. "It has certainly taken you long enough to get home."

Now and again Branwen pretends to take her role here at Argadnel's court — as emissary for her brother, Fergus of Cleave — seriously. I'd find it entertaining, if I could trust her, but I can't. She's a flake of the first order.

"Well, I'm here now."

"You should have been called back days ago. Why didn't Summer send for you?"

I frown. "She had her reasons."

"Hmph. Bedeven's reasons. Or that horrible Gormala's."

"No, Summer says Mom didn't want to worry me."

Now it's Branwen's turn to frown. She and I are still trying to figure out whether we're friends. Sometimes I actually like her and other times I'd gladly strangle her. Either way, she's an important link to my former life on Earth, when I was plain old Emma Sweeney and she was in the form of a man called Albert Maxim, who lived on the farm next to ours. Now she spends most of her time in the huge greenhouses Mom built in order to grow the lush orchidlike black plants called Stygia Mantles, which have both ornamental and medicinal properties. Mom and Branwen plan to sell them to other worlds. All this work keeps Branwen out of our way most of the time. Now she's looking genuinely puzzled, a rare occurrence, and that worries me.

"But I did get an anonymous message to come back immediately," I say. "Do you know who might have sent it?"

She looks at the wall as if it's suddenly fascinating. "None at all. But I'm glad they did. Your sister is so emotional, so ... *human*. It's downright unnatural. Comes from living too close to so many of them for so long, I suppose."

"Well, looks like someone did me a favor," I mutter, convinced by her evasive manner that it was her. But why would she do it? Her next words give me part of the answer.

She slides her eyes left and right and lowers her voice. "I'd keep my eye on that Gormala if I were you. She may be your sister's servant, but she's in Bedeven's pocket. Something is going on between those two. A lot of whispering in corners and midnight meetings. Be careful, Emma."

I feel a zizz of alarm slide down my spine. "You think they might be behind Mom's illness? Or plotting against Summer?"

Branwen backtracks immediately. "Well, I don't know about *that*. Summer is watching your mother's care like a little falconet. And the people of Argadnel are determined to keep their new Suzarain safe on the throne. All I know is that those two spend far too much time together."

"Maybe they're attracted to each other," I say, making a face.

She laughs. "Gruesome thought, isn't it?" But her smile vanishes as she adds bitterly, "Bedeven thinks he can come and go in your mother's room whenever he likes, but he insists I stay away from her. Unfortunately, your sister has agreed with him. And Gormala's like a vicious guard dog. Belldam Leto would be glad to know we'll soon have a bumper crop of Stygias. Would you let me sneak in with you to tell her?"

I'm tempted, because Mom might be cheered by knowing the greenhouses are doing so well. On the other hand, Branwen could be up to no good herself, especially if she's jealous of Bedeven's growing power in the castel. "She's not well, Branwen. I'll tell Summer to let you visit with her in a few days, though."

She looks slightly mollified. "Bedeven has no right to dictate what I, Fergus's emissary, can and can't do. I'll certainly report this to my brother. I'll be in the greenhouses if you need me." I think she's going to say something more, but instead she nods to herself and walks back the way she came.

I wait until I hear the door to the greenhouses close, then I run down the three flights of stairs to the main-floor hallways of the castel's bartizan. As I wander along the winding corridors, I decide to go to my favorite spot on the island and take some time to think things through before I put forward any kind of a plan to Tom, who's waiting in my tower room. But as I turn the corner near the side exit, I see Gormala and Bedeven sitting on a window seat. They're arguing. He tries to put a hand on her shoulder, but she shrugs it off and strides away in the opposite direction from me. I wait for Bedeven to leave, too, but he settles back down on the seat. Blast it!

I go into Watcher mode and transmute invisible. I'll have to be very careful unlatching the big ebony door. I wait until Bedeven's head is turned and then inch the door open and creep out, letting it fall shut with the barest whisper. I move down the hill toward the edge of the island. For just a moment, I feel free and light as air.

There's no beach in sight, as Argadnel is lifted high on its massive pedestal at night, but I can hear the waves crashing below. I run up the path to my left until I come to the hidden trail I made months ago behind a thick wall of prickly gorse. It takes me another ten minutes of climbing through the shadowy darkness, but I finally reach my resting place.

No one would ever know this curved wall of moonstone harbors a border cave, where two worlds meet. I've been to a number of border caves as part of my training. Sometimes you have to actually enter the cave from one of the worlds to see the other realm that shares the border cave. But as far as I know, no one has any idea that Argadnel shares a border cave with another domain. There is no mention of it in the history binnacles in the castel's library, although I checked thoroughly. I discovered it by pure chance the week I arrived on the island. I'd come up here to explore, sat down, leaned against the rocky wall and, suddenly, a majestic city appeared in the air. It took my breath away.

I settle on a small ledge beneath the moonstone rock. The smell of Argadnel's sea is soft and light in my nostrils. I take a deep breath and feel knots unwind inside my small body. I love this place. I touch a clouded spot in the luminescent stone and a small cave opening appears beside me. A thin light emanates from the opening, slides down to the edge of the island and veers off into the sky to my left. It's a flat light, like on a movie screen. As the screen solidifies, it reveals as always this strange world I've discovered.

Sometimes I see the huge, magnificent city — all swirling peaks and astounding colors; other times, it's like flying high above a wide vista of carefully planned landscape with huge stretches of ornate pools or long winding mazes or magnificent dwellings; and sometimes it's just an endless and silent garden, lush with dark blue foliage. It's like looking at beautiful paintings seamlessly joined together. There is an indigo moon in each scene, but I don't know if it is one moon I'm seeing or many.

I've never attempted to pass through this border world by entering the cave. I have to wait until I'm ready. I don't know when that will be. But it's not yet. The curious thing is, I've never seen any creatures or movement in this baffling place.

This time, though, an unfamiliar scene appears on the border light — a yellow sea, unlike the flat silver ocean surrounding Argadnel. Am I seeing a different world? Or is it part of the same one? The yellow surface undulates in great heaving rolls that never fully break into waves. It's as if there is something of great power moving underneath. The awful sense of what I have to do to make Mom well seems to be reflected in the vast lurking menace under that swelling surface. The sight of it is thrilling, soundless, unnerving. I touch the wall and the light vanishes. The flat pewter sea of Argadnel returns.

I usually feel exhilarated after I've been to my secret place, stronger ... better able to take on the worries of my family and my training. It's as if this strange new world gives me a spiritual blood transfusion. But tonight that yellow ocean has rattled me. I am suddenly anxious to talk to Tom. As I run out of the screen of bushes, footsteps patter on the stone path ahead of me, moving swiftly. Sometimes Summer's hound, Tobar, is allowed outside the castel at night. He has large webbed feet that slap the rocks as he bounds around. Is it him? I run to catch up, but no one is there.

5

A large barn owl sits on the sill of the only window in my tower room, looking out into the misty clouds of the Argadnel night. The face he turns to me is a pale heart with two intelligent gray eyes. I close the door firmly behind me and lock it.

"How is your mother?" the owl asks.

I shake my head, trying not to cry. "Oh, Tom, she's so sick. We have to help her."

He doesn't answer, but his eyes are full of compassion. Sometimes, we don't need words.

When I first met Tom, he was a new student at my high school. He was big, ugly and always scowling, and he wore white T-shirts and black jeans, a thick copper band on each wrist and a leather strap around his neck. Tom made everyone nervous, even the teacher. When he started hanging around the cow field watching Dad build his Plexiglas henge, I sensed something was wrong. I figured he was out there to make fun of Dad's goofy sculpture, but instead he ended up working for Dad.

At first I didn't like Tom. I didn't trust him. He kept showing up when I least expected it. I even saw him hanging around the farmyard a few times at night, and twice I caught him hiding in the barn. The second time, I followed him, and that's when I learned for sure that my family was in danger and Tom was somehow part of it. But what kind of danger? Not long after that, Tom told me that Fergus's group was about to kidnap Summer and take her back to Argadnel. Tom's job, as their Watcher, was to keep an eye on my family's movements. By transfiguring into a barn owl every night, he could easily watch over us.

At some point, I'm not sure exactly when, something changed between Tom and me. I still don't know why it happened, but it was as if Tom was suddenly bound to me by something deeper than his loyalty to Fergus. I can't explain what it is — even to myself. It's just *there*. He proved it by changing sides in the middle of the Game and becoming my ally, my friend, my protector. He even tried to help Summer and me through the circle gate in Dad's henge to the safety of Argadnel before Fergus or Rhona caught up to us.

We didn't make it.

Tom was shot and, I thought, killed. Even though I hardly knew Tom, I missed him almost as much as I missed Dad. I didn't understand why. I just knew that something really important had gone from my life.

We'd been on Argadnel only a short time when one morning a barn owl landed in the tree where I was sitting watching Summer play on the seashore. Tom.

I couldn't believe it! Tom explained that when he was revived back at Cleave, Fergus was so furious at him for helping me and my family that he punished Tom by not allowing him to transfigure back to human or Watcher form. Fergus then had his Druvid, Mathus, put an owl cunning on Tom. Until Fergus commands Mathus to remove the spell, Tom must remain an owl. When they finally allowed him to leave, he returned to the Watchers Campan and Histal gave him permission to come to Argadnel — to me.

The only way Mathus will lift the cunning is if Tom does something of great importance on Fergus's behalf — which will never happen. I don't know why Fergus let Tom live after he'd betrayed him. He was Fergus's Watcher, and a Watcher never, ever leaves the being he's guarding. But Tom did just that. Maybe because Tom had been his faithful Watcher for many years, Fergus showed some leniency. Or maybe Fergus simply enjoyed seeing Tom punished. Who knows? I asked Tom once. He said he didn't know, but looked uneasy and a bit furtive as he said it.

Now and again I see a faint image of the dark, intense boy from the farm hovering behind his owl form, but I know it's just wishful thinking. And every time, I'm reminded that it's my fault he'll never be Tom again.

Tom, whose Watcher name is Tamhas, was a skillful transmuter and shape-changer who'd passed all the Master levels. Now he can't do a lot of the things a half-trained Watcher can do. He can still talk, still telepath, and he *can* fly through semisolid things like mesh screening on windows, and even transport to a few places, but he can't transmute invisible or shape-change. I know how frustrated, how angry he gets, and it's all my fault.

The curious thing is, I've never seen him in his Watcher state except for a glimpse of dark green eyes ringed with pure white and hair as pale as moonlight a few seconds before we made a run for Dad's circle gate. I suppose he would look a bit like I do in Watcher mode. As Emma, I have short pale hair over blue eyes, a narrow nose and wide lips, but in Watcher mode I become a strange unearthly creature. She — I — turn into a tiny, slender, white-skinned humanlike creature with long white hair fanned high above a narrow forehead, a thin arched nose, strangely pointed ears and long fingers. My eyes are bigger — - dark green and rimmed with white. I don't think she — *I'm* — ugly or anything, but just so different it's scary. Yet I like the way I feel as a Watcher, especially when I'm transporting — as if all of my bones are filled with air and I could skim the surface of light.

Tom's eyes are hooded now, his owl gaze intense. "You can't," he says.

"Can't what?" I say.

"You can't do it, you know. Histal will punish you, if Fergus doesn't kill you first."

I glare at him, then bluster out a huge lie. "I'm not scared of *them,* okay? Besides, neither of them will *ever* find out." Then it dawns on me. "Wait a minute — what *can't* I do? What do *you* know about it?"

He laughs, a deep throaty sound that ends in a low hoot. He swoops over my head and lands on one of the two chairs in my room. "I was flying around the castel —" he begins, but I interrupt.

"— listening at windows again, of course."

There is a long silence while he blinks at me. I give in sheepishly. "Sorry. Go on."

"Okay — *listening at windows again* — and I happened to pass by the servants' quarters and I heard that your mother is seriously ill. Naturally I took a leap in logic — or should I say *illogic* — and put two and two together and came up with fifty-six. You've told me how much she misses your father. So I figure you were crazy enough to promise to track him down. I hope I'm wrong."

I put my hands on my hips. "I am going to do it — with or without you."

We try to outstare each other. Finally he sighs and says gently, "I should tie you up and throw you in the closet and keep you there until it's time to return you to the Watchers Campan."

"I don't have a closet."

"Well, I'd find one."

"Birds can't tie knots," I say triumphantly, and immediately feel terrible.

He chuckles. "I wish you'd get over all that guilt. It was *my* fault — and Fergus's and Rhona's — that this happened to me … to you and your parents. It was not yours, Creirwy."

I asked one of my trainers in languages once what "Creirwy" means and she replied, "It means 'little dear one.'" She'd said it in the usual cold, analytical way they say everything; but I'd gaped at her, realizing for the first time the meaning of Tom's pet name for me.

I lean my forehead against Tom's. When I close my eyes, his voice is that of the boy he once was, and I can almost see his rough face, his strong hands. "But will you come with me?" I ask.

I don't mention my hope to find Mom's birth child. You don't know how scary this particular owl can be when he's really angry. "I need you, Tom. To help me find my dad."

He says ruefully, "It's dangerous. You shouldn't do it. But … where you go, I go … as always, Creirwy. After all, I have to save you from yourself, don't I?"

6

"We have to plan carefully," Tom says. "And we'll have to try to keep Bedeven and Branwen sweet. So they don't suspect anything."

"Bedeven is already cheesed off big time," I say. "Which means he'll be watching me like a hawk. We'll have to go to Earth now ... *today.*"

Tom nods solemnly. "Even so, you should talk to him first, Emma. If you suddenly leave Argadnel with no explanation, he'll become even more suspicious. The servants know your mother has asked if there's any way of checking on your father. They're not stupid. Your mom's sick. Suddenly you disappear. This two and two won't be hard to add up, even for them."

"So what should we do?"

"We could simply tell them that Histal called you back to the Watchers Campan and that Summer will let you know when your mother is close to death so you can return."

I think this over carefully. "Bedeven might accept that, Tom, because he has no understanding that a human would never leave a loved family member who's dying. But I'm not sure that Branwen will swallow it. She's seen firsthand on Earth how close my family is."

"Listen, I'll go to the Campan and talk to Histal," Tom says. "I'll tell him that you'd like to leave the island to practice some of your new skills, and that Bedeven and Branwen will likely put the wrong spin on it. He knows the problems here. I'll get him to assure both of them, if they ask, that you're in special training under his orders and can't be disturbed. As long as I go with you, I'm sure he'd agree."

"Histal will *never* agree, Tom. I'm just an apprentice. And a pain in the neck most of the time. He'll know you're lying."

"I don't think so. I noviated with Histal. He has no loyalty to Cleave or Fomorii. In fact, he disdains both tribes."

"Then why did he allow you to be Fergus's Watcher?" I ask. "And why doesn't he demand that Fergus take this stupid, horrible owl cunning off you?"

He shrugs. "One doesn't question Histal. He never sees the short term, only long range. He's the Pathfinder's right hand, after all. They have their own plans, and no one will ever know what they are."

"But, Tom, the Master Watchers don't *ever* seem to worry about the rightness or wrongness of an Obligation." This is not a new argument between us. But I never receive an answer.

He gets the usual closed look on his owl face and says, "I've told you time and time again, everything is not as it seems, Emma. Leave it at that."

"Leave it?" I sneer.

He just glowers.

"Which of course I won't," I add. "Not until I figure out some answers. If I can't find a good reason why Watchers continue to be part of the Game and accept Obligations from cruel and greedy Game Players, how can I believe that being a Watcher is a good thing?"

"Believing has nothing to do with it. You *are* a Watcher, Emma, whether you like it or not."

"Sort of like some religions on Earth, huh? You're born into it. Don't ask questions. Doesn't matter anyway, because no answers are given. But the questions are still there. The Masters are like the leaders of those religions. They make it all very mysterious and puzzling, and one is just expected to accept it. Well, *not me.*"

He sighs. "Enough, Emma. Your training will answer many of your questions in time. Let's get to the job at hand. Finding your father."

I nod and say coldly, "Yes, let's avoid everything else."

"The point," he says patiently, "is that Histal *could* be giving you secret training. He's told the other Masters you have the potential to be a really gifted Noviate. Don't get a swelled head about it, okay? It all depends on your behavior in the future. But Bedeven and Branwen know Histal is taking a personal interest in you. They'll believe him. I'll return as soon as I can."

With that, he flies toward the mesh window, dissolves into a cluster of tiny flashes and is gone. He'll have to do some fancy talking to get Histal to agree. I'm always an idiot around Histal, the highest Master in the Campan. The only being higher than him is the one they call the Pathfinder, who no one ever sees. I can't believe Histal told Tom I've got potential as a Watcher. He sure doesn't act that way around me.

When I arrived at the Watchers Campan four months ago, I was homesick, scared, defensive, angry and lonely. Needless to say, I didn't get off to a good start. But Mom had encouraged me to go — she wanted me to reach my full potential — and Tom had arranged with the Masters to take me on as an apprentice.

The Watchers Campan is a secret place. Before Tom took me there, he asked me to put on a special cloak and hood. I was no sooner wrapped from head to toe than we were there. Well, *somewhere*.

I was standing alone in a dark box with curiously illuminated walls that seemed to be shifting all the time.

"Tom?" I called in a shaky voice. "Where are you?"

"I'm here," he called back. "See if you can reach me."

"But where are you?" I cried. "I can't get to you if I can't see you."

"Yes you can," he said. "Try."

I looked around. No window. No door. Just those strange pulsating walls.

"I — I can't. Why are you doing this?" I said, my voice quavering. "I don't like it."

"Remember when we were at the market in Bruide and I told you to use your inner eye? When you looked at Albert Maxim you saw that he was really Branwen in disguise."

"Yes."

"Well, look at the walls with your inner eye. Go on. Try."

Maybe it would work if I stared at the walls like a "magic eye" puzzle. My heart was pounding, but I let my "concentrated" vision loosen up and my eyes relax. I focused on one wall. For just a second I saw treelike shapes before it changed back to shifting blankness. I turned and tried the next wall. Slowly the shape of an owl emerged.

"I — I see you, Tom!"

"Well, then, come on, what are you waiting for?"

I kept the owl's shape in focus and walked to the wall, right up to it — and through. On the other side I found Tom and nine strange beings — long-faced creatures with fine snowy hair and green eyes. They looked a lot like my Watcher self. Seeing them

I felt like Snow White with the palest dwarfs in Fairytale Land. Their garments flowed and changed as they moved, sometimes body-hugging, sometimes loose, woven of silk and metal and light — glinting gray and blue in the dimness of the room.

One of them was taller than the others, with a narrower face and a thin mouth. He reached out and placed his hand on my shoulder. "You were right, Tamhas. It looks like this one might be worth the trouble. Welcome, Emma. We hope you will be with us a long time."

Those were the first words that Master Histal said to me. And the last encouraging ones.

I've worked hard to be a good Watcher, but they keep trying to get rid of my "human" emotions. I asked Tom once why the Masters want to drum any sign of *caring* out of me, considering that I'm being trained to keep beings from harm.

"It's so you don't get too involved in the Obligation you've been sent to complete," he said. "Look how you've bonded with Summer. It's rare for an untrained Watcher or Noviate to bond with a being they are sent to watch over. But if it does happen, the Noviate must be specifically trained to break that connection, so he or she can move on to other Obligations."

"They can't break the connection between me and Summer — with any of my family."

His eyes smiled. "No. The Masters have met their match in you, it seems. But they'll keep trying."

They won't succeed. And if they keep pushing me and not answering my questions, I'll choose my own road. My own life. And it won't be as a Watcher.

7

Tom returns in less than an hour and, to my amazement, tells me that Histal has agreed to do as we've asked. An owl's face doesn't have much expression, but I've learned to read Tom's, and he has his shifty look on. I'm not going to ask why Histal gave the okay. I don't want to know how many lies Tom told him.

"Do we go to Earth through the border cave between Cleave and Fomorii?" I ask eagerly. I'm determined to leave immediately.

Tom shakes his head. "I'd rather we go directly, so we don't set off signals in the cave; but you're not skilled enough. We don't even have an artifact as a guide." He looks at me intently and says, "Reconsider, Emma. It's not as if you can bring Dennis Sweeney here to live. And if Bedeven finds out and tells Fergus and Rhona ... we'll be in deep trouble. I really think we should —"

"What's an artifact?"

"Something that belonged to your father. We only need it once — we can use our inner compasses if we ever have to go back. But we left Earth so quickly —"

"Would a sweater do?"

"You have your father's sweater?"

"Mom was wearing it at the market the morning we left Earth. It's got Canada geese flying across the back." I run to the small alcove where I keep the few personal items I'm allowed and pull it out. "See? Now we can go."

A knock on the door makes me shove the sweater out of sight.

"Emma. Open up!" Summer and her hound, Tobar, burst through the door as soon as I turn the lock.

"You're going without me, aren't you?" she says accusingly.

"Going where?"

"You know perfectly well *where*."

I lean out the open door and look down the dimly lit stairs. Is that a flicker of a shadow descending? I push Summer aside and follow as fast as I can. No one is in the gloomy corridors, but to be on the safe side, I wind my way around to Bedeven's quarters and hide behind a pillar — just as Gormala comes out of his room.

She is speaking in her thin, sharp voice. "I told you she was the only one who could do it. You now have your proof."

Bedeven snaps impatiently, "Yes. Yes. Go now, so I can think."

Bedeven's door slams and Gormala walks quickly away, muttering. It couldn't have been her on the stairs. When I get back to my room, Summer is sitting on a chair, Tobar at her feet, both looking theatrically bored.

She says, "You are *so* paranoid, Emma."

"That's a joke, right?" I answer. "Someone *did* follow you."

"Gormala walked with me partway. I told her to go back. I didn't want Bedeven or Branwen to know I was here."

If Gormala was with her, they'll know soon enough, Tom telepaths to me.

"Why do you keep Gormala?" I ask my sister. "Don't you know that she can't be trusted? I just caught her coming out of Bedeven's room. And earlier this evening I saw her huddled with him in the hall. Something's up with those two."

Summer rolls her eyes. "I think Gormala likes Bedeven, so what? She's always trying to talk to him or be with him. Not that *he's* capable of liking anyone."

"I don't like *her.*"

"Gormala was good to me when my first servant vanished. I still don't know where Tally is. She was just a kid. We were starting to be friends. I've had two of my people searching for her full-time. At least Gormala is older, and able to take care of herself."

Or she's responsible for Tally going missing, Tom whispers in my head.

I lean into Summer's face. "Promise me you'll be careful around her."

Summer bristles. "She's a good servant. And *I* trust her. She hasn't done anything to make me mistrust her."

Don't argue with her now, Tom telepaths. *When we get back, I'll keep a close eye on that Gormala. I'll find proof that she's a bad one. Proof that will even convince Summer.*

You're right, I respond. *I'm just scared for my sister, that's all.*

"You're mind reading with that dumb bird, aren't you?" Summer says, shaking my arm. "Stop it. I command you."

"You are getting to be a big fat pain with that commanding stuff. I'm Emma, remember? Your sister."

"You're not *really* my sister," she counters nastily.

Her words slice through me. How long will it be before Gormala, Bedeven and others, like Allopath Bachod, turn her completely against me?

"Gormala's really getting to you, isn't she?" I say coldly. "And that snake Bedeven. Does that mean Mom isn't your mother, either? That Dad isn't your father? You don't really need to worry about *him*, right?"

Summer throws her arms around me, the little moonstone clusters in her ears clicking. "I'll never say that again, I promise. You *are* my sister, Emma. It's just that I feel I have no *say* in anything you do. Take me with you. Please."

Gently I pull her arms off me. "I can't. You know that. If you suddenly vanished, all hell would break loose."

Emma, Tom says urgently in my head, *you didn't tell her what we were doing, did you? She can't be trusted.*

I say out loud, "If we don't trust one another completely, then what's the point of any of this? Summer?"

She wipes her eyes and nods.

"You won't say a word to anyone?" Tom demands out loud.

"I promise," Summer replies. "I know it would put Emma and you at risk. I *do* understand, Tom."

"Tom and I are going to telepath to you now. Just listen and nod or shake your head, but do *not* speak out loud. We'll be able to read your thoughts."

Summer nods again.

I'm definitely going back to Earth. Tonight, I telepath. *To see if Dad's okay.*

Her face lights up, then changes to open-eyed excitement mixed with fear.

We'll be gone only a few hours. I need you to tell Mom that I've left for the Watchers Campan and that I'll come back when I can. Then, when no one is looking, I want you to wink at her. They don't know what that means, but she will. Okay? It's very important — I can't do this without you, Summer.

She thinks a moment, then nods uncertainly. "I'm sorry about what I said before. I know this is something you have to do, Emma."

And I want you to solemnly promise that you will say nothing about this to anyone. Not Bedeven, not Branwen and especially not Gormala.

She hesitates, about to argue. Both Tom and I stare at her.

It could mean life or death for Tom and me, Summer.

"Okay, Emma," she whispers, then she nods again, more firmly. "Yes, oh yes, I truly promise." I can see in her eyes that she means it.

And when they discover that we've gone, you must insist they talk to Histal.

"Yes. Yes, I promise. Oh, Emma, I wish I could be as brave as you."

She hugs me hard, and I say out loud, "Oh, but you are. Every day. You've gone from a sick little girl who's only fun was to paint each fingernail a different color to the strong and beautiful Suzarain Elen."

She grins and holds out her hands. Each nail glistens with a different bright color. We burst out laughing. When we stop to catch our breath, I hear a stone tumble down the stairs outside. Tobar bounds to the door and growls. I move quickly and swing it open.

Bedeven is on the other side. Behind him, a beaming Branwen says, "See? I told you she would be here."

Bedeven says in his syrupy voice, "We've been looking all over for you, Suzarain Elen."

"Why? Is it Mom?" Summer and I say together.

"Oh no, she's the same," Bedeven says. "No … it appears that when your bed-servant came to prepare you for sleep, Suzarain, you were not there. An alarm was sent out and the whole place is being searched. It was very irresponsible of you not to tell anyone where you were going."

Branwen adds, "I insisted that Bedeven and I come here first. In your concern for your mother, I thought you'd want to talk to Emma. When we spotted Gormala lurking on the stairs, naturally my instincts were proved right."

She looks triumphantly at Bedeven having no idea he was just talking with Gormala. Lucky for us, they don't like or trust each other. It would be a real problem if they started to work together against us.

Bedeven croons, "Branwen, why don't you escort Suzarain Elen to her chambers. I'll follow shortly. She needs her sleep and is looking rather pale, I think."

"Why? What will you say to Emma that I can't hear?" Branwen demands.

"Yes, what?" Summer echoes. She likes Branwen. Another problem — especially because I'm inclined to like Branwen myself and know I shouldn't. I have to keep reminding myself that she's no more trustworthy than Bedeven. She's Fergus's sister, after all.

I telepath to Summer, *Go with Branwen. I'll be fine.*

Bedeven's eyes narrow speculatively. Telepathing is absolutely forbidden in the castel, like being invisible — mainly because he and Branwen can't do either and don't want anybody moving around or talking in total privacy. Makes sense when you're running things like you're the CIA.

Summer lifts the red hood of her chiton over her head and says, "Okay. But I want to see Mom first to say good night. I also want to ask your advice about something important, Branwen."

That throws Bedeven off — he looks torn between staying and following them. Good move, Summer.

As they leave, I telepath to her, *Tell Mom not to worry.* Summer doesn't look back, but she lifts her hand slightly and I know she's heard me.

Bedeven crosses his arms, and his pale eyes gleam. "You are upsetting the young Suzarain and the Belldam. Stirring things up. As always, Watcher."

"I'm going back to the Watchers Campan tonight, so I'll be out of your hair. Master Histal has ordered me to special training. I'll return when Mom — when Belldam Leto fades. There's nothing I can do here, and my training is important." I speak in the clipped, cool tones of my Masters.

He searches my face with his sharp eyes. "No. I

think you will not go anywhere. You will remain in your quarters until I send for you."

"Histal will tell you where I am at any time," I say, lying through my teeth. "Besides, you have no right to —"

"You will remain *here*." He opens the door to reveal three Argadnel guards.

I stare at him, puzzled. "But *why?*"

"I don't need to explain to you, Watcher."

As Bedeven turns to go, I can't resist saying, "My sister is asking Branwen for advice." I sigh dramatically. "It seems she no longer wants to share her concerns with me."

"I'm not a complete fool," he sneers. "I know what you're up to."

I say as cheerfully as I can, "You do?"

"You're trying to upset the balance of political stability between Cleave and Fomorii by making me turn against Branwen. As long as Fergus and Rhona are partners, Branwen and I remain allies."

I smile sweetly. "I won't need to try anything. You'll mess things up yourselves, eventually."

Bedeven swoops around, his chiton swirling like a gray cloud, and in a flash his marble blue eyes are inches from mine. His breath stinks of rotten fish. "You, Watcher, had better be careful. Mark my words. When we have what we want, we'll make sure the girl *cuts you loose*."

He whirls through the door and is gone.

8

Impressive! Maybe you'd like to give lessons on how to be a brilliant diplomat? Tom telepaths.

Oh shut up! It's hard to snarl telepathically, but I've learned — Tom gets me riled pretty often. *What did he mean by, "When we have what we want?"*

I suppose he meant when they have control of Summer and the island. If your mom should — you know …

"And now I've only made things worse?" I snarl out loud.

He chuckles. "Not worse than usual. But Bedeven's antennae are up. He's on the alert. Are you sure you want to go through with finding your father?"

I put my hands on my hips. "My mother is *not* going to die. Summer needs her now more than ever." I grab the sweater from the alcove and hold it up. "How do we make this thing work without alerting the guards?"

"First, change into Watcher mode and sit on the window ledge."

I do as Tom says, not looking at the chalk-white arms and long fingers that replace my human ones as I transfigure. The uniform of a novice Watcher neatly adjusts to my smaller body. I don't know what it's made of, but it's almost like a second skin of the softest material. It's a tight-fitting jacket and leggings made of many strips of the strange fabric in different shades of green, as are my boots, which stretch to above my knee. I carry only one thing — a silky yet tough, flexible pouch that holds my few personal possessions as well as a moon disc that the human Tom always wore on a leather strap around his neck.

I'm really only supposed to use this form when I'm invisible, transporting, in training or on an Obligation. At other times, Histal says, Watchers shape-change to the form of the beings they're living among. That's why I usually remain in Emma mode, even on Argadnel, where everyone has a humanlike shape.

Tom swoops down and lands on my legs. "Now wrap your dad's sweater around both of us. Like I said, we'll only need it once. After this, our Watcher instincts will take us there if we ever have to go to Earth again. Cover your head with it. Scrunch up your legs, Emma. I don't want to get kicked in the head by one of your boots when we land. Okay. Now, close your eyes. Imagine the farm. Then fly above it."

I close my eyes and, within seconds, a cold

breeze washes over me. When I open them again, my bones jump under my skin. I don't transport often and it's always a shock to find myself actually traveling through the air.

Directly below us is a patchwork of misty farm fields. Everything is brown and dirty white, the trees bare. For a moment I'm confused. I don't recognize anything. But then, through the haze, I see rows of small brown boxes set out in a wide circle. Mom's beehives. In the far left portion of the circle is the familiar shape of the farmhouse.

Tom calls, "Now, slide down to the farmhouse — not so fast! Glide ... glide down to it."

There's a quick terror in the falling, but a reckless ecstasy too.

Tom cries, "Slow down, Emma. Slow down!"

I squeeze my eyes shut again. We land with a thud. I try to drag air into my lungs. All I see when I pry my eyes open are stripes of light, until a pale heart face suddenly appears above mine.

"Almighty Ochain. If you'd landed the other way round, you'd have squashed me," Tom grumbles.

"W-where are we?" I whisper.

"How should I know? I closed my eyes for your incompetent landing."

I look around. Cold flat soil under me, slats of wood above ... which explains the stripes of light, but ... where? I glance to my left. Latticed wood panel.

"Criminy," I say. "We went right through the verandah. We're under its floorboards."

I push Tom off me and crawl forward. My hands land in frozen slush. The air has the smell of cold earth barely warmed by a thin spring sun. I do some calculating. It must be late March. Against the house, tiny spears of striped green poke through the cold soil. Mom's wild crocuses. I shiver in my thin garment. I told Histal that the fabric of my Watcher uniform is too light and that I get easily cold or hot in it, but he just looked at me as if I was a pathetic whiner.

"You'll soon learn to regulate your own temperature," he said, and I was left wondering if I had some little gauge inside me that no one had told me about. If I do, I still haven't figured out how it works.

"Put the sweater on. It'll cover most of you," Tom says.

I put it on, happy to feel its woolly warmth around me.

We agree that he'll wait on the verandah steps as lookout. The yard is brown under a thin layer of vapor, the grass plastered down and crusted in a film of ice. The light is shaping the slanted shadows of late afternoon. I edge up to the front door, my heart lurching. Everything is familiar and strange, like a dream of a place you *know,* yet nothing seems quite as it should be.

I raise my hand to knock when Tom's voice says in my head, *No. Don't alert them. They're at the back of the house. Open your senses, Emma.*

Chastened, I open my inner ear and pick up a murmur of voices. I turn the door handle slowly. The entrance is chilly and stuffed with muddy boots and mounds of socks that reek of damp dirty wool. Above them is a row of metal hooks covered in raincoats and jean jackets. My heart lurches when I see my old baseball cap hanging on the last peg.

The voices sound ominously close now. I recognize one of them — I could never forget that aggressive growl. It's Mr. MacIvor, who owns the ice-cream shop in Bruide. His wife, the local midwife, was the one who exchanged Mom's second child for Summer.

My hand, resting on the faded wallpaper near the kitchen door, turns clear, then disappears. As I slide closer, I hear MacIvor say, "— sick and tired of sending him free supplies, Keeper. The town council won't reimburse me anymore if —"

A snarling voice answers, "You complain too much, MacIvor. Best watch that. Ain't good for your health."

Mr. MacIvor called the man "Keeper." He must be the new guard Fergus and Rhona installed to make sure no one uses the circle gate. I hope he's taking good care of Mom's bees, too. Mom's father, Grandpa MacFey, was called the Keeper in town.

I'd always thought it was because he was a beekeeper, but last year I found out that he, too, had been the guard or Keeper of the circle gate.

Of course, Grandpa MacFey wasn't my real grandfather. And I hardly knew him. Like I said, we'd come to visit him during the last few weeks of Mom's pregnancy. The day after we got here, Mom unexpectedly went into early labor and Grandpa MacFey called in the local midwife. I was taken away until Mom's labor was over. I was only seven years old, but when I saw the rumpled face of my baby sister, I was filled with such fierce protectiveness that I wouldn't let anyone except family near her. Naturally, I had no idea that the little creature wasn't Mom's real baby but a changeling child that I was bred to watch over. Now when I look back on it, all the clues were there — and I suspect, instinctively, Mom knew it, too.

Is Leto Sweeney herself a human? I think so, but her father and the people of the town of Bruide were, and still are, linked to Fergus of Cleave and others like him. I just don't know *how*. I'm pretty sure that link goes back centuries. I know that Leto had a strange ability to sense changes in Earth's weather patterns and an uncanny ability to control her bees. She even tried to make them attack Fergus and his gang when they were trying to steal Summer from us. It was pretty amazing.

As for Mom's father, I'll *never* understand why he

did what he did. The day after Summer arrived in our family, I came upon Grandpa MacFey and the midwife, Mrs. MacIvor, talking in our kitchen. I stood on the other side of the door, just where I am now, and overheard Grandpa MacFey saying, "You've done the right thing, Ina. You've done what was expected of you. My grandchild will go to a better place. She will be honored, even revered. We're part of something bigger than either of us can comprehend. We must protect —"

He caught sight of me and stopped. The look he gave me was wary, alarmed, almost as if he was afraid of me. But then he smiled and waved me away. I stood in the hallway long enough to hear him say, "Now, *that* one is doing what she's supposed to do. You did the right thing there, too, Ina. Let's get you home. I'll watch over my daughter and her family."

The woman replied in a sad voice, "You're right, of course, Ewan MacFey. But the old ways are not easy."

I didn't know what they were talking about, but some instinct made me run upstairs to make sure Mom and the baby were okay. I found Mom, agitated and white-faced, packing our bags. She kept saying over and over again, "It doesn't matter, Dennis. Don't ask. Just *do* it."

When she was done, Dad, looking bewildered, carried our stuff downstairs, put me in the back seat of the car, and pushed the baby's car bed in beside me. He helped Mom into the front and we drove away from Grandpa MacFey's farm. We never saw the old man again. But, after his death, Mom wanted to move back to the farm, and that decision changed our lives forever.

Why did Grandpa MacFey let them steal away his own daughter's child and put a changeling in her place? And why did he never tell my mother? Did he really think his grandchild would be a special gift to another world — have a life she'd never get here on Earth? Maybe he knew where Mom's real child was sent, maybe not, but he never told Mom. I've often wondered … why did Mom keep returning to the farm? I don't know that answer, either. I think perhaps she just *had* to. And now, here *I* am … back again.

Mr. MacIvor comes into view carrying a box of groceries and drops them on the table — the same table where Mom and a pale, sickly Summer sat all those months ago labeling jars of honey for sale at River Market. A deep sadness washes over me, mixed with an agitated hatred for the beings that separated my family. Why couldn't they have left us alone? We'd have found a way to make Summer better.

Another man appears dressed in green work pants and shirt. He's heavyset and dark haired like Mr. MacIvor, but his face is broad with a wide shelf of forehead and small bearlike eyes. Something in me withdraws from the muddy brown aura and damp earthy smell rolling off him. One of Fergus's men for sure.

I clench my hands tightly to keep from bursting in there and demanding to know where my father is.

As if he's heard me, Mr. MacIvor says, "Doesn't he ever leave that damn barn, Keeper? What's he do up there all day long?"

The other man smirks and lets out a low chuckle. "He waits."

"For what?"

Another chuckle exposes brown stubby teeth. "He hasn't any idea. He just ... waits."

"Well, I'm going to tell the town council —"

Keeper pushes his face into Mr. MacIvor's. "What Fergus does with Sweeney is his business and none a' yours. One day Sweeney won't be here. I'm just waitin' for the word. So, you ain't gonna say nothin' to no one. Get it?"

One day Sweeney won't be here? Waiting for *what* word? I head for the barn.

9

Tom has moved to the top railing of the outside stairs that lead to the bedroom I made for myself in the barn in order to keep a close eye on the house and yard. I may be invisible, but it doesn't stop icy water from seeping into my boots. I bet Histal doesn't have to traipse through icy water in boots like mine! As my foot hits the bottom step, an engine starts up behind me. A minute later, Mr. MacIvor drives past the house in a battered red truck, heading for town. I look back and realize I've left footprints in the wet snow. We'd better move fast, before the Keeper sees them.

A few seconds later, the Keeper walks out the front door and follows on foot — straight along the muddy driveway to the main road. I hold my breath. When I see him duck into the entrance to Grandpa MacFey's wood, I run quickly up the stairs.

I push open the door and a smell like rotting dishrags hits me like thick smog. My bed is still here, but the sheets and duvet are gray with grime.

In front of the window that overlooks the farm is a large maroon wing chair — the kind that has its own footstool built in. Its right side faces me. A bony hand rests on the arm.

I transmute into Emma and knock on the inside of the door.

"Put the supplies on the floor, Keeper," a voice says from the chair. "I thought I just saw you go toward the road. Must've fallen asleep."

I feel like I've been punched in the chest. The voice is rough, as if it isn't used much, but it's a voice I know as well as my own.

"Dad?" I whisper and walk in front of the chair.

Dennis Sweeney was always thin, energetic and strong. Now, he's a cadaver with a scruffy beard and red-rimmed eyes that look if they've just woken from a hundred-year sleep. His sweatshirt, jeans and sneakers are filthy, his hair long and greasy. But he's still my dad — and he's alive. A huge tidal wave of relief roars through me. At least Fergus kept that part of the bargain.

I try to smile reassuringly, even though my mouth is trembling. "Dad?"

"Who are you?" he asks, squinting up at me.

"It's me. Emma." I can't help it, my voice cracks.

"I don't know any Emma." He looks past me out the window. He doesn't ask why I'm here.

I kneel down beside him and put my hand on his. He moves his head slowly, as if his neck is rusty. He stares at my hand, a frown furrowing the already deep lines of his forehead. I squeeze his dry fingers. This time he really looks at me.

I whisper, "I'm Emma. I'm your daughter."

Dad's eyes slant away and then back to me. "I have no daughter. No family."

"You don't remember your wife, Leto? Your other daughter, Summer?"

"Don't have a family. No wife. No daughter." But his focus is turned inward now, as if trying to sort out what I'm saying. "Funny name for a daughter ... Summer."

"*Daughters,*" I say. "Two. Emma and Summer. We lived on this farm with you. And Mom. She made honey. You built a henge in the field. Remember?"

His eyes seem to clear a bit. "I remember the henge. You know I did that? How?"

"Because I was with you when you worked on it. You called it Brute Energy of Bruide."

"I *did* call it that." His face tightens with anxiety. "Should I know you?" He reaches out and feels the wool of my sweater.

"This is your sweater," I say. "Do you recognize it?"

Dad chews his lip and I can see that he's trying to remember. I take off the sweater and cover him with it. He smells it, then looks at me, trying to see something in my face, but he shakes his head.

I hear a tap, tap on the glass behind him. Tom is hovering.

The Keeper is coming back, he shouts in my head. *Too late to run. Disappear!*

I change into Watcher mode and vanish as fast as I can. As I do, I say, "Hang in there, Dad. I'll be back. Try to remember Leto. She always wore your sweater. Please *try.*"

Poor Dad. As I disappear, he half sits up, then falls back against the chair with a sigh. The Keeper strides in and bangs the door shut. "Who were you talking to, Sweeney? Whose footprints are those leading to your stairs?"

"I thought I was — she said she was my daughter ..."

I can feel the hair on my neck stand on end. The Keeper snarls, "A girl? When was she here? She didn't pass me outside."

Dad looks befuddled. "She just ... vanished."

I quickly slip around Dad's chair toward the exit. I try to pass through the door, but I'm so frazzled that I bang into it, then wrench it open and pelt down the stairs. A loud shout and the Keeper's after me. When I turn around, he's hard on my heels. I look back. Oh no. My footprints are clear in the snow and mud.

Tom shouts, "Fly!"

"But — I — haven't — done — that alone yet," I puff. "Except — in — transporting."

"Emma, do it!"

I can almost hear Histal's voice in my head. He always talks so reasonably, so calmly. *Let your feet leave* the ground, Emma. You are the only thing keeping you attached to it. Refuse to touch the ground and you won't.

I know I don't have to go very high, just enough to keep my footprints from showing.

I concentrate and, suddenly, I'm skimming above the ground, arms whirling to keep my balance. "Where — are — we — whoops! — going?" I shout.

Don't call out! Telepath. We'll have to get to Fergus before the Keeper does, Tom shouts in my head.

That jolts me so hard that I just catch myself from touching ground. *I — I can't. Fergus will kill us!*

We have no choice, he calls to me. *Head for the circle gate. Once we're safe in the border cave, I'll close it off so the Keeper can't get through for a while. I can tell by your voice that you're too low, Emma. Come on. Higher — fly higher!*

I feel like I've got lead weights in my boots. The trees of Grandpa MacFey's wood loom up fast. If I don't get more elevation, I'll be caught like a ragged kite in those sharp branches. I close my eyes and will myself up, up, *up.* With a great thrust, I fly straight skyward. When I open my eyes again, I'm high above the trees, terrified, skittery and exhilarated. I look back. Wow! I did it. The Keeper is standing in the middle of the road looking back and forth, scratching his head.

Tom sounds in my head, *Where are you?*

Here!

He swoops past me. *Look at him! What an idiot. Fergus picked a dumb one — aren't we lucky?*

As Dad's henge comes into view, I can see that many of its original pieces are missing. Others have fallen over, and kids have sprayed the few remaining Plexiglas stones with graffiti. We land near the center and I transmute visible. The circle gate looks like it wouldn't transport a fly.

"Does it even work anymore, Tom?"

Tom hops onto the graffiti-covered socle that holds the entrance to the circle gate. "I can feel it buzzing. But it looks like the Keeper's pretty lazy. He should have got rid of anything that hints of the existence of a portal by now. Let's go, Emma. We have to get to Cleave ahead of him."

"Can't we just return to Argadnel?" I beg. "If the Keeper's so dumb, he won't figure it out."

Just then, I see movement at the fence around the henge's small pasture. It's the Keeper, his face tilted up, like a bulldog sniffing the air. With amazing agility, he leaps the fence and lopes toward the henge.

"Whoa," I cry. "He's *coming.*"

"Jump up beside me."

As soon as my bottom hits the plastic socle, it's like we're on a jet-powered toboggan heading straight into oblivion.

10

We no sooner start down than we reverse and head straight up. Then a somersault and my body tightens into itself as we go through something hard.

"Oof!" I sit up and rub my hip. "Will I ever learn to land properly?"

Tom, who hasn't a feather out of place, says, "Doesn't look like it. I think you get worse each time."

We're inside the border cave between Fomorii and Cleave, facing the portal to Cleave. Vines have tumbled through the shadowy opening and wind around two wooden columns on either side of the entrance. I know there's a hall at the back of the cave that leads to the world of Fomorii, but I have no intention of ever going *that* way again.

I look around the small space. The only interior light is a sliver of purple that slides up into the roof from a small stone table in the middle of the floor. I know from my training that this is a converge light — a kind of intersection that connects with other worlds.

Tom says, "Quickly. Give me my silver moon disc — in your pouch."

I dig it out and he uses it to block the light. "I'll leave that in place for now," he says. "It'll slow the Keeper down, but he'll find a way through to Fergus, so we'd better get a move on."

"I'm scared of this place, Tom. Really I am. Can't we just go back to Argadnel? So what if Fergus finds out someone was at the farm. He won't know it was us."

"You don't really believe that, Emma," he says. "There's only *one* girl who'd come to the farm to talk to Dennis Sweeney. Only *one* girl who can move around as an Invisible, and that's the Watcher from the bee farm. One of the terms of your going with Summer to Argadnel was that you, your mother and Summer would *never* return to Earth. By going to see your dad without Fergus's permission, you've broken that rule. You have to understand, Emma, the rules *must* be abided by. The Game is nothing without its rules."

"Yeah — stupid, pointless rules, from what I can see," I snap. "But, Tom, they can't know it was us for sure —"

"Emma, please don't make things worse by blathering a load of nonsense. Be quiet and listen."

I glare at him.

In a slow, patient tone that sounds just like Histal, he says, "Even before we got back to Argadnel, the

Keeper would be telling his side of things to Fergus. Fergus is obsessed with the rules he lays down. It's how he keeps control of his Players. He would catch up with us and likely chop us into little bits and feed us to Rhona's fishes. *Do you understand?*"

"So now what do we *do?*"

"Don't be deliberately dim, Emma. We get to Fergus *first*. He'll be raging mad at us. You'll have to appeal to his newly softened side — the one that's courting the beautiful Rhona again."

"You're kidding, right?" I sneer. Suddenly the reality of what I've done makes me feel sick. What will happen to Mom — and Dad? I have only myself to blame. I take a deep breath. "Okay. *Okay*. Let's get it over with. Should I go in Watcher mode? Or as Emma?"

Tom's heart face tilts as he assesses. "As Emma, I think."

I slip into Emma's skin. Tom looks at me intently and says softly, "Fergus really did like Emma."

"We *hope*." I flush at what I think I hear in his voice.

To hide my uneasiness, I stand in the vine-covered arch and stare at the swinging bridge that leads down into the gloomy jungle. The last time I was here, I had only gone a short distance when it started to thunder and rain, and the vines of the bridge suddenly started growing, winding like snakes around me. I had to fight for my life to get away, and I swore I'd never come back.

I shiver and look up. The night sky is murky. An orange moon hovers high above the treetops. The dense odor of damp soil and plants chokes me.

Tom's reassuring weight lands on my shoulder.

"Ready?" he asks gently.

"What should I say to Fergus when — if — we find him?" My chest is shaking, my heart is pounding so hard.

"We won't find him," Tom says. "*He'll* find us, and when he does, you'll flatter him, grovel if you have to, appeal for forgiveness. Anything to put him in a good mood. He likes to think he's a forgiving type — as long as the beings in disgrace plead long and hard enough."

"What if he simply orders his Players to kill us — doesn't wait for an explanation?" I ask, my voice high and thin.

"He won't. He'll want to hear what you've been up to first. Above all else, he's nosy. So make it good. Remember, if you don't entertain him, he'll just get madder."

"But we're dead anyway, right?"

"Not if you think on your feet. Remember, he likes you. And remember that your mom and dad need you."

I clutch my head with both hands. "I've let them down. And now you're in trouble, too! I hate this," I wail. "Why can't I just be plain old Emma living on the farm? Why can't things go back to the way they were? Just Mom, Dad, me and Summer. Why do I have to be in this horrible, scary place?"

"You'll do great, Emma. Be strong." Tom's talons tighten on my shoulder. "I wish ... If I were Tom now, I'd be more help and ..." His voice trails off.

I touch his wing. I wish he could be Tom, too. I want Tom's big warm presence, his physical strength. But I don't say it.

Once I asked Tom what it felt like to have no set physical form. "I've seen two Toms, but I've caught only a glance of the third, your Watcher self. How many more Toms are there?" I asked him.

"I've been many things," he said. "Underwater creatures, four-legged and winged beasts, any number of beings from any number of worlds, but I *am* the Watcher Tamhas. The other forms I've never held for long — except this one, but this is not by choice." He shook his feathers.

"So you don't think of yourself as the human Tom?" I asked, disappointed.

His owl eyes became half lidded, the feathers around his face fanning full.

"I use that humanoid form quite a lot and always feel very much at home in it. After all, many of the beings from other worlds have a number of human characteristics. Even someone like Rhona, although she is as far from human in nature as any being I've known. But when I met you — as Emma — I recognized something I'd never acknowledged before — in *me,* that is."

"What was that?"

"I've never put it in words before. Let me think about it," he said enigmatically.

I guess he's still thinking. What difference does it make anyway? We won't be alive much longer. My heart is heavy with guilt and sorrow and fear.

"I know what you're thinking, Creirwy," Tom says close to my ear. "But you can get out of this. I know you can."

The light outside the cave is growing dim. "I guess we can't put off going out there any longer."

"No. But remember this," he says, his voice earnest, "don't fight anything or *anybody* that you come into contact with before we get to Fergus's castel. Just let things happen. *Don't fight it.* Okay? Promise?"

"I promise. Now let's do this before I lose my nerve completely."

I step onto the bridge. It crackles with an energy that surges through my feet. When I clutch the vine handrail, the thick stalk shudders and slides like a snake under my hand. As I move forward, all my senses are alert — for anything — but especially for signs of rain or thunder. The jungles of Earth, on television, always seem to be crowded with the sounds of birds and animals. But Cleave's jungle is dark and silent, except for the swish of leaves as we brush past them and the strange slipping sounds of the vines as they slide and twist along the bridge.

The bridge slants down in a slow, winding circle

like a smooth spiral staircase, until it vanishes deep into the undergrowth. It doesn't take long to reach the thick fronds of the treetops. I take one last wistful look up at the dim cave entrance — now just a speck in the high wall of brown stone.

Tom touches his soft head against mine.

I pull myself together, take a deep breath and plunge into dark, heavy air. The slope of the bridge is very steep here; at times forming itself into shallow steps. It's getting harder and harder to breathe. I feel as if someone is pushing soil into my lungs. My ears pop. Blood thuds hard in my head.

Tom says quietly, "Adjust for this, Emma, or you'll pass out."

I struggle, the way you do when you're under water, then I open my lungs and the suffocating feeling eases. My heart slows down. I take in a few deep breaths. I keep forgetting I can do things like this as Emma. But if Tom is right, I'm not really *Emma*. I'm a Watcher no matter what shape I take. Will I ever fully accept that I'm no longer just Emma, but some strange other creature as well?

I can't see far into the jungle. The trees, vines and leaves are a woven wall of dull green, brown and patches of black. Suddenly, just ahead of us, the bridge has become a sharply edged staircase veering down into a dark yawning hole.

"We don't have to go underground, do we?" I squeak.

"It won't go much farther. Keep moving."

Tom's right. The steps stop about ten feet below ground level at a tiled floor. No doors, no exit. Just walls of mud that rise straight up. I wander around for a few seconds, then some instinct warns me to head back to the stairs. But before I can make it onto the first step, they clatter upward and vanish over the lip of the opening.

"Now what?" I cry, pacing back and forth, fists clenched. "Am I supposed to climb these muddy walls? It's impossible. And I'm sure I can't fly in this heavy air. But *you* can."

"No I can't. And I wouldn't let you, even if you could," Tom murmurs from his perch on my shoulder. "Whist. Listen."

A faint rustling comes from ground level, followed by a fluttering of shadows around the rim. Then a swishing sound as something drops into the hole. I can't see what it is but, a second later, I feel a tug on my foot. I jump back and stare at a glistening rope that has wound itself around the toe of my boot ... a rope with tiny eyes like glistening blue beads along its back. Another slides up beside it, the tip wavering toward my other foot.

"Uck!" I cry, pulling away. "What is it?"

"It's a helminthes ladder," Tom says.

"A what?" I squawk.

"A flatworm ladder."

"Worms? You've got to be kidding. This is stupid.

I'd have been perfectly happy to discuss things with whoever's up there. There was no need to dump us in a filthy great hole with worms!"

Tom chuckles. "They had to check us out. The Barrochs are shy."

"What are Barrochs?" I demand, hands on hips. "Worm people?"

He sighs. "You'll see soon enough, Emma."

The ends of the two slowly writhing flatworms stretch up to the hole's surface. Their skinny bodies are dark brown, circled with pale blue.

"They're really worms?" I ask, gulping.

"Hey, you're not going to be a *girl* all of a sudden, are you?"

That gets me. I shout loudest when I'm lying. "No, I am *not!*"

"Well, go on then. The ladder won't hurt you."

I edge toward it. "But, Tom, the worms have made only one rung between them. That's all. And look, it's bright red. Yuck."

"Just put your foot on it and grab both sides at once."

"How can I climb up if there's only one rung?"

"It's no wonder you drive Histal crazy. You just never do what you're *told*. You just *have* to argue. Put your feet on the blasted rung. And remember, just let things *happen*. Don't fight — please, *please*. Promise me."

"Okay, okay, I promise. I just wish you could

climb this thing and I could sit on *your* shoulder. Why can't you fly up there and talk to them — tell them the steps would be much easier?"

"Emma …," he growls from my shoulder.

I reach up and wrap my hands around the two long rope worms, shuddering and grimacing at their cold, dry skin. At least they're not slimy. The muscles of their long bodies quiver in my hands.

Muttering "Yuck, uck, blerk" over and over, I put my foot on the rung. Immediately, the bottom of the pit drops away. We plunge down with it and, as if on a giant slingshot, we're launched straight into the air. As we fly past the rim, a row of dappled knobbly faces stares up at us from under piles of gray leaves.

We land on the ground, Tom on top of me, and before we can catch our breath, a spidery net falls over us. A hundred busy hands turn us around and around, like a cocoon. I have a thin shroud over my face, so I can breathe — and I'm able to see shadowy moving shapes, but I can't move. As they work, the creatures make soft crackly, grunting noises. I open my mouth to shout, but Tom, bundled up in my arms, whispers, "*No!*"

We're lifted and carried a short distance to what looks like a narrow box hitched behind two dark lumpy animal shapes with jutting spikes along their backs. There's a creaking like a door opening and we're shoved inside. It's dark. My back is resting against something hard. I hear a slapping noise outside and we lurch forward. Mewling clicks and croaks follow us. I wiggle until the netting around me loosens enough that I can sit up. Tom's head is just under my chin. I'm able to squeeze my fingers along his feathery body far enough to tear a small hole in the veil over my face. Through the hole I can see that we're in a sort of leafy box with small leaf-shaped windows.

The jungle is going past very quickly, a blur of muted green, gray and brown. When we suddenly come to a halt, I almost fall on my face. Tom grunts and whispers, "Try not to crush me. I'd like to live at least until Fergus kills me."

The sounds of rustling and soft clicking close in on us again. Dark shadows fill the windows and become mottled heads with small red eyes. With a sickening lurch, I realize their faces are made of overlapping leaves. More rustling, and a dull light streams back into the box. Have they gone for good? I peer out the window. All I can see is the wall of jungle. But then the wall shimmers and, with a loud crackle, it splits down the middle and opens, like a heavy curtain on a stage, revealing a narrow road that leads down a steep hill to two huge doors.

The carrier box lurches to the right and heads toward the open curtain, then stops. What now? I stick my head out the window as far as I can in this stupid cocoon. The leaf beings suddenly appear again, swarm the lumpy animals, unhitch them, and lead them away past my window. The beasts are dark orange, with thick lugubrious faces and nervously rolling pink eyes. Along their scaly backs are harnesses with sharp wooden spikes. When they're gone, silence falls. I wait.

"What's going on?" Tom asks, his voice muffled.

"Listen!" I whisper. Is that the squeak of wheels? Is the coach moving forward? It is! On its own?

"Get ready!" I cry, just as the little carriage rumbles quickly down the hill — aiming straight at the doors.

11

Just before impact, the carriage careens to one side and we topple out onto the ground like a big pale slug.

"Are you okay?" I gasp.

"Yeah, just get me outta here."

I struggle inside the cocoon. "I can't shift it," I say desperately.

"Think, Emma," Tom says.

"I tear this hole bigger and we crawl out. Right?"

"Emma ...," Tom says in an exasperated voice.

That's when it dawns on me. I quickly change into my smaller, Watcher form. The cocoon loosens immediately and it takes only a minute for both of us to wriggle out.

I stand up shakily. Tom hops around, flexing his wings. I'm sure I hear rustling not far off and feel a thousand eyes on my back.

I look up at the structure we almost hit. The doors are ten times — no, twenty times — taller than a man, almost touching the foliage high above.

If I didn't know better, I'd say they'd been cut into a monstrous tree trunk. Most of the structure is covered in vines, but the parts that are visible, as well as the doors, are carved with elaborate designs of leaves and roots, similar to the ones Branwen painted on the walls of the farmhouse when she lived there as Albert Maxim.

As we walk closer, I see that the design includes dense clusters of carved leaves dotted here and there. Each cluster forms a ghostly face. Hundreds of these leafy faces seem to be looking right at us.

When I change back into my Emma self, Tom flies onto my shoulder and says, "Okay. This is it — Fergus's castel. Ready?"

I nod, but the faces are giving me the willies, especially the ones at eye level, which seem to be quite ferocious. On the one nearest me, the leaves are twisted into knots over its eyes, giving it a look of angry torment. I touch its leafy cheek and it erupts from the wall, straining toward me, its mouth grimacing and stretching as if trying to talk to me. I leap back and, just as suddenly, the face returns to its savage wooden stare.

I hear a distant creak and look up. The doors remain shut. There's a faint rustle behind us and I look over my shoulder, but nothing moves in the silent forest, either.

"To our right," Tom whispers.

I scan the long wall and see that one of the small panels is open. A gray-green leafy face is peering out at us.

"Hello," I begin. "We're here to —"

The strange little being shoots a gnarled hand out of its pile of leaves, holds it up for silence and says something in the same grunts and crackles of the creatures that kidnapped us.

"Sorry?" I say. "I can't —"

Open your inner ear, Tom says urgently in my head. *Let your brain compute what she says.*

I let my Watcher machinery do its work, and when I speak, it feels as if I'm speaking English, but small clicks and grunts come out instead. "I am Emma Sweeney and I've come to talk to Fergus of Cleave."

The creature speaks and this time I understand. "I know who you is," it says. "Come along, come along. He don't like being kept waiting, now do he?"

As we enter a dim entryway, I say, "Are you a Barroch, too? Tom says the creatures that brought us here are called Barrochs. How do you know who I am?" Tom tightens his grip on my shoulder and I let out a muffled "Ouch."

The creature looks at me. "I know. I be of the Barroch tribe, the first tribe ever here. We be slaves to Fergus and his people. This once be our castel."

"Slaves?" I am astonished. "Do you ... have a name?"

The creature's face comes closer. Its red eyes search mine. I can smell the acrid odor of decaying leaves. "I be Cill. But don't you be saying it aloud, now. Come along, come along."

Tom warns me telepathically not to talk to her

because it could get her into trouble, so I stop …
for now. Cill opens another door at the end of the
small entryway and we walk along a wooden ramp
that hugs the wall of a long narrow hallway. Not far
along, a small platform juts into the long open
space that runs parallel to it. Beside the platform is
a large woven basket suspended by vines attached
to something in the dim recesses of the ceiling.

"Don't tell me," I say in Cill's language. "We have
to ride in that."

Cill climbs in and gestures for us to follow. The
basket sways. I clutch the sides with a death grip.
Cill releases a lever and we coast along, high above
a black trench.

The smell of earth is thick and heavy, but the
place is so beautiful I hardly notice. The walls are
green and gold, with carved leaf faces all along
them, but here the leaves are made of gold, inset
with gemstones. We pass by many ramps and a
number of long corridors. Each ramp has a door
beside it. Cill takes a number of turns and
switchbacks until a large gold door looms ahead.
We slow down and bump gently against its ramp.

Cill climbs out. She opens the door and ushers
us ahead of her. "You be waiting in here until he
come." Then she's gone.

We're in a huge round room, the leafy faces here
larger and even more elaborate. In the center of the
back wall is a mammoth gold humanlike face.

Fergus, Ruler of Cleave. Trust him to have his scary mug made into the biggest mask of all.

Below his mask, on the floor, are two black tree stumps. No furniture. The floor is made up of tiny squares of colored stone, more leaves, more faces.

A loud bang makes Tom and me jump. It's followed by the tramp of booted feet. When the tramping grows earth-shatteringly loud, a door suddenly appears at the far end of the hall and a line of leather-draped men and women carrying lethal-looking weapons and shields of all shapes marches in. They circle us and, with a synchronized one-two foot stomp, halt.

Into the rustling silence slides a breathy whine that skims higher and higher until it makes my ears hurt. A tall man slowly marches through the door carrying a brown leather bag shot with gold and spiked with horned tubes, the longest tube in his mouth. His face is scarlet from blowing into it, his eyes unblinking. He passes by, then marches up to the golden face of Fergus of Cleave where, thankfully, he stops torturing the air.

I'm so frantic, I almost laugh out loud. "A *bagpipe?*" but Tom hisses at me to be quiet just as the gold mask cracks in two. As each half slides away, a wooden stepped platform rises up. At first I see only a glimmer of gold, but then Fergus appears in all his awful glory. The panic almost bursts my chest when I realize that Rhona, Queen of Fomorii, is standing beside him.

12

Fergus looks just as I remembered — in thick brown leather with green scrollwork, his hair a black halo around his head, wide bands of gold edged with snarling wolves' heads on his wrists and around his neck. His dark skin is marked by an ugly snake of a scar on his right cheek. His features are flat and hard, eyes under thick brows jet black with no whites showing. He's not tall, but he's muscular and solid.

Rhona is taller, and beautiful in her frightening, icy sort of way. She's wearing a flowing blue garment that changes shade with every movement and reveals the outline of her slender figure now and again as if she's surrounded by spirals of water. A vibrant green collar stands like an open fan on her shoulders, framing the elaborate twisted-silver headpiece that fits over the back of her head and sweeps past her face in flashing finlike wings.

Behind them, two familiar figures emerge from the shadows. They're always hanging about in shadows, watching, assessing, calculating. The tall bald man dressed in leather as black as his skin is Fergus's Druvid, Mathus. Gold glints in his ears, and when he smiles, gold flashes there, too. The other man is taller and very thin, in slashes of vibrantly colored eelskin studded with pearls and underwater gems. His hair is long and gray under a skullcap of blue shark skin, his arms and half his face smothered in tattoos. All his movements are followed by an eerie echo of greenish light. This is Rhona's Druvid, Huw, the man who tracked us down at the market where Mom was selling her honey last summer, the man who tried to grab Summer from Tom and me. He didn't care two pins about Summer. He was only determined to beat Fergus by getting to Summer first. He's not a native Fomoriian, but a Celtoi, the tribe whose roots lie deep in Earth's ancient soil. Is that what the people of Bruide are? Some kind of ancient Celt? However, Huw has no allegiance to Earth. He is devoted only to Rhona.

Fergus and Rhona move down the stairs side by side, Fergus holding his left arm out so that Rhona can rest her hand on it. She has a stiff, uneven gait, but she's as powerful and deadly as a sea viper.

The Druvids remain at the foot of the stairs while Fergus and Rhona walk to the two tree stumps. Fergus leans toward Rhona, who says something to him in her strange tinny voice. The second they sit down, the tree stumps sprout shafts of foliage that twist and twine in the air with snapping noises, turning into two magnificent thrones.

Rhona's hands rest on the braided arms of her chair. Her scaly gray right hand is circled at the wrist with a jeweled bracelet. Under the elaborate headdress, her pale azure features are narrow and sharp, and I know from experience that when she smiles — which is rare and usually because she's enjoying someone else's discomfort — her teeth are icy blue. One of her slanted eyes is a dark, intense green, the other the milky dead color of an opal. I expect my blood to freeze in my veins, but I'm not prepared for the look on her face when she glances at me. Instead of her usual flat expression, she looks surprised — no ... worried, if that's possible. Why? Just as quickly, I'm convinced I'm wrong, for her expression is now its usual one of haughty disinterest.

Fergus suddenly booms, "Well, Watchers, we meet again."

I nod and try my most charming smile.

But Fergus isn't charmed. He growls at Tom, "Watcher Tamhas. I told you I didn't want to see you unless you were ready to return to the Game. Now you come to me with the little Watcher in tow. This can only mean you have allowed your apprentice to get into trouble, and you are here to wriggle out of it. Am I right?"

Fergus always calls Tom by his Watcher name.

Tom shifts on my shoulder and his head dips in a deep bow. "Thank you, sire, for allowing us a hearing."

"Hmph," Fergus grunts, then turns to me. "And what do you say, little Watcher? You're in trouble, are you?"

I'm frozen with fear. Tom whispers in my head, *Bow!* I bend like a robot from the waist.

"Well?" Fergus asks. "Gromand got your tongue?"

"Yes, I guess I am in trouble — sort of," I say stiffly.

He leans back and scans his people, as if to say, See? These two are complete idiots, are they not? Then he growls at me, "*Sort of?* What does *sort of* mean?"

"Well, sire, it's just that I don't think I've done anything all *that* wrong."

"Is that so ...," Fergus now says musingly to the ceiling.

Tom is shouting warnings in my head about how this man could kill me right where I stand and not think twice about it. He needn't bother. I'm already terrified.

I rack my brain — how to start again? Humbly, I say, "Actually, sire, I've come for your help."

Fergus tosses back his head and belly laughs. The people surrounding us titter. Even Rhona smiles — a look that should ice-pick me to the floor.

"You?" Fergus hoots. "Ask for my help? What do you think, Rhona of Fomorii. Do we let her speak or do we slice off her little white head?"

Rhona looks at me speculatively, and I know she'll probably go with the second option.

Fergus says in a patronizing croon, "Tell me, Watcher, what *have* you been up to that you now seek my help?"

Rhona touches him with her left hand. "I don't wish to hear a meandering childish tale, Fergus. I will send for Bedeven to escort them back to Argadnel." Her voice always sounds like she's speaking through an electric synthesizer.

Did I hear right? Send us *back?*

Fergus echoes my thoughts. "But why? They've broken a very important Game rule, my dear. I'm waiting to hear them admit it. Were you not telling me that you were bored, Rhona? Perhaps the little Watcher can amuse us." He glares at me. "Well?"

I tell him how sick Mom is and how I promised her I'd find out how Dad was doing. "I wanted to — to see him so I could tell her he was fine."

"And how did you intend to find out how *fine* Sweeney was?"

"My mother, the Belldam Leto, is *dying,* sire and — er — madam. I'm just trying to help her. You both said how important it was to keep her at Argadnel, as the mediator between your two emissaries and Suzarain Elen, my sister, Summer. If Mom — the Belldam — dies, I'm afraid that everything will fall apart. I was hoping I could bring Dad, that is, Dennis Sweeney, to her — that seeing him would make her well again." I add hastily, "But it was all *my* idea. Neither she nor the Suzarain knew what I was doing."

"How did you plan to accomplish this, Watcher?"

I know he's baiting me, but I keep going. "I — uh — planned to transport to Earth and search him out."

Fergus looks contemplative, tapping his finger on his thin lips. "And?"

"I went to Earth and found him."

"So ... you've already been to the farm. And how was he?"

"He's sick, sire. He's dirty and thin — and he's forgotten me." I bite my lip hard. I *won't* cry.

"And I suppose that you raced here ahead of my Keeper? To get your version in first?"

I'm getting really nervous now. His questions sound interested, almost kindly.

My voice shaking, I say, "Yes, sire. I'm sorry —"

"Against my specific orders that you and the Belldam and the Suzarain were never to go to Earth again. You all agreed to it. It was made an official term of the Argadnel Game. *A rule.*" His voice has become a low growl.

"Mom is *sick* from missing Dad. If she could just *see* him, I *know* she'd get well again. I didn't think you'd mind. It seemed a small thing, really, if one looks at it in Game terms."

"Oh, that's what you think, is it? A small breach of the rules?"

"Well … yes … sire." I blink rapidly, waiting for the blast.

"So …" His voice continues in that low even growl, "Tamhas? You broke another of your promises to me, did you not?"

Tom shifts on my shoulder but doesn't speak.

I telepath to him, *Say* something, *Tom. We're dead otherwise.*

He says nothing.

"It's all my fault, sire," I say. "I made Tom come with me. Please, sire, could you return my father's memories to him and let him come to Argadnel to be with my mother? I'm sure she'll recover, and it would be *good* for Argadnel."

Fergus leans forward, his black eyes on my face. Slowly, and with an ugly smile, he says, "If the Belldam dies, Watcher, we can guide the young Suzarain ourselves."

I try to use my training to stay calm. But my heart is sinking to my knees. He's right. They don't really need Mom. At first they did — to keep the new little queen happy and to make sure Bedeven and Branwen kept to the rules. But now that Bedeven has wheedled his way into the confidence of Argadnelians like Gormala, Mom's *definitely* dispensable. The island may be too small and unimportant to take over completely, but if it's needed during one of their Games, Fergus and Rhona would sacrifice the whole place without a second thought. Argadnel is like a small property in Monopoly. You never know when you'll be able to use it for an important trade.

What should I say to convince him that Mom is important enough to keep alive? That it wouldn't harm anything if Dad was allowed to see her? I telepath to Tom.

But, once again, Tom doesn't answer. His eyes are hooded, dead looking. Why isn't he helping me? I know I have to try to be careful, to be diplomatic. I know I have to flatter Fergus, if nothing else.

I take a deep breath and blurt out, "How can you think about letting an innocent person die, Fergus, when you have it in your power to help her? How can you do something so — so wicked, so *evil?*"

Uh-oh, wrong thing to say. Not careful. Not diplomatic. And definitely *not* flattery. Why can't I keep my mouth shut? Tom's talons tighten on my shoulder.

I try to think what to say next, before Fergus explodes. His face is a dark mahogany red, his hands two hard fists on the arms of his chair. He's about to rise when Rhona sneers, "Surely you can't be serious, Watcher. The Belldam is dying because she *misses* someone? That's ridiculous." She smiles thinly.

I don't care what I say anymore. "Wouldn't you miss Fergus if he was taken away from you? Wouldn't *you* get sick from worry? If you really *love* him that is."

There's a hiss of sucked-in breath around the room. Rhona's face darkens to a dull purple. Her green collar leaps into orange flames that swirl around her head. "How dare you challenge me? Never, *ever* challenge

Rhona of Fomorii." With that, she stands and points at me. A shaft of sizzling light crackles off her scaly fingertips. "Get her out of my sight! She will die at star time." She sits down suddenly, as if she's surprised at her own words, and the look she gives me is a strange mixture of confusion and fury.

Fergus stares at Rhona, the anger drained out of him. I can't tell if it's because she's taken away his thunder by ordering my death, or if he's wondering why she didn't answer my question. He nods at someone behind me, who grabs my shoulders and aims me toward the far door with a hard shove. Another guard grabs Tom and tucks him under his arm, dropping a leather hood over his feathery head.

"No!" I cry.

Emma. Please. Not another word, Tom telepaths.

I telepath back, *Now you find your voice. Transport us back to Argadnel!*

I can't. They'll have closed off the portals.

We have to do something.

Challenge him! he calls to me.

Just as we're about to be marched away, I turn and shout around the guard's body. "Fergus of Cleave. In front of all your Players, I challenge you to a game of Fidchell. I'll beat the socks off you. And if I win —"

A hand clamps a smelly cloth over my nose and mouth. I try to breathe, but I melt away into silent blackness.

13

I push up through a thick murkiness into dim light. My nose and throat hurt. I roll over and throw up on the floor. Then I ready myself for the dark comfort of sleep, but someone's cold hand grasps my chin and yanks my head to one side. I blink blearily at Huw's long face hovering just above mine. The swirling blue tattoos on the left side of the Druvid's face make me feel sick again.

"You little fool," he snarls. "What are you playing at?"

I gasp out, "Nothing. I had to —"

His fingers tighten on my jaw. "Who *told* you to go to the man Sweeney? Who is controlling you? What are you really up to?"

I can't answer him. Everything is getting darker. Am I dying? My body seems to be floating up from the bed, the room spinning with shadows.

"Tell me," he hisses.

"Drop dead, freak," I whisper, and allow the hovering darkness to suck me away.

The next thing I hear is a distant swishing. Then

a gentle voice says, "You be fine soon enough."

I open my eyes to find Cill's ugly leaf-strewn face looking down at me.

She gently wipes my mouth clean with a warm damp ball of leaves that smells of lavender and lemon.

I sit up. "Tom." The room spins. I fall back with a groan.

"He be right here, don't you see?" Cill says, pointing at a low-hanging beam. Tom is crouched in a wooden birdcage too small for him, the leather hood still over his head. Other than the cage and the cot I'm lying on, the only piece of furniture is a small chair made of woven twigs.

"Oh, Tom," I say, holding my aching head. "What are we going to do?"

Tom mutters in my head, *He'll come, Creirwy. Your challenge was a good one. Be prepared. Don't give an inch. We now have nothing to lose.*

Cill washes the floor with great care, then gathers up her bowl and prepares to leave.

Can I trust her or is she a spy for Fergus, this bundle of leaves and woven grass — all gray and brown with threads of dark green? I decide it doesn't matter.

"Will you send Fergus a message for me?" I ask.

I can't read her small red eyes, and her facial expression never changes. "I not one to do that. No one listen to me. No one notice me. I once be daughter of king, but now I just slave."

My face must show my disappointment, for she reaches over and touches my shoulder. "I be nearby."

She raps on the door. It swings open and she's gone. I have to think. I have to plan. First of all, I have to free Tom. Maybe he can fly to safety. At least one of us should try to make it out alive.

Very slowly, I raise myself onto my elbows. My head woozes, but it doesn't fall off or spin like a top. I try standing up. My legs belong to someone else. I concentrate, one step at a time, around and around the circular room until I get my balance. There's one small window and I stop to look out. We're off the ground, but how high I can't tell, for there's no vista to look at — just graceful leaf fronds and ropy vines. Now and again, I can see the hairy brown bark of the tree trunks that support this tangled mess.

When I'm certain my head is solidly on my shoulders, I push the small pallet bed under the birdcage. Just as I lift it off its hook, the door swings open again and Huw strides in.

"What do you want now?" I ask.

"Get down," he says sharply.

"I have to get Tom out of here," I say, putting the cage on the bed.

"Leave it. Come with me," Huw snaps. "Don't worry, I'll bring you right back."

Go with him, Emma, Tom telepaths. *I'll be okay. Don't get him angry.*

Huw pushes me through the door.

"Where are you taking me?"

He grabs my arm and drags me down a wooden corridor damp with moss and oozing water. It smells like a root cellar. I sneeze twice. He's tall, so I'm on my tiptoes all the way. We swing around a corner, go down another hallway, up a set of stairs carved out of solid wood and along a hall heavily covered with elaborately painted carvings of fish and other sea creatures.

He pushes open a silver door and we enter a high-arched cave room. The ceiling and walls are dark blue and dimly lit, with wavery splatters of light dappling across them. The stone floor is black and glossy, divided by a long, narrow waterway. The water is covered in flowers — striped, spotted, thick-veined — some standing on stems above the water, some half-immersed, others centered on red- or blue-splashed lily pads with small purple toadlike creatures cricking and leaping back and forth across them. Every now and again, the smooth water is rippled by an ugly fat-lipped fish with pale blotchy scales. A gentle burbling fills the room and echoes with a hollow emptiness that reminds me of an indoor swimming pool. On the other side of the narrow channel is a stone seat with wide curving arms of giant conch shells.

I stand, hands on hips. "Why did you bring me here?"

"She wants to talk to you," Huw says. He's now wearing a tunic of plain orange eelskin, his leggings a dark blue, tucked into soft, short snakeskin boots. He stands in front of me, tattooed arms crossed over his chest, long thin legs apart.

I stare him down. His eyes change every time I see him, sometimes jet black, other times a strange, cold gray-blue. He grins. I tilt my chin higher. I hate him, remembering how he chased Summer, Tom and me across the farm fields as we desperately tried to make it to the circle gate.

"You appear to have set up a small Game of your own," he says, breaking into my thoughts. "Whatever it is, I hope you're prepared to take the consequences."

I bristle. "I'm not involved in any *Game*. I just want to make sure my father's safe and that my mother gets well again."

"Mmm. Is that what you *think*? Then perhaps, Watcher, this new Game goes on *around* you."

"What Game?"

"You had better be wary," Huw says. "There are those who seek something, and I want to know what it is."

I don't understand him. "Rhona and Fergus's Game is over. They're partners now. If a different Game does come up, they'll be allies, won't they? Besides, I'm not important enough to be involved in anything they do."

"Then why are you here?" he asks with a malevolent grin.

"I just told you why," I snap.

He strolls toward the narrow waterway, his curious green echo hanging in the air behind him. "Their Game will never end, Watcher. They're like two of your Eorthe panthers, wary, uneasy, yet strongly attracted as well. He had this chamber built just for her — to make her feel at home."

"Maybe he loves her," I mutter, but I don't add "as amazing as *that* is."

"Oh, I doubt that … infatuated, perhaps — but mostly he's trying to dupe her into believing he cares more than he does, to keep her off guard. She, in turn, *pretends* that this is all she needs." He laughs. "No, this is just a temporary lull in the Game. One that can be broken at any time by either of them."

"Did you tell her that Fergus is duping her?"

"She's no fool."

"But you're her Druvid. Isn't it your duty to tell her?"

"You're wrong there, Watcher. Lately I've learned to keep my own counsel. I watch and wait."

"But surely you *have* to tell her that Fergus isn't to be trusted. Your job is to be loyal to her and only her." I know I'm going to regret saying this.

He raises one eyebrow. "I am a Celtoi. My ancestors came from Eorthe. They bred with other beings from other worlds, but our blood is still Celtoi blood. I follow my own way."

Shocked, I say, "Does Rhona know you're not loyal to her?"

"My dear child, you come from a place that *pretends* to honor fair play and loyalty above all else." He sweeps his hand through the air. "The worlds I travel through honor the Game above all else. Fair play and the Game rarely coincide."

"Does that mean —," I begin, but I am distracted when the strip of water begins to undulate. The flowers separate and a dark creature slides just under the water. A green-silvered tail slaps the surface, like a beaver before diving. With a sudden surge, two slim arms appear, followed by a rush of foam and bubbles as the creature lifts out of the water, twisting quickly to sit on the stone chair. It's Rhona. Her long silver hair flows down her back. She pulls it up and lets it fall with a wet slap against her blue skin. Tiny shells wound through its tendrils click and tinkle.

She lifts her face, breathes the damp air in the room and sighs. "I shall go home to Fomorii soon, and I shall spend a full mooncrest lying in my perfumed sea bed breathing in the smell of my beloved ocean. This is pleasant, but … small. Poor Fergus. He tried." She looks around disdainfully.

Huw says, "Madam, I've brought you the Watcher. We'd best move quickly. Fergus will soon be looking for her."

Rhona looks me up and down with her strange

mismatched eyes. I wonder what she can see out of the fish eye, with its thick opalescent whiteness. The long olive-green tail lifts above the water, then swirls through it. I'm mesmerized. I'm actually seeing Rhona as a ... *mermaid?* One hand is dead gray and scaly. I also notice pale red slits that ripple open and shut along her neck. Her torso is covered in wide translucent fish scales that rise as high as the fluttering gills and surround them in a deep bluish swirl. She is so fantastic looking, I can't take my eyes off her.

"I have decided not to have you killed," she says in her synthesizer voice. "You will be returned to Argadnel, where you will remain under Bedeven's watchful eye."

"I doubt Fergus will agree to that," I say, "although it would be fine with me. I'd soon have to go back to the Watchers Campan anyway. I promised Histal —"

"Histal, the Beholder, *really* knows that you are here?" she asks. Her tail swirls through the water, as if she's trying to be nonchalant.

"Well, not exactly *here*," I admit. "But I have permission to — uh — do some exploration on my own."

Huw laughs. "*Someone* is not going to be pleased, is he? Better you than me when he finds out."

"Leave her be," Rhona orders.

I frown at Rhona. Why is she being *almost* nice? So I ask, "Why are you sparing my life?"

She shrugs. "Perhaps, as a thank you, you might share something with me."

"What?"

She looks at Huw. "Leave us."

He stares back at her, his face darkening.

Just as she is about to speak again, there's a loud thudding on the door behind me. Huw opens it, says something to the urgent voice on the other side, and closes it again. "He's on his way to the Watcher's cell, madam."

"Damnation," Rhona cries. "Take her away. But when he's done with her, I want her back here, do you understand?" With that, she slides into the water, her tail slaps once, hard enough to spray us, and she's gone.

Huw returns me to the cell, where Tom is still crouched inside the wooden cage. As Huw shoves me into the room, I say, "What was she going to ask me to do for her?"

He growls, "Say nothing about seeing her if you value the life of your owl." And he's gone.

14

Tom asks. "Where did he take you?"

"Rhona wants something from me — I have no idea what. I'll tell you more when I get you out of there," I reply, pulling at the thin wires that tie the cage door shut. One of them cuts my finger. "Ouch! Stupid thing. That Fergus. I *hate* him!"

"And you, Watcher, are a *tribulation* to me, as well," says a voice behind me.

I whirl around. Fergus seems amused, rather than angry. He takes the cage, opens it, lifts Tom out and removes the hood. Man and owl look at each other eye to eye.

Fergus shakes his head. "You, my old friend, are a mystery to me. I know you would never have gone against me before you met this one. I'd have staked my life on it. What is this loyalty you have to this small creature?" Fergus always talks loudly, as if his listener is across the street. It hurts my aching head.

"This is what I am meant to do, sire. I cannot change it," Tom says.

"Even if you die for it?"

The two continue to stare at each other intently, and it dawns on me that they're telepathing — and they've blocked me out. Why? And why was Tom so silent in the throne room, leaving me to take on Fergus and Rhona by myself? What's going on between them?

Suddenly Fergus shakes his head, throws Tom into the air and shouts out loud, "No. I have fulfilled that duty!"

He's heading for the door but stops, turns and glares at Tom. He says, "That was a long time ago, Tamhas. I have done what I agreed to — I owe nothing more."

I have no idea what he's talking about, so I try to help. "When we first arrived, Rhona said she was willing to send us back to Argadnel. Couldn't you just do that? Who would it harm?"

Fergus's blunt finger almost touches my nose. "You have broken *my* rules. Not *hers*. I'm judged by my Players on my ability to control. No one can keep this much power if they don't govern by the *Game rules*."

"But —"

He dons a maudlin face. "You've done something very troublesome, Watcher. I have no personal desire to see you die. I like your gumption. But even so, you cannot be seen to break my rules and get away with it."

Tom says, "Emma challenged you to a game of Fidchell, sire. Surely ..."

Fergus holds his hand up for silence. Then he paces back and forth. He puts a finger on his lips, thinks, nods, then narrows his eyes. "Yes … yes. You challenged me to a game of Fidchell. If I refuse that, my Players may wonder why."

He glowers at the floor, then claps his hands so loud I almost jump out of my skin. "All right," he booms. "Let's strike a bargain. We'll play one round of Fidchell. If you lose, which you *will,* you both die. If you *win* —" He laughs. "What does it matter? You couldn't even beat me at that beginner's game we played on the farm."

"But if I *do* win —"

"Name your prize, Watcher. Anything you want."

I throw caution to the wind. Fear does that to me. Makes me a bit crazy. Besides, Fergus is right. I'll probably lose. But when I played Fidchell with him on the farm, I came very close to beating him each time. I've been in Watcher training for months now. Surely I've learned enough strategy skills to have some kind of chance. Either way, I may as well ask for it all.

"First, whatever happens, Tom stays with me and you don't harm my mother, dad or sister. They had nothing to do with what I've done. If I lose, *only I die.* If I win, then my father not only gets his memories back and is allowed to come to Argadnel, but you also tell me where my mother's human child is and allow the child to return to my mother."

I hear Tom's strangled voice in my head. *Oh, Emma, why didn't you tell me you'd made another promise to your mother? Will you never learn?*

Silence hangs in the room like an executioner's ax. Fergus stares out the window for a moment, then turns and crosses his arms over his chest. Suddenly his laughter booms around the room.

He wipes his eyes. "You are truly amazing. When I was on Eorthe, the minute you walked into my room with Branwen, I knew you were going to cause trouble. And after you did your best to create havoc *there,* I allowed you to go to Argadnel with the woman and the little queen. I protected the man Sweeney because you begged me to. Why? Because I liked your mettle. Few creatures stand up to me and live to tell it. I should have known it wouldn't be long before you'd be messing around in things that didn't concern you."

He grins. "You have an inner core of recklessness. You leap into things without thinking. And that mouth of yours ... well ... it seems you still spend too much time talking yourself *into* trouble and not thinking your way out of it. Your trainer, Histal, must be at his wits' end." He blasts out a huge chuckle.

"He is a bit frustrated with me," I admit sheepishly. "Sire, will you not agree to play for the stakes I've laid out? I'm the one who started all of this. If I lose, I'm prepared to pay for it." Fergus is hard to pin down, one minute angry, the next acting like a kindly uncle. Either way, he's totally untrustworthy, but I still have to try.

He throws his hands into the air. "You go to your death, Watcher. It almost saddens me to do this to one with so much spunk. But … *you will not win.*"

"You have little to lose or to gain with this game, sire. But I have *everything* — to lose *and* to gain." My voice is raspy with emotion. "I *have* to beat you, you see."

"Oh Great Ochain, save her. She's killing us," Tom whispers.

Fergus chuckles again, pats me on the head and says, "This is too good to pass up."

He knocks on the door and Mathus walks in carrying two wooden boxes — Fergus obviously planned to play Fidchell all along.

Mathus puts one box on the floor and touches a medallion in its middle, and it springs up into a small table. He puts the second box on top and bows to Fergus, who looks at me with a Cheshire cat grin and says, "Shall we begin?"

15

A knock on the door surprises us all. It's Huw. "I saw Mathus waiting with the game board. I wish to observe. Queen Rhona would expect it."

Fergus looks as if he's about to refuse, then nods. "Why not? I don't mind an audience watching me win at Fidchell."

Mathus opens the game box. Fergus grabs the chair, motions to me to sit on the edge of the bed and puts the table between us. As soon as I look at the board, I realize this Fidchell game isn't the one we played on Earth. It's much bigger and the tokens aren't the same. They're clear glass lumps with vague indiscernible shapes. The trees, buildings, rivers, deserts and mountains are three-dimensional, but they keep altering shape as I look at them. When I lean over the board, I feel like a bird flying high above tiny but very real landscapes that flow into one another, ever moving, ever changing. Oh criminy, what have I done?

"I — er — I thought the board would be the one

we played on at the farmhouse," I say, my voice quaking.

"What would be the fun in that?" Fergus says, grinning wickedly. "Besides, that was a younger's game, not a grown-up Fidchell board."

My mouth is so dry I can hardly speak. I never thought to demand the same board we played on in the farmhouse. "What do we do?"

Fergus says lightly, "Oh, much the same as with the other board, little Watcher. Like all games in life, Fidchell can get boring if the board never changes. Mathus is the Creator of New Boards."

"Is *that* why you never lose?"

Fergus glares at me, then growls between his teeth, "Take care how far you push me, Watcher. Where would be the sport if I could never lose? Mathus sets games that can outwit even me. But I am the best player in all the worlds."

"If I do win, just by chance, will you agree to my terms?" I ask in a high piping voice.

He shrugs. "We will discuss them *if you win,* which of course you won't, so it doesn't really matter. But I will abide by them — with minor alterations. Come, let us begin. Mathus, explain."

I'm not sure I understand what Fergus just said. Has he agreed to my terms or not? But Mathus is talking and I have to pay attention.

"This is a form of Fidchell that we call a Seeker Game. There are five worlds on this board," he says.

"A single amulet is here in this farthest realm. It is this that you seek." He touches a small ebony box, which sinks into the game board and vanishes. "We start here — in this world I call Manx, which remains stationary. You must find the amulet and take it to a place that will show itself when you draw near it."

He points to a green and brown world thick with trees. Cleave?

"How can I take the amulet to a place I have no way of seeing?" I ask, my voice trembling.

"This and the other worlds you'll encounter you can't know about until you arrive there," he says. "Even then, you can't be sure they're what you think they are."

"This is gobbledygook!" I cry. "It makes no sense."

He continues in a smooth tone. "As in all Fidchell games, there are a number of obstacles, puzzles and skirmishes to face and win before you reach the amulet, claim it as your own and find the finish point."

I'm still trying to figure out how I can move about in the game if I don't know where I'm going.

Fergus rubs his hands together. "You go first, little one. I'll move past you in no time."

He touches the largest of his glass players and it becomes a kingly figure. He has nine other tokens, which he touches in turn. Nine soldiers appear, dressed like the men and women I saw in the big throne room.

The last time we played, I had four men including myself. This time, I have six. Like Fergus I touch each one, but only two change into recognizable shapes — the first to a tiny creature with long fingers and large eyes, like I had in the last game, and the second is a small owl. Tom and me? Is this Mathus's idea of a joke? My other four are cloaked, faceless figures. Suddenly Mathus picks all four up and drops them on the board. They vanish.

"Hey!" I cry. "That's not fair."

"You must gather the others as you go, along with a number of small game pieces — a sword, a key and a looking glass ... among others."

"Does my main token have the same powers as the last game?" I ask. "Or has that changed, too? Maybe I should wear handcuffs and a blindfold while I play!"

"You have the same powers — more or less — but you may find that you're a little more agile this time."

"Oh that's good," I say nastily. "And the other four? Where did they go? Who are they?"

Mathus shrugs. "You must find them. They will become what you make them."

I have no idea what he's talking about, but I know that as the tiny Watcher, I have certain abilities the king doesn't have, which I hope will compensate for the number of soldiers that surround him.

Who am I kidding? This game is already over and it hasn't even begun.

Because it's so confusing and because I'm so anxious, I have trouble hitting my stride. When I touch the little Watcher figure, everything on the board swirls — tiny worlds pop up and vanish again. The board is a living thing. That unnerves me. All I can think is, if I fail, I die. And if I die, will they also kill Tom? What about Mom and Dad? And Summer? She'll be left alone to face that terrible Gormala and others like her.

I have to concentrate. I *have* to win.

My hand trembles as I move my two players through an ash-gray forest. There I pick up a third player, who remains unformed. I'm so distracted that, within the first few minutes, I almost lose the tiny owl to a king's player that I should have spotted right away. The soldier skulks along behind us, and just as it's about to leap out from behind a tree, I manage to get my little figures and the owl to safety inside some kind of pointed building.

That close call forces me to focus — I have to make it a good fight. Soon, I completely forget about the tiny prison cell in Cleave. The gray forest melts into a dark hole that we have to fight our way out of. As soon as we do that, I smell the rush of hot sand in a desert wind that twists into the winding force of a deep river. Under a dark misty light, I move to the loneliness of a windswept mountain. Each world is more elusive than the last and I can barely keep up. Somehow I've picked up three non-player pieces — a small sword, a tiny cup and a silver bottle. I've also gathered all four of my figures around the owl and me, but they remain indistinct — all I can make out is a hand here or a wing there.

"Why aren't my figures taking shape?"

Mathus shrugs. "I cannot answer you while the game is in play."

Fergus takes that opportunity to slide one of his soldier tokens past me.

I don't know how long we play. It feels like days. I've fought tokens that popped up out of the undergrowth, I've battled through a throng of birdlike creatures, I've hidden in forests, and I've slid past Fergus's tokens that appeared out of nowhere — but I think I know where the amulet is hidden and am now determinedly winding my way toward it. I keep only a small part of my consciousness on the whereabouts of the king and his men — I concentrate on getting past all the hazards — and to my utter amazement, I do find the amulet's ebony box first. Inside is a small carved snake with a wolf's head.

When I grab it and begin to travel down the other side of the board, I glance at Fergus. He shows no sign of being upset. In fact, his eyes seem to be glittering with good humor.

What does *that* mean? What does he know that I don't? Why am I sure he let me reach the amulet before him, that he is somehow manipulating me?

I've been moving my pack of figures back the way we came. For some reason — I don't know why — I feel compelled to move my little gang in another direction. When I turn them away from my set path, I glance once more at Fergus. He no longer looks amused, and a deep flush stains his neck. I look over at Tom who is resting on the window ledge. He winks one eye slowly. I notice that Fergus's men are scattered across the board, not much use to him. Yes! I've thrown him off!

It takes Fergus a long time to make his next few moves. Up to now, I've barely finished my move before he makes his. I decide to change direction, backtrack, then return the same way. He tries the same thing, but his men can't catch me. Yet.

The game speeds up. Unformed tokens I hadn't seen before — perhaps they'd been hidden by the trees on the board — circle me and my men but don't hinder us. Whose tokens are they? It doesn't matter. I don't have time to worry about them. I move quickly, Fergus moves, I move, he moves ... and suddenly my six little players are headed toward a dark-brown square that has risen out of a misty corner. I race past the king figure with the amulet, the little owl and my other figures close behind. I don't remember much after that. I just keep moving. Finally, Fergus and I stare at the board, stunned.

It's over.

And I've won.

16

Fergus slowly raises his eyes and gazes at Mathus with a perplexed frown. For the first time, Mathus looks uneasy. Huw leaves the room with a gleam in his eye, shutting the door silently behind him, no doubt to tell Rhona that I beat Fergus.

I'm too scared to say anything. I glance at Tom. Even for an owl, his eyes are huge. I feel as if all the blood has drained from my head.

Fergus breaks the awful silence. Patiently, he says, "Mathus, did you plan this Seeker Game so the Watcher would win?"

"Of course not, sire." Mathus sounds appalled. "I would never do such a thing."

With a loud crash, the game flies across the room. "Then how did this happen?" Fergus bellows.

I flinch, but Mathus stands his ground.

"Once a Fidchell board is set, I have no control over it, sire. You know it can be used only for random play."

"But how could this … this inexperienced *creature* beat me?" blusters Fergus.

"Perhaps she outwitted you, sire, just as she outpowered your players on the board." Mathus looks innocent, but I can see a flash of defiance in his eyes.

"Outwitted me? Outpowered *me?*" Fergus says. "I've won dozens of true Games — I've gained three more worlds in less than twelve mooncrests. *No one* can outwit or outpower me."

"Perhaps —" I begin.

I hear Tom's warning and stop.

"Perhaps ... what?" Fergus grinds out.

I shrink away from his distorted features and say in a small voice, "Perhaps it was a fluke? Just luck?"

Fergus thinks a moment, then stands up and says, more calmly, "Yes, that must be it. Whatever this word is — *fluke*. A lucky mistake?"

I nod.

He lifts one shoulder. "We'll have to play again."

Is this how it works? He gets to play until he wins? Anger flushes my face.

"No way. We had a deal!" I stand up and face him. "No matter how it happened, I still won."

Silence falls like a thick blanket. I stand as still as Fergus of Cleave, my head high, my face as set as I can make it. He glares at me. I glare right back. If he shouts again, I'll probably faint.

I ignore warnings in my head from Tom to be quiet. "Sire, I know you are angry now," I say, "but I also know that you are a Player of your word. That the rules for a Game Player of honor are as important as the Game itself, even in a mere game of Fidchell."

Fergus's face is black with anger. He raises one hand and I force myself not to step back.

His voice is choked. "You were lucky, that's all."

I nod. "True. But I had my family's lives in my hands, so I had to win, don't you see?"

"I've never had a family and I rule many kingdoms. And what should this so-called family matter to you? They aren't even of your *blood*."

"But they're of my *heart*." I *won't* let him see me cry. "I'm responsible for them being safe and happy. And I know you'll honor your word."

We stand eye to eye. I don't know what Fergus sees in mine, but he pushes his hands through his hair, walks to the window and looks out. "You are a curious little creature. But I *am* a Player of my word. When I set terms, they are set."

Unless you can get away with *un*-setting them, I think, but keep my mouth shut for a change.

He turns and leers at me. "I've been rather bored of late. Why not an amusing diversion? Rhona and I have big plans for a War Game, but that won't be for a while yet. Meanwhile I can send you off to play Fidchell ... for real. And this time you'll be lucky to survive."

I find this toothy smile as scary as his anger. "What do you mean?"

He cocks his head. "I will let you go ... for now. So you can find your mother's Eorthe child. How's that?"

"Find her? You mean you won't bring her here? You said you'd agreed to my terms ... except for a few minor —"

"*I* set the rules!" he shouts, slamming his hand on the table. "You listen."

I shut up.

Fergus growls, "Your quest will be to *seek out* this Sweeney child. You will bring it to me within one mooncrest. Then and *only* then will I give you the way to Sweeney's memories. A *real* Seeker Game, you see? You win this Game and I'll help you with the Sweeney problem." He shrugs and smiles wickedly. "It's the only bargain I'll strike. It's open for ten breaths."

Mathus intones, "Ten, nine, eight —"

"Do you agree?"

"Seven, six, five —"

Tom whispers in my head, *Emma, listen — before you —*

"Four three, two ..." Mathus says ominously.

"Yes. Yes, I agree!"

17

What have I done? One mooncrest is only eight Earth days. I hear a small snort. When I look up at Mathus, a secretive smile hovers on his lips. He turns quickly and points at the scattered game pieces. They rise and float over to the small wooden box, then drop neatly into it without being touched. The lid snaps shut. When Mathus flicks his hand at the small table, it folds itself into a second box. Both rise and settle on his outstretched hands. In an instant, they shrink to the size of two decks of cards, which he then puts in a leather pouch.

I'll never get used to what they call "magick." Histal says that it's not "magic" at all — it's simply matter moving matter, no different than picking something up and moving it with your hands. But I grew up on Earth, where everything is heavy and plodding and little is truly magical, even for those who wish it so.

Fergus says, "Mathus … the brooch."

Mathus opens his hand. On his palm is a brooch — a small posy of brown, dove gray and purple feathers gathered around the long pointed head of a wolf whose silver body winds around a muddy-colored oval stone, ending in a curled snake's tail. Fergus takes it and clicks it with his thumb. A small dagger as sharp as a fillet knife snaps out. I step back quickly.

Fergus grins and presses the brooch again. The knife vanishes. He pins the brooch to my sleeve, saying, "I'll allow you one weapon. This can also be shown to those who doubt our connection in the Game. It is the emblem of a Cleave Player. To win the Seeker Game, you must find the child as well as smaller Game pieces, as in Fidchell. Let's see, I'll make them a shield, a silver talisman, a key, an airship or other vehicle, a mirror or magnifying glass and a mask."

I ask, "How do you know I'll even find these things? Do you plant them?"

He gives a sneaky laugh. "You clearly are bursting with questions. I'll allow you five — but we won't count the last two, as they are not the right kind of question."

I look at Tom. His eyes are half shut, as if he's closed himself down again.

"He can't help you," Mathus snarls.

I take a deep breath and ask, "Well then, where do I find this child?"

Fergus guffaws. "Wasted question. *Answer* ... how should we know?"

"But you're the ones who took her."

Mathus answers, "We don't do such menial work. A Taker removed the child."

"A Taker? What's that?"

Fergus grins. "Question two? *Answer* ... they are used when needed. And paid off in kind."

"What does *that* mean?"

"Question three ..." He's really enjoying this. His face is as bright and full of mischief as a child's. "*Answer* ... they're given a changeling. They put it in the place of the other younger, which they take as payment."

"These Takers got my mother's child as *payment?*"

"One assumes so," Fergus says brightly. "That's standard. That was a question but I won't count it." He smiles a patronizing smile.

"And what does a Taker do with the child he steals?"

"Question four," Fergus hoots. "This is most enjoyable. But, Watcher, you're wasting your questions. *Answer* ... A Taker is allowed to do with the younger whatever they wish."

I look at Tom, but he just looks miserable.

Suddenly it clicks into place. "Oh, now I get it. I'm allowed five questions, but you don't have to answer them truthfully."

Mathus says firmly, "They've been answered truthfully, if skimpily. If you wish a more elaborate response, I can give it to you, but it won't help. Yes, the children removed by the Takers become their property to do with as they wish. It's our understanding, from hearsay of course, that the Takers sell the youngers as workers and get paid in riches, food, land — anything they can't grow, develop or make in their own world. No one knows much about the Takers. They do a needed service in disposing of the awkwardness of trying to place all sorts of youngers from different worlds. Some youngers are even human — *they* are nearly *impossible* to get rid of."

I can't believe what I'm hearing. "You hire Takers to put a changeling in place of another child and their *payment* is the kidnapped child? That's *horrible*."

"That is enough information, I think," Fergus says calmly. "And your opinion is irrelevant."

"I still have one last question," I say, knowing that, whatever it is, it won't help me figure out where to begin my search.

"Well?" Fergus asks archly.

"Why don't you care about what happens to the children taken from their mothers and fathers?"

"That is not an information-seeking question," he says, his cheeriness gone. "The Game begins as soon as you and Tamhas depart Cleave."

I decide to goad him. "Will you tell Rhona about this Seeker Game?"

"She has nothing to do with it."

"But she's your partner in any new Game, isn't she?"

"This is not our Game, Watcher, it's *yours,*" he growls.

"Sire," Mathus offers, "surely Rhona will want to know why these two weren't killed."

Fergus pretends he hasn't heard his Druvid.

Mathus continues. "Perhaps, sire, you could tell her that you sent the Watchers on ahead to the new War Game site to scout for both of you. In exchange for their lives."

Fergus says hopefully, "Do you think she'll believe that? I can't afford to fall out with her. We have this new Game set to begin in two mooncrests and I need her and her best Players."

Mathus shrugs. "Does it matter? You are the supreme ruler of Cleave. It's your decision." Why are they talking so freely in front of us? Is it because Fergus is used to talking in front of Tom? Or is it because I'm irrelevant, like Fergus said.

A knock on the door and Mathus swings it open. Cill is on the other side. "Oh, I thought you gone, sire. Queen Rhona want girl Watcher summoned to her. *Alone,*" she says in her crackly voice.

Fergus gets a hunted look on his face. "Why?"

Mathus says, "Perhaps she wants the enjoyment of seeing them put to death. The Beheader is ready at all times."

Beheader? My neck suddenly feels small and bare.

Mathus continues, "Perhaps you will have to kill these two just to placate her."

"No!" I cry. "You *promised*." I point to the brooch on my sleeve. "You would never go back on a bargain set with *this*." I'm not sure this is true, but it's worth a try.

Fergus nods slowly. "The Watcher is right. I am bound to uphold my bargain."

Mathus raises his eyebrows. "But, sire, I suspect Rhona feels she has every right to be involved."

Fergus snarls, "I am the ruler here. She'll just have to accept my decision."

"Or you could lie," Mathus says.

"Or I could lie." Fergus's familiar wicked smile returns. "I will say these two have been sent as scouts to our next Game zone. It's a dangerous place and they'd probably be killed, so no doubt Rhona would approve of that. Meanwhile, let's get these two on their way. You, Watcher, have one mooncrest in which to accomplish this task. I will send a time keeper with you."

"I don't want one of your *people* tagging along. They'll try to screw things up. That's not fair." I'm not sure, but I think I hear Tom choking.

"Don't push me, Watcher," Fergus threatens. "Here … you …" He points at Cill, then at Mathus who clips a gold disc with black markings onto her knobby wrist. "You will go with them. I can replace you later if you don't do the job right. Keep a close watch and report often. The Seeker Game ends in one mooncrest. Use the time marker. Someone will also keep time here. Understood?"

I didn't think Cill was capable of looking surprised, but the leaves fan out on her face, and her tiny eyes stretch. "Me? Go with Watchers? To other worlds? I be chosen?"

"You three will leave now. The Seeker Game has officially begun," Fergus says.

Mathus lifts one hand, and a sharp pain goes through my head. I feel as if I'm being pulled by my hair through a keyhole at a thousand miles an hour.

18

We're back in the border cave between Cleave and Fomorii.

Tom is lying on his back, talons straight up in the air. I panic and lunge toward him, but he says in a surly voice, "I'm okay. Dizzy. Mathus is a lousy transporter. Worse than you and that's saying something. Leave me be for a bit."

The bundle of leaves next to me stirs, and a thin crackly voice says, "Ooo dear. I be all inside out."

I look Cill over. "You look, uh, the way you did before, I *think*."

She presses her gnarled fingers to her face and moans. "Thank be to Oak-Looh."

The opening to Cleave is closed off by a wall of stone.

Tom rights himself, shakes his feathers and says, "So? Where do we go from here?"

"What do you care?" I snap.

"What's that supposed to mean?"

"You weren't much help back there. Why didn't you *help* me?"

"I *couldn't*," he says miserably. "Mathus telepathed to me the whole time that he'd kill you where you stood if I didn't keep out of it." His voice breaks. "I had *no choice,* Emma. I had to hope you could pull it off on your own. They were the worst moments of my life!"

I rub my hands through my hair. "I'm sorry, Tom. I'm all mixed up. Let me think a minute."

He watches me silently.

"I guess we go back to Argadnel first. Tell Mom I've —"

"I don't think that's a good idea, Emma," Tom says after a quick glance at Cill.

Cill says, "No worry talk. I not *ever* reveal." She presses a gnarled finger to her lips to seal her promise.

"Why isn't going to Argadnel a good idea?" I ask Tom.

"Bedeven could trap you, threaten to hurt your mother to keep you there. Fergus won't tell him where we've gone, that's for sure. Why would Rhona want to send you home, unless she, Huw and Bedeven are up to something?"

"And whatever they're up to, Fergus isn't included," I say, remembering that she was about to ask me for something when I had to leave her water chamber to face Fergus.

"Things aren't going too smoothly in Gamers' paradise," he chuckles. "I think we should seek out the child now — before Bedeven, Rhona and Huw figure out what's happened."

"But what could they want from me?" I ask. "I have nothing they'd be interested in. I think they're all just bored and making up intrigues for something to do." I shake my head. "Even so, I have to tell Mom I saw Dad. It will give her strength. And Summer has to know what's happening, too, so she won't worry. If she starts to fret, Bedeven will really get suspicious. Don't worry, I'll stay invisible."

"Summer will beg to come with you," he says.

"Please, Tom. Just a quick visit. I won't be able to concentrate if I don't see Mom."

He sighs. "Cill and I *can't* be invisible unless you make us so, and then only for a very short time — if we're right next to you. Damn this feathered pincushion cunning. If Cill and I are captured, they'll hold us until you're *forced* to appear."

"I'll hide you in my room. They won't even know we're back."

"What about the time we waste? We only have one mooncrest — eight days — for this Game."

Cill looks at the gold time marker on her wrist. "One mooncrest — eight Earthly day. Twenyfourth Earthly hours in one Earthly day. That make one and niney-two Earthly hours. We use up one Earthly hour and one quarter. That leave —"

"Okay. I get it. Look, we'll be really quick. I'm not changing my mind," I say.

Tom lowers his heavy eyelids and sinks his head deep in his shoulders. "Why do I bother arguing? I never win. If I was Tom the human or even Tamhas, I'd —"

"You'd still help me," I say earnestly.

He looks at me and, for just a second, I see Tom's intense dark eyes. I reach over to put my hand on his heavy shoulder. Instead, my hand brushes the soft feathers of a wing.

"Oh, Tom," I whisper. "What have I got us into?"

"Time is flashing by. Come on. Let's get this visit over with so we can begin the Game."

He flies to the small table, removes the silver disc with his beak and gives it to me — the purple light streams upward. "We all have to be touching."

Cill grabs my arm. Her hand is dry and leathery. I hold on to Tom's wing. He puts his head in the thin stream of light and off we go — straight up through the cave's ceiling.

19

We're in my garret room in the tower. Cill checks her time marker. "We use up one more Earthly hour now and —"

I lean into her face. "Don't keep talking about it, okay? Just let us know every six hours or so. I'll go nuts if you do it all the time."

Cill nods and scuttles to the door. "I got good ears. I let you know if anyone coming."

Tom looks at me and smiles. "I know I sound like Cill, but you've got one hour to see your mother and get back here. We still have to figure out how to begin this Game."

"Okay," I say. "I'll be right back."

I transmute invisible. Cill gasps. "If I could do that, I teach my people and we all vanish away from Cleave."

I open the door and slide out into the dark hallway. I run quickly down the curving stairs and through the serpentine corridors of the castel. But I'm brought up short when I turn a sharp left. Three circles of light are moving toward me. Under the hovering glow spheres are three people. I immediately recognize Gormala and Bedeven, but the third person is ... Huw? How did he get here so fast? And why?

"If you would tell me why you need the Watcher here, I might be able to understand the urgency," Huw is saying. He and Bedeven are wearing gray chitons that flutter around their ankles. The glow spheres give all three of them a blue pallor. "Does it have anything to do with the crop of Stygia Mantles? Argadnel will reap a goodly profit from them, but what has that to do with the young Watcher?"

Bedeven tilts his head as if paying respect, but his words belie his action. "I cannot say. If Queen Rhona does not wish to keep you informed, Druvid, I cannot help you. All I know is she's furious that Fergus sent the young Watcher and Tamhas on this implausible scouting mission. It could take some time to track them down."

"So a crack *is* forming in the alliance," Gormala says with a self-satisfied smirk.

Huw turns on her. "You may leave us, mistress. Your opinions are of no value."

She stops almost in front of me, bristling with anger. I press my back against the wall. "I have every right to be here — and have opinions. I am the representative of Suzarain Elen and I —"

Huw sneers, "Oh, is that your pretense? *Go!*"

Gormala pulls her black chiton to one side, as if touching him would contaminate her, and sails regally down the narrow hall.

Bedeven sniggers. "As trustworthy as a ringed ferret. All teeth and nastiness, that one. But she has her uses."

Huw puts one hand on Bedeven's shoulder. "You, Queen Rhona and I must be together in this, my friend — if, in fact, our queen is designing a Game against Fergus. We cannot keep secrets from each other, or things will go amiss."

Bedeven moves out from under the hand and bows. "We must find the Watcher and hold her. That is all you need to know. When our queen is ready to confide in you, she'll do so."

It's Huw's turn to bristle. "*I am Rhona's Druvid,* closer to her than anyone. I think perhaps you are gulling her with some fantasy goings-on here at Argadnel. If you have nothing to back it up, I shall enjoy watching you fed to her razor sharks."

With that, he turns on his heel and goes back the way they came. Bedeven is now so close to me that I can smell his dense fishy stink. I try not to breathe. He looks at Huw's retreating back, then he grins widely and walks past me with a jaunty swagger. I sigh and take a deep breath, but catch it when a silent figure emerges from the shadows of a deep archway. It's Branwen, wrapped head to toc in dark brown, only her eyes visible. She waits for a moment, then moves quickly down the hall in the direction Huw took.

20

What is this all about? And what do Bedeven and Gormala need me here for? I run as fast as I can to Mom's room, open the door a crack and slide through.

Her bed is empty.

I quickly check around the room, then run up a flight of stairs and push open my sister's door. Summer's room is filled with toys, painting tables, chairs and a desk covered in books and papers. The walls are lined with bookshelves half full of books, the rest with keepsakes she's found roaming the beach and gifts given to her by her people. A large reproduction of the island stands on a heavy table. Her education is important, according to the council that watches over her, especially her knowledge of the island. Against one wall is a silver four-poster bed mounted with huge moonstones. The bedcovers are of the finest silk (unlike my small pallet with its single plain coverlet). Summer wanted to give me a bed like hers, but as part of my deal with Histal, I agreed to keep my things simple here, like at the Watchers Campan.

I stand at the foot of the bed and choke back tears of relief. Mom's skinny arms are stretched out on the coverlet. Summer is curled on her side, one of her hands resting on Mom's shoulder.

I may be invisible, but Summer's hound, Tobar, knows I'm here. He sits up and whines. Summer stirs and mutters at him to shut up, but he only whines louder. I check the room. No servants. No Gormala. I become visible, just as Summer opens her eyes. "Emma!"

I crouch beside her. "How is she?"

"She isn't waking up much anymore," Summer says, her face as pale as the Argadnel moons that circle the island. "I'm keeping her with me now."

"Can she hear?"

"I don't know. Sometimes I think she hears me, but other times ..." She swallows hard. "Did you see him?"

I nod.

She sits up and grabs my hand. "How is he?"

"He's forgotten us, but I'm going to get his memories back."

"How?"

I lean close and telepath what happened. Her grip tightens. "Oh, Emma, anything could happen to you."

"I'll be okay. Look, I've got to get going. Bedeven

and Huw are looking for me. Rhona wants something from me but I don't know what. I've got to get enough of a headstart so they can't find me."

"What do they want with *you?*" she asks, eyes wide.

"I don't know — I can't figure it out."

"I won't ask to come with you, Emma. I can't leave Mom."

I hold her close. "Thank you, Summer. Will you tell her that I was here and that Dad is alive and that I'll be back in eight days? I hope to bring him with me when I return."

"Really? You think you can?" she asks excitedly.

"I hope so. Promise you'll tell her that he's okay, but don't tell her about my plan to bring him here. I can't be sure. Not yet."

"Yes, I promise. Take —"

Suddenly the door bursts open. I dive under the bed.

"I heard you speaking to someone. Who was it?"

I transmute invisible, slide farther under the bed and come out on Mom's side.

Summer says, "Huh? You woke me, Gormala. I must have been talking in my sleep."

I'm standing beside Mom. Gormala looks around the room with her sharp eyes. Tobar is staring right at me and I pray she doesn't notice him. I bend over to kiss Mom and I'm just turning to get the heck out of there when from the corner of my eye I see

Gormala pick up a dish. She runs around the end of the bed and sweeps her arm through the air. A spray of fine powder flies straight at me. One of my hands sparkles lightly where it has struck.

"I've got you!"

Gormala lunges, but I dodge past her and out the door. I frantically brush at myself and race down the corridor toward the side door that leads to the sea. I wait until she's in sight, open the door wide, let it shut and hide behind a pillar. It works. She opens the door and dashes outside. As soon as it closes behind her, I pull across the wooden slat that locks it. As I take off again, I can hear her pounding and screeching on the other side. With luck, no one will hear her until I can get back to Tom and Cill.

I crash through my door. "Gormala knows I'm here, which means they all know I'm not on any scouting mission for Fergus! We've got to get away. Now. Tom! Where do we go first?"

"To Histal."

"We can't go to *him*," I cry. "He'll send me to that jail thing he calls a confiner for … for disobedience. He gave you permission for me to do some practice stuff while I was visiting Mom, but he'll never —"

"You know he's the only one who can guide us through our next step."

I pace, frantic and undecided.

"Okay," Tom says sarcastically, "let's just sit here and they'll come for us and we'll never even *start* this Seeker Game. Histal is the only one who —"

A tap on my arm, and Cill whispers, "Chances must be, no?"

I nod reluctantly. "Yeah, chances must be. I'm dead either way."

From my pouch, I take my Watcher medallion — the device Watchers use to get back to the Campan. All three of us touch it. Just as the door bursts open behind us, we drop through the stone floor.

21

We land in the Entry Ring of the Watchers Campan. Three Watchers guard it day and night, usually Warder Whinge and two Noviates. Cill lets out a sharp cry and all three guards leap to their feet. The two Noviates grab her.

She stares around wildly, crying, "Where we be? I see nothing."

I've forgotten that only Watchers can see the Campan. Cill can't see the pale blue floor we stand on or the misty walls shifting and changing around us.

"It's okay," I assure her. "You're on the island of the Watchers. But you can't see it or the guards. Close your eyes and it won't be so scary. Don't worry, no one will harm you."

Warder Whinge growls, "I haven't been shown any special authority to let you return. You're in trouble, Watcher Tamhas. I allowed you to push your way in, just one day past, but this is too much ... and to have the audacity to bring in an Outsider. Unbelievable

---

arrogance. Punishment will follow." He sprays out the last few words with joyful vindictiveness.

Warder Whinge is tired of guarding a gate where no strangers come to challenge his authority. Now we've brought an Outsider. His big chance to show off.

Tom begins to explain, but Whinge snarls at him, "Silence. Until you have been identified."

Tom sighs and nods. One of the Noviates takes my voiceprint by having me talk into a long piece of crystal, while the other checks out the metal band around Tom's leg by holding what looks like a tuning fork next to it. I can hear the low hum from both.

"Please, we must talk to Master Histal," I say.

Whinge is the Master of the Gate and I've only had one short training session with him. He's impatient and arrogant and always ready to tell you what you've done to make his life a misery. He thinks he's made for bigger and better things than minding the gate, so he pushes his weight around at every opportunity.

Tom says in a firm voice, "Warder Whinge, it was necessary to bring the creature from Barroch here. She is a slave of Fergus of Cleave, and he has commanded that she accompany us. If you wish to hold her while we go about our business with Histal, then do so. We won't be long."

When Whinge speaks again, there's an unnerving eagerness in his voice. "You can't go anywhere without my permission. I am the Master of the Gate!"

"I have no doubt that Histal, who is also *your* High Master, will be very angry if you don't let us through," Tom says with great calmness. "You know me, Warder. You know I do not come on trivial matters."

Whinge glowers, then disappears through a shifting archway, only to return a few seconds later looking as if a bee has stung him somewhere tender. In a choked voice he says, "You may pass. But the creature from Barroch remains with us."

I turn to Cill. Her eyes are tightly shut, and she is letting out a string of crackly little mews.

"We'll be right back, Cill," I say. "Don't be afraid. You can't see it, but you're standing on a floor with walls all around you."

She opens her eyes and nods, then closes them tightly again with a little squeak. "I be here. I go nowhere. I be nowhere I *can* see."

Tom and I walk quickly down a long corridor of shifting walls. Sometimes they become wavery bushes and trees, sometimes high blocks of sandstone, sometimes open sky and clouds. I have no idea what the Watchers Campan really looks like, as it continually changes. Only a High Master such as Histal can stop the constant shifting and make a place solid and real, so that a Watcher can train.

We keep walking, knowing that at some point Histal will make himself known. Around a corner, a dark blue door appears. Thousands of tiny worlds and stars are scattered across its surface. They swirl slowly, constantly changing. Tom touches a small constellation that has two six-pointed stars and a pale purple moon (like the tattoo on his wrist when he's the human, Tom Krift) and the door opens. I have a tattoo on my wrist as well, two crescent moons with a small arrow joining them. But I've never seen my tattoo on Histal's wall. Not yet, anyway.

On the other side of the door, Histal stands in a cloudy, white space. He's never raised his voice to me — he's almost always patient with my stupid questions, and yet he scares me silly.

Histal is the tallest of all the Masters, but still small by human standards, not much taller than a ten-year-old boy. His face is long and white under the thistledown hair. His eyes are deep green circled with a line of clear white. As usual, I find it hard to figure out what he's wearing. It looks like a cloak of metal, and silk, and threads of light.

"So, you have been to Eorthe, Watchers," he says solemnly.

I'm shocked. But I shouldn't be. Histal always knows everything, it seems.

Tom and I answer nervously, "Yes."

"And to Cleave."

"Yes."

"And no doubt you had a good reason," he says with great politeness.

"We believe so, Master Histal, we —" Tom begins.

"I don't want to hear from you, Watcher Tamhas," Histal snaps. "Because of you, I told the Argadnel emissaries, Branwen and Bedeven, that you were on an Obligation for me. I am deeply disturbed by your abuse of my trust. I expect a clear explanation. But you and I will discuss that later, Tamhas. No ... I wish to hear from the Noviate."

I clear my throat. First I tell him it's my fault that Tom lied to him. I take full responsibility. Then I tell him almost everything that happened. I leave out the part where I talked to Rhona and how I overheard Bedeven and Huw, because I want to stay focused on Mom, on how I have to find her child. I figure I'll tell him the other stuff later.

"And so you see, Master Histal, if I don't play the Seeker Game, my mother — that is, Belldam Leto, will die."

Histal replies, "Yes, alas, the Belldam is fading. But what of it? These things are part of the cycle of human life, is that not so?"

"But I've found a way to help her, Master."

"You agreed with Fergus of Cleave to go on a Seeker Game without your High Master's permission. In fact, you have made me an accomplice to your little scheme — a *dupe*, if you will."

My scalp tightens. I never even thought of that. We *are* in huge trouble.

"Well?"

"I felt I had no choice, Master Histal," I say.

"But you *did* go to Eorthe, expressly against the orders and rules of the Game that you, the Belldam and the Suzarain all agreed to. Once again, you have let your human emotions rule your Watcher's head."

What can I say? He's right.

Histal walks around a low table of clear glass that floats out of the mist. On it are a hundred or more small spinning orbs of all colors. One of them is a swirling blue — with dark ugly chunks corroded away.

He points at it. "The Belldam — your mother, as you call her — comes from this place. Eorthe. *Earth.* A world of great beauty that is being destroyed by the ones who should be caring for it. The tribes have always let emotion rule their logical side. We have avoided direct contact for many centuries. Their war games, like those of Cleave and Fomorii, are pointless and ugly and endless. Their greed demands the destruction of all other living things. Soon this world will be a rotting hulk folding in on itself and those who caused its destruction.

"A number of these other worlds that you see before you, thanks to the Pathfinder's Mission of Enlightened Tutelage, have seen that the Game is not necessary, that curiosity, exploration, knowledge, experimentation, discovery and creativity make their lives exciting."

"Then why do you continue to send Watchers on

Obligations to places like Cleave and Fomorii to help with their Games?" I ask.

Tom growls in my head to shut up, but Histal says, "I am not prepared to answer this to a mere Noviate. We have our strategies. You ask questions, Noviate ... too *many* questions. This is your one great flaw as a Watcher. You must rely on the wisdom of your Masters as to what is right and what is wrong. Questions will only lead you into trouble."

"But you just said that curiosity is —"

"Silence!" His voice echoes through the room, and a fierce wind forces me to close my eyes.

What is the matter with me? Why do I keep asking questions when I know he hates it?

"Yes," Histal snarls, "why *can't* you hold your tongue?"

"I *try* —" I begin, but he holds up one hand, sighs and says, "That did not require an answer, Watcher."

My bottom lip is trembling, but I bite it and try to look contrite, which isn't hard. Then I say, "Please don't punish Tom. Punish me. It's all my fault."

Tom's talons tighten on my shoulder. Actually, they gouge my flesh. I know he's telling me I'm talking too much.

Again, Histal sighs. "Hopeless. Utterly hopeless. To *continue* ... the woman you call your mother *is* unique as a human. Her influence has been good for the island of the new Suzarain. The young queen has greatly benefited from the tutelage of this Eorthe

woman. The island has steadily grown more stable.
The Belldam has developed a Stygia Mantles industry
that is helping the island economy, as well as bee
farms that will use the flowers to make a unique
medicinal honey. This woman has an ancient gift —
one that tames the bees, even bees of other worlds."

"So you see?" I say eagerly. "My mother has done
amazing things. It's important that she become well
again."

Histal shakes his head. "If the Belldam is fading,
we'll need to do some careful maneuvering to
protect the island's stability."

My heart shrinks. What is he saying? "But if you
could show us where to start the search, I could
find my parents' child and Mom would be well
again. Then —"

"But they are *not* your parents, are they?" he
says, not unkindly. He looks at Tom. "The Noviate
misses the point — as she often does. Argadnel can
now be managed without the Belldam. She is no
longer needed."

"No!" I whisper.

Histal says, "That is all. Now, report back to
your instructions immediately."

"No, wait. Aren't Watchers protectors? Don't
you want to save someone *good* when it is in your
power?" I grab his sleeve. It slips out of my fingers.
"And what about Mom and Dad's child — stolen
and lost? What about *her?*"

A great force slams me and I fly through the air, landing on my backside.

"Ooph!"

I rub my shoulder and elbow. I'm in a stone cell — the confiner. It's over. I won't find Mom's child. Dad will never get his memories back. *Mom will die.*

I shout, "I don't care what you do to me! I hate this place. I'll get out of here somehow. And I won't come back. I'll find my mother's child all by myself. You're no different than Fergus or Rhona. You're a ... a ..." I search for the right word. "... a *monster!* I thought you were different. I thought you ... you *cared!*"

My shouts are instantly swallowed by a deafening silence. As I pace the floor, something deep inside me stands still and takes stock. Then an inner voice tells me I've been a fool, I've gained nothing by being emotional — by allowing my human behavior to beat down my Watcher's logic. I stop pacing. How do I fix it? How do I make Histal understand that I really *am* trying to be a good Watcher, but that I'm also deeply committed to my family?

I close my eyes and in a calm voice, I say, "Master — if you're listening, I know that what I've done is wrong. Please let me explain once again why it is *logical* ... why it is *imperative* that Belldam Leto be made well again. For the sake of Argadnel. Please let me have one more chance to explain. I did it all wrong. I —"

A loud crack followed by a terrifying rumbling sends me into a corner, where I cover my head with my arms. The walls dissolve and I topple over onto my side.

Histal reaches down and grabs me by the collar. His green eyes are black now, the white line a bright yellow.

"You will *never* shout at me again. *Never.* Do you understand?"

I nod madly and try to hold myself straight and firm.

"Your emotional outbursts, Noviate, are *inexcusable.*" He pushes me away. I try not to blink, for if I do, I know that tears will come. His voice when he next speaks is low and even. "Yet ... I *sensed* a change — perhaps you've learned something about being a Watcher?"

Again I nod, trying not to beg with my eyes.

He twists his thin mouth to one side, as if assessing me. Then he sighs and says, "Because of this change — and because of a careful, *logical argument* from your Watcher Tamhas — I am willing to give you one last chance. You will be given passage to *one* place. Tamhas and the Barroch will go with you. The rest is up to you."

I'm about to thank him, but he puts one long white finger in the air for silence. His deep-seeing eyes become as blue as a prairie sky, and in them I sense a tender sadness, but it's gone so fast I'm not sure I actually saw it.

"Go," he whispers, "before you say something and I'm forced to change my mind." In a swirl of blue, he's gone.

I struggle to my feet. I don't know how it got there, but I'm holding an oval magnifying glass with a handle made of the finest filigreed silver. I realize I've collected the first Game piece on the list Fergus gave me — a glass. My Seeker Game has begun.

22

Tom and I are escorted by a Noviate back down the hall.

"Wow, I can't believe you won over Histal like that, Tom," I say out of the corner of my mouth so the Noviate can't hear me. "I tried to explain, but —"

"For once, just shut up," Tom snarls.

I shut up. We collect Cill, who holds my hand tightly but won't open her eyes. "I check my time marker," she hisses. "Sixteen hour since we leave Cleave."

"Almost one whole day gone," I whisper. "How can that be?"

Tom mutters, "If we'd gone straight to Histal after Cleave —"

Warder Whinge snaps at us to stand under an amethyst light in the corner of the room. Behind him is a map of all of the worlds in Histal's room painted in glowing light.

"You *do* know where you're going?" he asks us.

I shake my head. I have no idea, but Tom says

formally, "Yes. Master Histal has given you the co-ordinates, has he not?"

Whinge grins, touches a small gray sphere and says, "Better you than me. *This* one is a lunatic."

We slide up through the purple light and land lightly on soft sandy soil. He may be a creep, but Warder Whinge is a champion transporter.

We're at the edge of a small gray forest. The sky is slate gray, the smooth tree trunks like old pewter. It's as if all color has been wiped out of this world. Kind of like the first place I landed on the Fidchell board, but different too. That one had a pointed building on it.

Cill is crooning happily, "I see this place. I feel ground. I see trees. Lovely, lovely trees."

Something moves through the forest behind her. A bluish shadow slides quickly behind some bushes and is gone.

"Did you see that?" I ask.

"What?" Tom looks around.

"I think there was someone over there in the forest."

Tom flies off quickly, his pale form floating silently in and out of the trees. He returns and says, "Nothing there. Relax, Emma. No one followed us."

Since the owl cunning was put on him, Tom's Watcher powers are much weaker. I'm *sure* I saw something. One of Rhona's people? How could it be? Surely only those at the Watchers Campan know where we are.

"This is where a Searcher named Gyro lives," Tom says. "Histal told me it was the best place to start."

"But it's nighttime. Can we wake him up?"

"It's always night here," Tom says. "No one sleeps in Hafflight."

"It's always like this? No sun? I'd *hate* that."

"Well," he says, "you don't have to live here, Emma, just visit. Gyro's a recluse who uses his own eccentric searching devices, but Histal says he's brilliant. And this is a difficult search."

"But how do we know he'll even —"

"Enough questions. Follow me."

Tom slides through the air toward a brooding hill in the distance. I have to run to keep up with Cill. When we reach the hill's base, Tom floats in circles above us.

To my right, at the edge of the trees, I see another flicker of movement.

Cill whispers, "Your eyes real big. You see someone?"

"I don't know. I thought I did … never mind. I don't see anything now."

"We got big hill to climb." She points up at it.

I have an idea. "Can you fly?"

"Fly? Me?" She laughs, dry crackling snorts. "I be of ground. I burrow. I dig. I climb trees. But I no be bird or flying bug. You go before. I be fine."

I sigh. I was hoping I could practice flying up to the top. "No. I'd rather we stayed close together." I glance nervously over my shoulder. The movement was probably just an animal. Or a bird. Or a breeze moving the gray leaves.

Tom calls out, "Come on, you two. *Move.*"

We struggle about three-quarters of the way up the hill along a winding path, where we find Tom sitting on a metal fence as light and airy as lace. Gray pearls threaded on hundreds of thin wires create a curtainlike gate in the strange twilight. Two curious statues, with eagles' bodies and foxes' heads, sit on pedestals on either side of the entrance. I push the pearls aside and Cill and I walk through. We no sooner drop the curtain than the pearls sweep against one another with high pinging noises and the statues emit piercing screeches. A second later someone shouts, "Stay as you are. Don't move!"

A tall gray mecha-drone humanoid appears out of nowhere and stands in front of us, a steel crossbow and arrow aimed at my head.

"Don't shoot," I cry. "We come from Master Histal. We won't harm you. I'm a Watcher from the Campan Island."

"Prove it," the mecha-drone says, then adds, "if you don't mind."

"Prove it?"

"Show him your Watcher self," Tom calls from above our heads.

Quickly I change into my Watcher form and just as quickly back into Emma. I can hear Cill whisper, "Yes. That do it, I sure."

Tom swoops down onto my shoulder as the mecha-drone raises his bow skyward and releases the arrow. As he lifts his bald head, I see that it's actually a riveted helmet with a flap over his right eye. In the flap is a tube that looks like a miniature telescope.

The arrow bursts into hundreds of tiny blue eagles with red fox heads that fly silently toward the pale stars and vanish in bursts of purple light. Then all is gray again.

"Wow," I cry.

The mecha-drone bows with a sweeping gesture. "I'm still working on it, but it makes a nice display, does it not?"

"And if that arrow had hit me?"

"Oh, my dear younger, I would never *shoot* anyone with it. Come, come. Follow me. And bring the bird and the leaf creature. I believe I've seen one of those leafy beings before — the Barroch, if I'm not mistaken. A peaceful race, protectors of the forest, if I'm not wrong. One of the *lost* tribes because of those dreadful Games, am I right? And the owl is a Watcher, too. But of a higher station, it seems to me. I heard him direct you. I understand all your languages, even the most archaic. You see, I have my all-purpose translator in my ear. I invented it … a long time ago." He points proudly at a piece of coiled metal sticking out of his ear. "One never knows who will drop by for information. I am *always* prepared, as one should be."

"I'm Emma, this is Tom and this is Cill. And you're Searcher Gyro?"

"You are not incorrect. Follow me, if you will."

Without waiting for an answer, he marches toward the hill.

23

The mecha-drone creaks with every step, as if his joints haven't been oiled for a long time, like Dorothy's tin man. Tom grips my shoulder, Cill grabs my hand and we follow. On the other side of the hill, rising out of a shallow valley, are two glittering pyramids on tall stilts with a long noselike shape between them, like another pyramid lying on its side. The whole thing looks like a giant fox head with pointy ears. The pyramids are covered with pale twinkling lights. Every now and again, a light breaks loose and fires off into the sky with a sizzle of color. Each time this happens, the metal man laughs with delight.

I feel a squiggle of a shiver when I remember the Fidchell game. So there are pointed buildings in this real-life Fidchell, too. As we move down into the valley and get closer to the structure, it becomes clear that the stilts are made of the same lacy metal as the fence. It also covers the surface of each pyramid "ear" and the "nose." As the mecha-drone waits for us at the base of one of the stilts, I realize he's wearing a similar, though finer, lacy metal, cut into armor with all sorts of angular pieces sticking out. No wonder he creaks when he walks.

When five or six lights suddenly shoot off the pyramids into the sky, leaving trails of dusky green smoke, I breathe, "It's so beautiful."

"Why thank you, how nice of you to say," Gyro cries. "I have many more things that will astound you, I suspect."

He waves us toward an enormous bicycle-like thing with a huge wire box kite attached to a series of back wheels. He directs us to climb into the kite, assuring us it's perfectly safe ... as far as he *knows*. Doesn't he ever say anything for *sure*?

Is he a mecha-drone or a *real* being? As far as I know, mecha-drones, which are fully mechanical creatures, aren't common because Players don't like to use them in their Games. They're too easy to destroy, and I've heard from the Masters that they're rather stupid as well, programmed only to take orders. Yet I see that this metal "man" has hands of real skin and bone and seems intelligent ... so far, at least.

"Please, climb aboard my conveyance," Gyro says with a wide silver smile.

Tom mutters at me, "Do it — and don't quibble."

"Sheesh, at least let me quibble *first* before you tell me not to," I mutter back.

Cill whimpers, but climbs in after me, clinging to the steel rods inside the kite. Gyro climbs onto the bicycle seat and begins pedaling. Of course, we go nowhere. I stifle my giggles, but before I can laugh out loud, we're in the air, circling the sparkling pyramid. Clutching to one of the steel rods and ignoring Cill's pitiful cries, I pinch myself to make sure I'm not dreaming. (I've been testing myself like this for months now — and the pinches always *hurt*.) I keep expecting — hoping — I'll wake up in my little room in the barn and Mom will call me down for breakfast and everything will be normal again. But it'll never happen.

Through the steel lace of the "kite," I see rolling gray hills surrounding the pyramids, with dim misty lights in the distance. The kite-cycle banks sharply and we enter a yawning triangular door in the nose between the two ears. The craft clatters to a stop.

We're in a storeroom so crammed with junk that we have to climb over rusting metal pieces, boxes full of steel balls, chunks of glass, nails, screws and all kinds of tools to get to a clear space. Gyro waves proudly at a long table. Every bit of its surface is covered with more junk and at least fifty different machines with dancing lights.

"Behold my *newfound passion*," he says, and his face breaks into a grin, displaying steel teeth. When he turns his head, light glitters off his nose, which looks like a small doorknob.

Gyro sees me looking at his nose and fingers it. "I've been rather forced to rebuild myself in bits and pieces, I'm afraid. Because of my experiments, you see. I lost the old beak in one of my most interesting trials and had to make a few new ones. I can change it whenever the mood strikes me. See?" He pulls off his doorknob, reaches into a small box and smacks a long pointed nose onto his face, giving him a definite foxy look. "Do you have a preference regarding noses?" he asks solemnly. "I have many more."

"I — er — think I like that one," I say.

"Good choice, I believe." He says it like he's the head waiter and I've just ordered the most expensive meal on the menu. "Now, before you tell me why you're here, let me show you a few of my latest devices. I don't get many visitors, as it happens."

Gyro creaks over to a low tub of water. A clear ball with a metal fish speared through it bobs on the surface like a minnow caught in a bubble, its head poking out one end, the tail out the other. Tiny openings along its body look like windows on a small jet.

"It's a boat of some kind?" I ask.

"Yes, and it can float on any liquid in any world and will never sink, as far as I know. And it will provide the atmosphere of any home world too. And that …," he points at what looks like a flat windmill on a floating platform in the tub, "… *that* is a Weather Preventer Platform. If a wind comes up, this device will avert it and send it *packing* ... at least in my trials it has." He's getting excited now, his arms creaking around like tiny windmills. A couple of small bolts fly off him and clatter onto the floor. "We could put dozens of these platforms on waters all over the worlds to keep them open and safe for passage ... or so I hope."

"Have you made any life-sized ones?" I ask. "I mean that actually work?"

"Er — not as yet," Gyro says, sounding defensive. "But I'm waiting for the right time to present them — perhaps at the next Worlds Enlightenment Ponderate. But one has to be very careful because these ideas could affect all the worlds and," he lowers his voice, "whoever controls them could become quite powerful. So I have to think about things very carefully ... yes, lots of *thought*." He looks around anxiously.

"We need your help, Searcher Gyro," Tom says. "Histal told me you're the best Searcher in all the worlds."

"But that's not my *calling* anymore, you see." He explains patiently, as if we should already know this. "No need to call me Searcher. Gyro is good enough. I've stopped searching. I never really liked it much, as it happens."

"But Histal said —" I begin.

He interrupts. "I haven't announced my change

of pursuit, as I've been much too busy. But I can't help you, you see, to my infinite regret. My calling, my *passion,* you must understand, is to *concoct.* I even dabble in alchemy." He looks around furtively. "But of course, I must be wary of that as well, as the Mages and other sorcerers don't like dabblers moving in on their work. One has to be very careful not to overstep other Contrivers' boundaries. They're a very jealous bunch. But I just want to make things that will better the worlds for everyone. I need to … to express what is really *me.*"

Tom tries this time. "But Histal said —"

"I am now doing something so exciting I can hardly contain myself, if I may put it that way." Gyro turns quickly and another piece of metal flies off him so fast that Cill has to duck.

Tom sits on the table, hunched and gray. Gyro doesn't notice he's getting angry.

"I have been struggling with the concept of combining time spans, durations *and* binnacles," Gyro announces, "if you grab my meaning."

"And what *meaning* is that?" Tom growls.

"Why, to travel through *time,* if you understand me. I call it my Time Mover."

I say, "Hey, that's what people on Earth have always wanted to do. I'm from Earth. Or … sort of. I'm surprised someone in one of your worlds hasn't figured it out by now."

Gyro looks anxious again. "Well, they haven't.

But I believe *I* am very *very* close. I've only been to Eorthe once and I found it a rather stupid place." He laughs. "Surely I have no fears of being outdone by someone from *there*. Why, the next time you come to see me, I could very well be ten thousand mooncrests in the past, perhaps."

He frowns deeply and adds, "I only wish I didn't have to do it all on my own. I lost my nose trying it before it was ready. But, you see, I can't trust anyone else. There are too many jealous Contrivers around, I have found, willing to take someone else's work."

"Don't you have friends who could help?" I ask.

He shakes his head sadly. "I've always been on my own, and with all these *worlds*-altering things I'm discovering, I fear to make friends." He sighs. "It must be nice to have *someone*. I *am* rather lonely at times, if I were to admit it."

He looks so sad that I try to distract him. "When were you last on Eorthe?"

"Oh — I believe it was in the year of 1720 or thereabouts. I am very old in Eorthe years."

I laugh. "You must be. Things have definitely changed since then. We've — they've — split the atom and sent people to our moon and —"

He stares at me, then slaps his leg with a clang and laughs. "Surely you're teasing me? It simply cannot be true, can it?"

I say earnestly, "It's true. Really."

"But they hadn't even figured out how to find where they were on their own globe when I was there. It was so ... basic. I wanted to help, but no one would listen, as it happens. Rather *stupid* ... if you'll forgive my bluntness."

"A man named Harrison figured it out — longitude, we call it, Searcher Gyro," I say. "I learned about it in school. Harrison worked in the 1760s."

"Well, I *never,*" Gyro cries, then his voice drops to a near whisper, as if someone might be listening. "But they can't go backward or forward in time yet? You're certain?"

"I *know* they can't."

He slaps his leg again. "Well, that's all right then. Let me show you how close I am."

He takes us to a part of the table that has one small area clear of stuff. Sitting on a piece of silky material is a tiny square box of dark silver. He touches a lever on the side and the top snaps open. When I look inside, there's nothing there, just a white emptiness that seems to pull me toward it.

Gyro snaps the lid shut. "Did you feel its pull, Watcher? I believe you might have."

I nod. "You closed it so fast, though, it was hard to really tell."

"Can't be too careful." He taps his nose and instinctively I check to make sure mine is still there. "I am working on a very small scale right now," he continues "to avoid accidents, if you understand.

I've sent tiny objects into it and they've vanished. When I reset it, they came back." He clears his throat. "Unfortunately they were slightly *altered*. But never mind — I'm sure it only needs a tweak or two."

"Will you sell it?" I ask. "You could ask anything you wanted if you sold it to a leader like Fergus, say." Then I shut up. The shock of what Fergus might do with something like this is too horrible to contemplate.

From the look on his face, Gyro agrees with me. "Oh no. I could never *sell* or barter it."

"But imagine the power this could give *you*," I exclaim. "Everyone would want it."

He looks frightened. "I — oh no … I don't want to have that kind of power." He glances at the small box as if seeing it for the first time. "Oh dear …"

"Well, you *might* use it to become the Supreme Searcher of all the worlds," I say, trying to offer him something.

He looks surprised. "I could *what*, you say?"

"Just think how it could make being a Searcher so much more exciting and easier. You could go back in time to find things that beings have lost. Or unite beings that have been apart for many mooncrests. It would be a very powerful tool. For *good*. And no one need know how you do it. That way, no one could abuse the power."

Gyro's face is open with amazement. "I never

thought of that, as it happens. You're quite right. It's a tool *made* for a Searcher, isn't it? I lost my interest in searching because I got so bored ... sitting and searching through the binnacles. But now, this. How perfectly imaginative of you. Still, I don't know ..."

I say, "Maybe it's important to do what you do best. To *accept* what you do best. Anyone can be a Searcher, I suppose, but a *Supreme* Searcher ..."

Tom telepaths, *Keep going, Emma. You're doing great ...*

Gyro is looking at me with interest.

I go for it. "And that's why we've come to you, Gyro. Please could you look for something? We're in terrible trouble and need your help."

"What have you lost that has put you in such trouble?"

I tell him what's happened and how we need to find Mom's child.

He thinks about it for a bit and says, "Let me make a deal with you, if you will allow me." He flashes what I think is a friendly smile, showing off his metal teeth.

"A deal?" Tom asks.

"What kind of a deal?" I add.

"If I do this for you, will you help me launch my maiden voyage into times past? Make sure I have someone to stand by, so to speak." He leans close to me and whispers, "I feel you are trustworthy."

Oh no — Tom telepaths.

He isn't asking us to go with him, Tom. Just to be here. What have we got to lose?

Tom sniggers. *Okay, but he'll have to go find us first.* Aloud, he says, "You've got a deal."

Gyro grins from ear to ear, his silver nose gleaming brighter than his teeth. "Follow me!"

24

Gyro leads us through more piles of stuff to a door that dissolves into a pyramid-shaped space. The sloped ceiling and walls are gray metal. Now and again I see flashes of light in the darkness above. The lower sections have shelving packed with papers, ancient tomes and metal and glass ornaments of different shapes and sizes. On the floor are more piles of stuff with walkways between them. There are three chairs and a three-legged table with a triangular top directly below the pyramid's point. Above it, hundreds of gray spheres spin through the air like a giant mobile without strings. I wind my way toward the table. Tom flies around the room dodging the spheres. Cill rustles close behind me making oh! oh! sounds.

The top of the table is covered with mirrors, glass balls, magnifying glasses, and other glass and steel pieces I can't identify. Right in the middle of the table is a small steel pyramid. About a hundred tiny dusky balls of various sizes circle its point like a solar system, never bumping into one another, even though they keep changing position and elevation — echo of the larger spheres above us.

"Why is everything gray?" I ask Gyro.

"So I don't become confused," he says. "Only the essences of life I'm searching for will glow with traces of true color, you see, when I bring them up. If everything else is gray, it makes it easier not to get false readings."

The stuff on the table is beautifully designed, incised or engraved with what look like old Celtic symbols. When I try to touch one of the glass ornaments, it becomes a puddle of liquid and slides away. When I try to pick up a magnifying glass, it spins so fast I can't touch it.

"Hey!"

"All of my inventions," Gyro says from behind me, "allow only *me* to touch them, as it happens."

"Wow. You *are* good," I say in awe.

He beams. "Now, Watcher ... some questions about times and locations, if I may."

Luckily, I know all the answers. I tell him exactly where and when Mom's real child was born.

He sits at the table and says, "To make sure I understand ... you say the child of Argadnel's Suzar and Suzarain was taken from the island world, placed on a farm in Bruide, Manitoba, Canada, Eorthe — uh — Earth. And that this *other* child was seized by a Taker and removed to another world, as far as one can tell."

"Yes, Fergus hired a Taker," Tom says.

"But which one?" Gyro muses.

"We don't know," I say.

"Let's see if we can find out," offers Gyro. "Let me just ..."

He leans over the small pyramid on the table circles a hand over the drab planets and touches one — it turns pale blue under his fingertips. A gray sphere above turns blue as well. A thin glass sheet rises out of the tabletop. On it is a map of North America, but without any roads or cities marked. He touches a spot near where Manitoba would be, and another sheet rises up as the first one drops down. He does that five times. When the last one slides up, I recognize the silver snake of the Brokenhead River as it curves past our farm. A small red dot pulsates just about where Dad's henge stands.

"Mmm," Gyro says, "there is a portal there. Still in use. The color and the spacing of the beats indicate this is one of Fergus of Cleave's sites."

He goes silent after that, collecting things around him. He peers into tiny glass pyramids that shimmer and whisper. He examines beads of light that appear on the glass sheet, with his magnifying glass held up to the telescope over his right eye. Finally, he takes one of the pyramids, flattens it between his palms and holds it up to the map of Bruide over the red light. He chews his lip. He pulls his nose on and off. He scratches his ear. He looks again. He pulls the telescoping eye back and forth.

"It's all blurry," he says. "I think they've put some sort of cunning over the area. My magnifiers don't work, or so it appears."

I reach into my pouch and pull out the small magnifying glass. "Could you try this one? Histal gave it to me."

Gyro examines the glass carefully. Then he holds it up to his eyepiece and sucks in his breath. "Yes. Clarity of the finest order." He twists this way and that until he's practically standing on his head.

Finally he sighs and says, "The child was — let me see …" He stops, squints, then looks at me out of the corner of his good eye. "It appears that the younger could have been taken by Yegg, known as the Night Flier. I can *just* see a trace of Yegg's essence — a kind of yellowish tinge. I'm quite sure of it. Odd, however. I wouldn't think even Fergus would use her, but that is what my calculations say. I hope they're not wrong."

I say eagerly, "How do we find her?"

"Yegg works alone. In the Rebuff area. Other tribes, such as the Ravans, Hobyahs, Bogles and others, come from ruins along those Tag-A-Long Isles. However …"

"However … what?" Tom asks.

Gyro stands up. "It's not an easy place to get to. I think I'm the only being alive who knows how to get to this particular Taker's realm. I was involved in a nasty incident with Yegg when I was a novice Searcher — I was just a younger myself. I lost an ear, thanks to her." He taps his left ear, which gives off a metallic ping. "Nasty business. I wouldn't advise going to her Hollow —"

"Could you take us there?" Tom asks.

Gyro is startled. "Oh no, I'm much too busy with my experiments. But," he adds magnanimously, "as my new — er — friends, and because you've agreed to help me when my Time Mover is ready, I'll give you my air sloop to take you there. You can return it when you come back to help me with my official launch. Come."

Cill pokes me. "Air sloop? In *air?*"

"Don't worry — I'm sure it's safe." I say it, but I don't sound very convinced.

"But it *his* sloop," she persists, tugging at my arm. "His ideas crazy. Time travel stupid. He *crazy*. I afraid of being up in air without trees."

I go nose to nose with her. "Cill, all you do is complain and whine. Either shut up and come with us, or go back to Cleave and tell Fergus you're too scared to stay with us."

I think what she's giving me is a look of total disbelief and hurt.

I pat where her arm should be, if she has arms somewhere under that pile of debris. "I'm sorry, Cill," I say. "I didn't mean to hurt your feelings."

The crisp mottled leaves soften a bit, but she doesn't look me in the eye.

Tom, on my shoulder, says, "Emma, I've never seen this Yegg, but I've heard of her. She snatches youngers who haven't even been asked for, just to sell them off. She's dangerous."

I look at Cill and then at him. "If you two want to back out, be my guests. But I'm going. So? Are you in or out?"

Cill pulls herself as tall as she can. "I no be a *coward*. I *go*."

Tom shakes his feathers and stares at me. I have my answer.

25

We follow Gyro through a triangular archway at the far side of the pyramid and up a narrow staircase. We climb and climb and finally come out into another pyramid, empty except for a small airship in the very center, formed of metal wires so fine they look like cobwebs. It's about the length of a mid-sized yacht. Rising high above it, near the bow, is a silver sail as delicate as gossamer, shaped like a huge umbrella with its center point forward. A much smaller sail, designed like a backward C is fashioned on the stern. The prow, of course, has the face of a fox. It dawns on me suddenly — an airship: I've found the second of the Game pieces on my list.

Tom says, "Gyro, have you tested this?"

"Oh yes, a few times," Gyro says. "It works very well, I believe." He leans forward. "I programmed it to be very sensitive to the desires of the pilot and crew. I'll also give you a small atlas device with many other worlds, including my own, on map membranes. But I'd advise you to be careful, as I haven't tested all these worlds yet. I wouldn't want you to get stuck — or crash-land."

"Crash? Fall down from sky?" Cill squeaks.

I glare at her and she shuts up.

Gyro climbs a ladder on the starboard side, and Cill and I scramble up behind him. Tom flies to the bow of the little sloop. A triangular open window is cut into the sail for the pilot to see out of. There's one seat at the window and four seats behind. Below the opening is a large glass pyramid, and below that ten glass buttons. To their left is a pale blue triangle with a black center, and to the right, a pale yellow oval with a green line through it, like the eye of a bird. Under the row of buttons is a single green triangle.

Gyro gives me a flat metal thing that looks like a simple square of grayish glass. "That's your atlas. Just touch the lower right and the list of worlds will come up in your language with the codes. This is the code for Yegg's island, Bakkon." Tom flies onto my shoulder to look.

I memorize the sequence, show it to Cill, who studies it, then I carefully put the device in my pouch. Gyro sits down in the pilot's seat. "The flight panel is simple. Each of these ten buttons has two or three symbols on it. Keep pressing a button until you find the right symbol, then move on to the next. The green switch will lock each one in. Dead easy."

"Yeah," I mutter to myself, "*dead.*"

As Gyro pokes away at the buttons, Cill and I watch carefully. Four shapes float up into the pyramid one at a time. I see a triangle with a green dot in the middle, another that looks like an upside-down T, a circle with a red-and-black line angled through it and finally a black ragged shape. Just like the little map device said. Gyro locks in each shape that matches the code.

"That sets the coordinates."

"You have created the most amazing things," I say in true admiration.

Gyro sits a moment, as if reflecting, then gets up and motions me to sit in the seat he's just left. He looks worried.

"What is it?"

"You should know there is a little black button under the pilot's seat. Don't touch it. Well, not unless it's an emergency. It has a limited number of pushes on it, so use them wisely, as it — uh — were. Three pushes at most, I believe."

"What does it do?" I ask.

"I've actually never tried it, as it happens. But I set it up to react to any emergency situation, so to speak. That's all I can tell you. Trust the little sloop. As I said, it is sensitively attuned to its riders."

"And that means?"

He shrugs. "You have to experience it to understand."

"So what next?" Tom asks.

"I'm going to leave the sloop and open the pyramid. When I give the signal, I want you, Emma, to press the blue triangle, followed by the yellow oval. Got that? Then hit the green again for takeoff. You must always use the three-color sequence for takeoff. In all likelihood, it will land itself when you reach your destination."

My heart is pounding. "*In all likelihood?* You can't guarantee it?"

Gyro's face crumples slightly. "I'm almost certain. Uh — yes, I can certainly pretty — uh — firmly guarantee it. Be careful."

I look at Tom, who nods. Cill whimpers. We have no choice.

Gyro climbs down the outside ladder and walks to a panel near the door. A crack appears in the wall in front of us. It spreads wider and wider, then it stops with a clang. Tom, Cill and I stare out of the opening at the gray sky.

I hear a shout and look over my shoulder. Gyro cries, "Now!"

I whisper, "No turning back." I lean forward, press my hand over the blue light and then the yellow, and then I press the green triangle. The little sloop begins to move forward.

26

I hear another shout as we slide out of the pyramid into the cool night air. Gyro is standing in the opening, his arms windmilling. I don't wave back. I'm too scared to lift my arms. Tom isn't scared, though. Through the triangular window, I can see him on the prow of the airship, his wings outspread. I'm afraid to move in case we tip. The sloop seemed to be slipping from side to side on takeoff. Who's to say it won't just flip over in a stiff wind? I look around and find Cill under the seat behind me, letting out fretful moans. I'd like to join her.

"It's wonderful. We're moving at a great speed and yet it's as soft and easy as floating!" Tom shouts. "Relax, Emma."

I try. I lean back and gaze around me. The gray sky is full of dull silvery clouds. Below, pockets of dusky forest, rolling plains and threads of pewter water slide past. Now and again, I can make out a clump of what looks like housing of some kind — villages or other habitation in this strange half-lit world.

We travel a long time. As the airship floats through the puffs of cloud, I have time to think … and worry. My mind keeps going back to my family. How are Mom and Summer doing? Is Summer keeping a close watch over everything? No doubt the dreadful Gormala is. And did that Keeper of Fergus's take his anger out on Dad? I can't dwell on any of these thoughts for long. They're too frightening and painful.

I didn't have a chance to tell Histal about Gormala's and Bedeven's attempts to keep me in Argadnel Castel. It's clear Bedeven is acting on Rhona's orders. I still don't know what they're all up to yet. Huw didn't know why they wanted me kept a prisoner there, either. *Why* didn't he know? I thought he and Rhona were really close. Yet from what he said to me, he may work for her, but his allegiance is only to himself.

Is that why Rhona kept this information, whatever it is, from him? One thing I'm learning in these strange worlds is that *loyalty* doesn't seem to exist. There's Rhona, living under Fergus's roof and plotting something behind his back. You'd think Mathus would have an ear to every door. Bedeven even mentioned the possibility of Rhona starting a new Game *against* Fergus. Why? Players usually start a Game for reward or revenge. What has Fergus done to make them set up a Game against him? More important, what do *I* have to do with *any* of it? It's too weird.

Summer may be the queen of Argadnel, but let's face it, Rhona and Fergus run the place. So it's not as if Rhona needs to fight Fergus for profits from the Stygia Mantles crop. I'll never understand these peculiar beings. I just hope they have no idea where we are.

But then I remember the shadow in the woods of Hafflight. If it was someone who was after me, they'd have grabbed me then and there ... wouldn't they?

I'm so deep in thought, I don't notice what's happening until I hear a faint "Oh, oh" from behind me. I open my eyes. Straight ahead is a sheet of dark yellow that stretches from horizon to sky.

"What's that?" I cry. "It looks like a wall."

"It's a border wall. I hope this thing can go through it!" Tom shouts.

I hear a gasping crackle behind me. "I no go through walls. I be solid, too," Cill wails.

Tom slides into the sloop through the open window.

"Get ready!" he cries.

The wall looms up with tremendous speed. I close my eyes and scrunch down in the seat. Suddenly, my face is pushed against what feels like a thick sheet of plastic wrap. I can't breathe. I try to push it away, but my hands bounce back from it. Lights flash behind my eyes. I'm going to pass out. As I spin down into darkness, there's a rushing sound, a loud snap followed by a burst of cold air and an explosion of flapping and high-pitched squealing. I can breathe again, but the lungfuls of air I gasp are rank.

"Eeew. Horrible stink!" Cill cries, then she pushes my shoulder. "Look!"

The sky ahead is dark yellow and swarming with jagged-winged creatures.

They rise and fall in twisting, teeming columns. The sloop weaves through them as if it has built-in radar. Now and again, dark green creatures smack into our sails, but most take off as fast as they hit. One, however, crashes near my face, spread out on the front sail like a manta ray. Its little feet try to grab hold of the sail's metal threads, its wings flap frantically, its thin nose and lethal teeth push and bite at the sail. Another one falls beside it. Then another and another. I look to my left. We're moving toward the largest column, sliding right into it.

I dive for the floor and crouch beside Tom under the flight panel. Cill scrabbles from her hiding place under the far seat, grabs my arm and pulls me close, then tucks Tom under her leafy cape.

"No worry. I hold you tight."

The ugly bat creatures swoop and slide around the little airship, some banging into the sails, others screeching past us. I can feel the flutter of air from their wings. The sloop tips to one side and we slide with it. I try to brace us with my feet, but it's no use. Cill's gnarled toes stretch out and grow into long strands of leathery brown that twine around the welded seats like sturdy vines and hold us fast. The sloop wobbles, then stabilizes for a moment. I'm about to take a much-needed breath when we drop like a stone and my stomach goes up into my throat.

Cill's arms tighten around us, her fingers growing into tendrils that strap us in.

Suddenly, the sloop twists sideways and turns around and around, all the while slowly, continually, heading down, down, down. With a quick rush, we slide forward and come to a stop.

The flapping and screeching has stopped, too. We sit in stillness.

I croak, "Where are we?"

"Might as well look," Tom says.

Cill doesn't move.

"We — uh — can't unless you let go, Cill," I say gently. She opens her eyes and nods. Her fingers and toes release us, returning to their normal length.

"That was great!" I cry.

"Great?" she asks.

"Yeah — you kept us safe. You were very brave."

Cill's face blushes like autumn leaves, and her eyes shine.

Tom and I edge toward the side of the sloop and peer over. We're in a cave, bobbing on a smooth watery surface. Sticking out of the steaming liquid are the tops of small volcanoes, spurting fizzes of light and a deep acrid stench. The roof is made up of gorgeously patterned stalactites. Some hang in various lengths above the waterline, while others dive below the surface like ornate columns. There are furtive movements and faint clicking sounds high above that make my skin crawl.

"Are those things bats?" I ask Tom, pointing to a jagged wing and sharp-toothed nose poking out from a rocky recess.

"I think they're like Earth bats, but I've never actually seen them before. They're called bakkes."

A shallow opening to our left shows us how we entered. To our right is a long passage with high rough walls lined with fire pots. We drift toward this passage and move slowly down its narrow length. It reminds me of the corridors in the lowest levels of Argadnel Castel. The liquid slaps against the walls, and the light reflects off its surface, dappling and fluttering. The corridor turns sharply at the end.

"Look," I say, "it's a landing of some kind. Do we dock here? Is it safe?"

Tom answers sharply, "What else can we do — other than abandon the whole Seeker thing."

"Thanks for stating the obvious," I snarl.

He says softly, "I just worry for you, Creirwy. I'm not much help to you under this cunning. And I think we may have bitten off way more than we can chew."

"But what else could I do?"

"You could have left things as they were," he says, "to protect yourself."

"You'd rather my mom die than risk your neck?" I ask incredulously.

Tom growls, "I have no fear of risking *my* neck. I fear that you will lose *yours* — because of this foolhardy bravery of yours."

The little sloop bumps into a shelf of stone — the time for conversation is over. We climb a set of steps that leads up to a wide shelf. Tom's talons grip my shoulder, and Cill hangs on to the tail of my jacket.

We must be the most foolhardy threesome in all the worlds.

27

A shuffling, dragging sound makes the hair on the back of my neck prickle. From a shadowy corner of the cave a hunched shape emerges. It's very large and very black — but as it comes into the light of a fire pot, its surface becomes a flowing mix of green, blue and blood red. As it scrabbles toward us, it makes a chitty, crackling noise, and I can see it's not wrapped in a cloak and hood as I first thought, but in its own heavily veined wings. A second set of jagged wings drags along the ground behind it.

We wait. I feel sick. My legs are shaking so badly that Tom is jiggling on my shoulder. He tries to send me soothing words, but I can't hear them for the blood pounding in my ears.

Slowly, the creature's wings rise from the ground, while the ones surrounding it unwrap and spread, creating a deep hoodlike shroud. Inside the darkness, I can see that its head is broad, wrapped with a strange headpiece of red silkiness that forms twin circles like flat rounded ears. The face is sooty and hidden in shadow, its features obscured. I can't really make out the shape of the body either, as it appears to be covered in layers of black fur.

The creature makes a number of high chittering sounds. I have to open my inner ear to translate, "From where do you come?"

I answer in the same weird language, "From Fergus of Cleave."

"Show it the brooch," Tom suggests, which I do, by holding out my arm.

The creature half bows. In a tight-throated wheeze, it says, "That does not impress me particularly. You wish to have a younger removed?"

Tom says, "We wish to *find* a younger. One that was stolen for Fergus of Cleave. A Taker named Yegg replaced an Eorthe younger with a changeling. We're on a quest to find this younger from Eorthe."

"I am Yegg. I remember. Rarely do I go to Eorthe."

I gasp. "You're Yegg?"

This ugly creature is the one who stole Mom and Dad's child. I can feel a rush of fury rise up from the soles of my boots.

Tom telepaths, *Calm, Emma, We'll get nothing from this being if you lose control!* Aloud, he says in a firm polite voice, "Can you help us?"

"If you wish to have a younger taken or replaced."

"What can we offer you for this information?" Tom asks.

Yegg laughs, a whistling painful sound. "I doubt that I require anything you can offer. You work for Fergus of Cleave. He still owes me a pledge. I give you *nothing*."

"But didn't you take the Eorthe child as payment?" I ask, my voice high and tight.

"I did. But Fergus of Cleave also promised me five good Game Players from his world. He withheld that payment. I will bide my time until I receive my lex talionis in other ways."

"Lex what?" I ask.

"That is one of the languages of your world. You are a human, are you not? And you don't understand?" Yegg sneers.

"It means revenge," Tom says.

I take a deep breath. I want to shout, "If anyone deserves revenge it isn't you, you revolting creature." But instead I say, "Maybe we can help you get your revenge."

The creature moves forward a few paces. Three yellow flashes glimmer in the darkness under the crimson headpiece. "Who are you to think you can help me do this?"

"We're on a Seeker Game for Fergus," I say. "If I find the younger that was taken from Eorthe within one mooncrest, I'll win the game. He's promised to give me something I need. I could ask him to give what you're owed, too."

Again Yegg laughs, and my ears almost flap in the

air currents. "How untaught and guileless you are, younger. I wish you good fortune getting even the eye of a mousel from *him*."

"It's a chance I have to take," I say. "That younger is important to my family. My mother is dying. The younger is her child. She needs to find her. Please help us."

"Mother? Family? I know these concepts, but I don't understand this bond — what is the point? It drives humans to do the most curious things," Yegg says. She comes closer. "You *are* human, am I right?"

I change to my Watcher form.

Yegg leans forward. "Ahh, a Watcher. But you call this Eorthe woman *mother?*"

"I — uh — I was also a changeling. Placed a number of Earth years before you brought the child of the Suzar and Suzarain of Argadnel to my parents' farm and took their child. I was brought up as a human, I'm not one. But I still love my mother. My *family.*"

"Your family! Drivel! You are a Watcher. Your only job was to watch over the Argadnel younger. Not the Eorthe younger. Love … family … they are of no value."

"But you know where the Eorthe younger was taken." It's all I can do to keep from screaming at her.

I hear Tom say, *You're doing great, Emma. Keep it up.*

"Perhaps I do, perhaps I don't," Yegg squeals. "What does it matter, Watcher? Give up the Game. You will lose."

"I won't. I've just finished beating Fergus at Fidchell."

Yegg's laugh careens around the cave. I want to cover my ears, but I won't allow myself any sign of weakness. "You are a tale-spinner, Watcher. No one beats Fergus at Fidchell. He doesn't allow it."

"But I *did* beat him."

For a moment, Yegg is silent, then she says, almost dreamily, "It *would* be like a receiving a gold moon to see Fergus brought down a world or two." Yegg sweeps a black claw through the air. "Yes, why not?"

I can't believe it. Is she actually going to tell us, just to get even with Fergus?

"We'll need to know exactly where you took the child, Yegg," Tom says.

"It's not difficult," Yegg sneers. "I gave it to the mask maker, Mirour, who lives in Cymmarian Market. He often places these youngers for me. Find him and give him this talisman."

She throws something at us. Tom catches it in his beak then drops it in my hand. It's a small silver bakke. A talisman. My third game piece.

Yegg says, "Mirour will know who gave you that. He may decide to tell you where the younger is. He may not. That is all I can do."

It almost chokes me but I manage to say "Thank you."

I take the little map device out of my pouch and hand it to Cill. She begins to look up the symbols for Cymmarian Market.

I can't stand it. I have to know. Before I can stop myself, I ask the Taker, "Why do you steal youngers? Aren't you ever sorry that you take them away from their families and homes?"

Tom shouts in my head, *We don't have a way out of here yet, Emma. Don't anger her. Shut up and let's go!*

But Yegg isn't angry. She's clearly puzzled.

"What is *sorry?* I only understand satisfaction. I am well paid. No one cares about the youngers. They are useful, but of no real value. You see, to move from a marginal Player in the Game to an active Player, I must *accumulate*. Land, riches, tradable items … what these things give me is *power*. When I accumulate enough power, I will be able to amass a strong group of Players, entice them from other Game Masters. And one day I will be the greatest Game Player in all the worlds."

"And then what?" I ask.

"I do not understand."

"Once you become the greatest Game Player in all the worlds," I say, as if she's a bit dim, "what then?"

Suddenly, the air shifts, growing darker. "The Game is the only worthwhile challenge in all the worlds! Surely even one as stupid as you knows that to be true!"

My next words are out of my mouth before I think. "I don't know it's true at all. How can anything to do with the Game be worthwhile? Game Players don't do anything that's worth … *anything* … do they? You and Fergus certainly don't!" I immediately want to suck the words back into my throat.

I hear Tom gasp, and there's a small whimper from Cill.

Yegg screeches, "It is *you,* Watcher, who do not know the value of anything. You think you have insulted me by comparing me with a Player of Fergus's ability. You have not. But I *will* beat him one day."

Apologize or we're dead! Tom shouts.

I bow deeply and back away. "Forgive my hasty words," I say formally. "We'll — uh — just get going now."

Her screeching bangs off the walls, searing my eardrums. "You have fifty breaths to escape my hollow in order to prove you are worthy of keeping the bakke. Let's see if you can make it before I or my little pets tear you to bits."

She moves forward, like a huge hooded snake readying itself to strike.

Tom flies to the sloop shouting, *Get over here and get these coordinates in place or we'll be bakke meat. That's less than two minutes!*

As we race on board, Cill pushes the map device into my hand. "I find code for Cymmarian Market. There. You fix it in. I get us moving," she says.

I run over to the lighted panel expecting Yegg to attack any second now, but instead I hear a loud screech followed by silence. When I look back over my shoulder, Yegg is trussed up in vines, like a roast ready for the oven.

"How did you do that?" I shout at Cill.

"Just put in code!" she calls back. "Tom and I get us out to cave opening!"

As I set to work, I feel the little sloop turn around. There are five symbols in the Cymmarian Market code. I press the first button, looking for a red circle with five blue dots in the center. It's not there. I press the second one and thank heaven it's the first symbol that comes up. I go to the next button, looking for a backward G with a tail. There it is. Now for a tent shape, yes … and now for an upside-down J with spikes. My hands are trembling. When will the bakkes drop on us? The final symbol is a starburst with a small face below it. I can't seem to get the green triangle to hold that symbol in place. It keeps sliding away. Above us, a low chirruping grows into loud chittering.

I can feel the movement of the sloop and look up. Cill has extended her fingers to the small columns that flank the hallway. Braced against one of the steel seats, she's pulling us along the waterway at a pretty good clip. Each time we reach a pillar, she points her other hand at the next one and the long fingers slide through the air. Tom flies nearby. If Cill misses, he grabs her vinelike fingers and winds them around the pillar so Cill can tighten her grip.

"We've got less than a minute," Tom cries.

We're now in the cave with the small volcanoes. I aim the bow of the sloop toward the small opening ahead. My hands are shaking. I work at getting the face symbol to stay up. Finally it works.

"I've got it!" I shout, locking it in.

"Push the blue, then the yellow, then the green again," Tom shouts. I push the blue one, then the yellow, just as a swarm of bakkes lowers like a black curtain outside the opening. At the same time, a small swarm falls from the ceiling and covers the flight panel. My hand misses the green button, and I can't get near it again.

"Oooh, we be dead soon," Cill wails. "You hide. I *fight*."

"Tom, what should we do?"

"Push the black button under the seat. Gyro said to use it in emergencies!"

"But it's never been tested!" I shout.

The flapping above turns into a thunderous pounding. Thousands of bakkes soar out of the stalactites. I hit out at the first one that tries to land on me, but soon I'm covered with so many, I can't fight them off. Razor teeth cut into my arms, my back. I can hear Cill shouting, too. I know I should use my Watcher training and vanish, but I can't leave Cill. I dive under the seat and push the black button with all my strength.

Everything blows up.

28

We're roaring through the air, the little sloop dipping and swaying. Behind us, a group of tattered bakkes recedes in the distance. I point at a scrawny green creature creeping out from under one of the seats. Cill grabs it and flings it into the air.

"What happen?" she cries, watching its lopsided flight. Soon it's just a speck. "How we get away?"

Tom, clinging to the big sail, says, "I don't know. It was all noise, and then the bakkes scattered. We flew straight out. You'd think the sloop had a mind of its own. It was as if it said 'Boo!' and scared the creatures away. It's *amazing.*" His feathers are ruffled and some are sticking out at weird angles. I check my hands. They're covered in red bite marks. Some of them are bleeding.

"Well, let's hope this little airship knows where it's going *now,*" I say, shaking my hands to try to ease the pain.

The sloop tips slightly from side to side.

Tom laughs. "It *does* have a mind of its own. I like that."

I check the flight panel. The settings are the ones I put in. I guess the black button acted like the final green switch.

"You guys were so brave," I say. "We wouldn't have made it if it wasn't for you two."

Tom turns his head to one side and winks at Cill and then at me. Suddenly I feel light as air. At this perfect moment, bites and all, I'm happy.

Cill says worriedly, "Now we go to this place Cymmarian Market. Maybe more monsters."

I give her a little push. "Hey, I think we can beat a few small monsters, don't you?"

She titters and Tom laughs softly. I'm just glad he hasn't brought up the fact that my big mouth almost got us killed back there.

The little sloop banks to the left, and suddenly we cut through a thin border wall into total blackness. There is no up and no down, just a cool, peaceful, anonymous darkness. Pale lights come on all along the sloop's handrails and the edges of the sails. I sit down on the floor, wishing I had a sleeping bag. The metal is hard and cold.

At least the air is sweet. Cill is standing by the railing, and I see her glance at the time marker on her arm. "We be well into second Earth day now," she announces.

"Plenty of time," I call back, knowing it's not true.

Her face leaves shift to a concerned frown, but then she digs into her body leaves and comes out with a pouch. It's full of small wooden boxes, tiny glass pots and vials. She opens one, dabs my wounds with a soothing cream, then pats me awkwardly and says, "You sleep, Emma Watcher ... need strength." She moves off a little way, lies down and closes her eyes.

I gaze at the pile of leaves and smile. Tom lands beside me and without thinking I whisper, "Why do you think we trust her?"

"Do we?" he asks uncertainly.

"For some reason," I say, "we've accepted her as one of us. But she *is* Fergus's slave — she relies on him for everything. How do we know she isn't a spy? How do we know she isn't relaying information to him through that thing on her arm?"

Tom says, "We don't. But we've been with her almost every second, and I bet Warder Whinge didn't take his eyes off her. When did she have the opportunity to talk into that thing or send a message?"

"Maybe when she's reading it, she —"

"I do no such thing," a gravelly voice cries. Cill is sitting up, leaves bristling.

"You heard us?" I ask, realizing we should have been telepathing. But I thought she was asleep.

"I be of forest. I hear feather fall. Your whispering nothing." Then she adds in a hurt tone, "And I no be spy for Fergus."

"Well, you must understand why we're wondering," Tom says, not unkindly.

Her face fans out into a leafy circle, her red eyes sparking. "I do. I be slave, but I not be *willing* slave. Fergus hold my people in tight fist. I no have allegiance to slave owner. This first time I free — even short time. You be my *friends*. But you no trust me now."

"That's not true, Cill," I insist. "But you can't blame us for wondering. Even so ... I mean ... we *do* like you."

"You just not sure *how* to trust me," she says sadly. "I understand. You take time marker. I not touch anymore. That way you know to be safe."

Tom and I look at each other. I feel ashamed. Our instincts have surely been right all along. "If we can't ever trust anyone, what's the point of *anything?*" I ask him.

"That's a notion that Fergus would not agree with," he says, laughing. "But, hey, I'll go along with it for now."

I grin at him.

"You keep your time marker, Cill," he says. "Emma says you won't betray us, and I'm inclined to agree."

Cill's leaves flutter and turn a gentle russet red. She lunges forward and hugs me hard, then gently taps Tom with one of her long fingers. Instead of the moldering smell I'd picked up when we first met her, she now has a scent like freshly mowed grass mixed with sage and nutmeg. She pushes me away, snuffles and returns to her sleeping spot, where she curls up with a sigh.

I no sooner lie down than I'm dreaming of horrible creatures with fangs, of flapping wings, of darkness and strange clamorous music.

29

I wake up to curious snapping sounds. The heat is overwhelming and I can't see a thing, the atmosphere is so clouded with red grit. A sandy wind hits the airship like crackling waves on an open sea.

Cill grabs my arm. "Hard to breathe," she moans. "Drying inside out. Look." She is covered with sandy red powder. Her face is curling up.

"Where are we?" I ask. "Where's Tom?" My open mouth fills with sand. I spit it out.

Tom calls out from the stern, "Over here. I fell asleep. I'm sorry."

As soon as the words are out of his mouth, the little sloop tilts sideways. A loud grinding noise is followed by a sharp downward tilt.

"Tom!" I shout. "What's happening?"

"Yeow! We going to crash!" Cill wails.

Tom battles toward us, his wings fighting the wind, but a gust pulls him up and away. He's a struggling speck, then he's gone.

"Tom!" I shriek. The sloop twists in circles. As we spin, a huge shadow rears up in front of us. We lurch forward and the shadow moves over us, eclipsing everything.

"Aiiyee!" cries Cill.

All I can see are red gills, monstrous talons and a long jagged tail that swings over our heads, then bangs against the metal sail. A loud boomph, a wail of pain and the creature drops behind us, vanishing into the murky tumult below.

"A drakon," Cill calls out. "That be killer!"

I've seen pictures of drakons — giant winged beasts with feathery chests and fierce faces like crocodile-birds. But I didn't know they were this *huge*.

For a split second, the air clears and I look for Tom. In the cloudy light, a vast desert of dark red sand dunes slides below. In the distance a large blue lake? No, it's gone in the next wave of sand. If I don't do something we will crash. I crawl to the flight panel. My fingers hover over the black emergency button. I'm afraid to push it. Gyro said it only had three "pushes" in it. Suddenly, a series of lights go on and off on the flight panel, and the sloop stands absolutely still. My hair is flying around my head, but the ship doesn't move. There's a deep pulsating rumble under my feet. We lurch to the left, and as I slide toward the edge, I reach out and press the black button. Nothing happens. The fine sand has locked it shut.

Margaret Buffie

I'm thrown against the seats when the sloop turns again sharply. To my horror, I can see the twisting shape of a drakon — the same one? — coming at us. The sloop tries to turn, but it isn't fast enough. We hit the thing head-on, carrying it with us like the plow on a snow-clearing truck. Clinging to the railing, I can see the dunes only a few feet below us. We're going to crash. The creature is roaring like a thousand wounded lions. I slide into Cill's soft body as the sloop hits the ground, churning sand high in the air behind it.

The wind howls furiously around us. I try to brush the grit out of my eyelashes. I choke and spit out sand and dust as dark as dried blood.

"Cill," I shout, "are you okay?"

A hand grabs me. "We die out here," Cill exclaims. "We need shelter. Come."

Before I can object, she's over the side of the sloop with me in tow. We run toward the bow. The head of the drakon is half buried in the sand.

"He dead?" she whispers. "I think he dead."

The beast is twice as big as our sloop. Its huge taloned feet lie sprawled, already covered with drifts of scarlet sand.

Cill moves around one enormous foot and leads me to a deep cave formed by its front leg and chest. She crawls inside. When I hesitate, she gestures impatiently. Inside the cave, the smell is strong but not repulsive — almost pleasant, as if the drakon's skin has been oiled with spices. We crouch in the relative quiet and watch the red sand skim past, the howling of the wind distant and less scary here.

I look at Cill. Her eyes are closed. The leaves have dried on her face exposing dark cracked lips. A pale green fluid oozes from the cracks.

"You're hurt," I say.

"I be needing moisture soon — I have my healing pots and bags, but not have time for water." She takes a small vial of thick yellow salve out of her pouch in her leafy skirts and spreads some on her lips. "We need fluids or we die."

I try not to think of the dryness in my mouth and throat. Tom is missing, we have no water, and we're stuck under the arm of a giant reptile. Despite the heat, I'm suddenly chilled to the bone with fear and worry. I rest my forehead on my knees. I now know we won't make it.

30

I drift into an exhausted sleep, I don't know for how long; but suddenly I'm awake, and every cell in my body senses something has changed. I lift my head. The wind has stopped. Thin clear moonlight shines into our drakon cave.

I push Cill's shoulder. "Cill. Look."

She opens her eyes. "Now we find water?"

"We'll try."

I stand up and my head touches the drakon's leg. I immediately fall onto my backside, my mouth opening and closing like a landed fish. "It — it moved."

"What move?"

I point up. Above our heads, the long stretch of greenish scaly skin is quivering.

Cill grabs my hand. We barely make it outside when a huge claw lifts into the air and crashes down right beside us. We run to the side of the sloop, just as it's pushed backward into the sand by the creature's back legs stretching. Behind us, the drakon's head lifts out of the sand and lets out a deep roar.

"Oh, jeez!" I cry. "It's alive after all!"

Cill grabs my arm and we stare mesmerized as another head — a dusty leather-helmeted orb topped with three black feathers — appears over the top of the drakon's nose. A black leather hand undoes the chin strap and peels away the helmet to reveal a beautiful dark green face with a yellow nose pointed like a beak and piercing blue eyes. Atop its glistening head is a big topknot of shiny black feathers. Its eyes widen when they see the little sloop.

"So this is what hit us." To my surprise, the creature speaks in Treidwij, the universal language for trade throughout the worlds. "Poor Lycias couldn't get his bearings. By bringing us down I believe you may have saved us from a terrible end."

The drakon lifts his head, but the birdwoman swats at it with her hand. "Stay put, Lycias." The creature groans and his head subsides. "I've once-overed him with my scanner." She holds up a shiny piece of coal-black glass. "He's sound. Just needs to get himself upright. Drakons are clumsy beasts on the ground but, aah, celestial sprites in the air."

The feathered head vanishes, and a second later the birdwoman appears around the end of the drakon's beak and rests her foot on it. She's at least seven feet tall and dressed in oily black leather from narrow head to slender ankle. Her feet are bare, the green toes long and bony, the nails yellow talons. Over her shoulder hangs a drawstring bag covered in more shiny hard feathers.

She strides up to the little sloop and stares at it intently. Over her shoulder she calls out, "Lycias — up!"

The great creature struggles, kicking up buckets of red sand, but finally rights himself. On his back is a saddle of black leather with streamers of black feathers hanging from it. Bulging leather bags are tied tightly to the saddle. The drakon shakes himself and roars. His green scales rattle, and the deep blue feathers on his chest billow out clouds of red dust. He stands up, his leathery wings trailing in the sand as he staggers around getting his bearings.

"I thought he was dead," I say in wonder. "We used his legs as a cave — to protect us from the sand storm."

But the tall creature isn't listening. "Where did you get this ship?"

"From the Searcher Gyro."

She turns her startling blue eyes on me. "I am Badba. I come from Ravan in the Tag-A-Longs. I travel to all worlds. From a Searcher, eh? You searching for someone?"

"My name is Emma, and this is Cill. Yes, I'm searching for my mother's child. She was taken and a changeling put in her place. We were heading to

Cymmarian Market. But right now, I'm worried about my friend, Tom. He's an owl — blown out of the ship. I'm hoping he was able to fly —"

"A bird?" She heaves the bag off her shoulder, opens it and lifts out a struggling pile of feathers. "This one?"

"Tom!" I cry, reaching out.

She lifts him high in the air. "Not so fast. I fancy an owl dinner. I grabbed him as he swooped by in the storm. They are rare beasts in my travels." She sucks her teeth. "A tasty meal for me and my drakon, I think."

"Put me down. I insist that you release me!" Tom bellows.

He swings his head to one side. Badba shouts and drops him. He flies straight at me. I hug him hard.

Badba whips out a long dagger and holds it up, ready to throw.

"No!" Cill cries, pushing herself in front of us.

Badba leans over and glares at her, shaking her bitten hand. Then she grins, displaying long yellow teeth.

"I have been to your land of Barroch many times," she says to Cill. "Even before Fergus took over. You aren't warriors. You don't scare me, leaf bundle!" This close, I can see that Badba's skin is actually made of tiny glistening feathers. Is she a bird or a humanoid? She has no wings.

Cill holds herself as tall as she can, her red eyes

gleaming. "I be Sover-reign of Barroch tribe. Put away your — *that* —" she points at the long knife in Badba's hand "— or I no heal drakon."

Badba laughs. "You — a Sover-reign? Of what? The slaves who toil and fetch for Fergus of Cleave?" Then she stops. "What did you say? My drakon isn't injured."

Cill points a long finger and says, "Then why his wing down, like it broken?"

Badba turns and we all look at the poor drakon wandering in circles, one wing dragging in the sand.

Badba dissolves, becoming a shadow that slides quickly over the sand, leaving a trail of purple light. Suddenly she appears beside the drakon. She looks him over before frantically waving. "Come! You! Barroch! Come!"

After Cill rustles away, Tom and I go to look over the little sloop. We push buttons on the flight panel but no lights appear. "It's broken. And I don't know how to repair it," Tom says.

"Maybe that Badba creature could —"

He whispers, "Be careful. She's a Ravan."

"Is that bad?"

"They're scavengers. They go from world to world collecting stuff to sell or barter at the world markets. They also do odd jobs for the more unsavory Game Players — spying, stealing, thieving. If we say the sloop is broken, she'll come back and strip it bare. We can't let her get the mechanism for Gyro's ship. She'll sell it to someone."

"But maybe we can use her in other ways."

"No," he says forcefully. "You can't trust Ravans, Emma. Let's make sure Cill's okay and then get as far away from that Ravan as we can."

We approach the drakon just in time to hear Badba command it to lie still. The huge creature lowers itself to the sand and closes its eyes, but the moans that come from its chest are pitiful.

"You not attuned to drakon," Cill says, shaking her head.

"Lycias and I are old friends. I would never neglect him," Badba growls. "I checked him over. He was fine."

Cill points to a thick viscous liquid trailing down from a deep gash in the drakon's wing. In the sand it turns to a dark purple goo.

Badba runs to the animal's head and throws herself on his hideous nose, screeching like she's being stuck with pins.

Cill pays no attention. She's searching through her pouch, pulling out three or four vials. "You there!" she calls to Badba. "Quit silly noise! You lift me up to wound."

Badba immediately does as she's told, sniveling to herself. Tom and I look at each other but try not to laugh. Soon, though, I can hear small irritated rumbles and hoots coming from his chest.

"What is it?" I ask.

"We should get going. It will be a long walk for

you and Cill to the market. I'll fly ahead and guide you, but we should leave now."

"She has to help the drakon. He's in pain, Tom."

"There's no guarantee the Ravan won't kill us afterward. She's dangerous — unpredictable."

"But if Cill doesn't help, then Badba *will* be angry and vengeful."

He backs down, grumbling how if he wasn't locked in a stupid bird's body, he'd get things done a lot quicker, and maybe — just once — I'd listen … and when she slits our throats maybe then I'd admit I was wrong.

Cill is dabbing the wing of the drakon with various oils. Soon the creature's moaning eases and a peace that is almost beatific descends on his ugly face.

"He be fine now," Cill calls. "All healed."

Badba, who has been crouched on the drakon's back watching Cill work, leaps into the air, does a backward flip, lands on her feet in the sand, and dances wildly in circles.

"Barbarian," mutters Tom.

"I will reward you all!" Badba cries, her voice a high screech of joy. "Come. Lycias and I will take you to the market!"

31

"There it is!" Badba calls out, pointing to a wavery blue oval cut into the red sand dunes.

A large lake riffles in the night wind and glows dimly, as if there are lights under its surface. I can't see a market though. I'm clinging to Badba's back, with Tom flying just above us and Cill hanging on to me. She's feeling better, as Badba gave us a few sips of water. The saddle is hard and slippery, and at first I had a few moments of breath-gulping certainty I was about to slip away into the hot air below. Cill bounces behind me. A minute ago she wrapped her fingers around the saddle horn and twirled her toes through the side straps, so I now feel fairly secure.

The sand swoops past below, and every now and again a tall thin funnel of red dust floats up beside us. Suddenly I remember a desert in the Fidchell game. Is Badba one of the glass figures? Is Cill? Does this mean Mathus has some idea where we are?

A spiral of red dust leans in, as if trying to grab us. "Dust snakes," Badba shouts, laughing as it tugs at Lycias's wing. Lycias ducks and weaves, then with a loud bellow shoots straight up in the air before leveling off.

"That blue area isn't water!" Tom calls out to me from above. "It's a tent of some kind!"

As we get closer, I can see that it is indeed a blue tent — perhaps half a mile wide and almost a mile long, with smaller green tents all along one side. As we swoop closer, Badba seems to be directing Lycias to an opening at one end of the green tents.

Lycias drops gently down to the sandy surface and lands in front of red sandstone pillars with a gate stretched between them. In front of one of the pillars is a dusty gatehouse.

The green tents are open on all sides, full of animals, drakons, camel-like creatures, sand sleighs of all sorts and many kinds of airships. The smell is powerful, like a giant's country barn — multiplied by a zillion.

"Hey, it's a parking lot," I say to Tom, who has landed on my shoulder. I slide down from the saddle after Badba. She directs Lycias to a large stall in the green tent nearest us and pays the stable keeper to take good care of him. Then we walk toward the gatehouse. A guard steps out of it. He has no hair or ears that I can see, but he does have three huge nostrils and warts all over his thick face. His eyes are lost in deep circles of sooty black.

He smirks at Badba. "So you're back then, Ravan.

Thought the market tribunal kicked you out. You got the token to show you're allowed back in?"

Badba gives him a shiny disc from her hip bag.

He jerks his head toward us. "What about them, then?"

She shrugs. "They're my helpers. Useless lot, but I have much to gather while I'm here."

The guard looks us up and down with little interest and waves us through. The gate opens slowly. The monstrous blue tent is cool and the light is strangely diffused, like twilight; but it teems with beings of all colors, sizes and shapes. The bombardment of music, voices, smells and sights takes my breath away.

Buyers are milling around the stalls that are ranged throughout, while sellers are shouting out their wares. Many shoppers are holding masks to their faces on slender colored sticks. The masks are fabulous, some grotesque with twisted or gaping mouths and crazy expressions, others serene and beautiful. Most are trimmed with feathers, jewels or long beaded fronds.

Somewhere under the babble of voices, there's the low beat of drums, the thin thread of a flute, a burst of bells and now and again short tight shouts and whistles. A small group of women dressed in cerulean cloaks and hoods flows in front of us like an undulating wave, leaving a low whispering chant in its wake. Just as they pass, I see someone standing nearby — a cloaked figure in sapphire blue, his face hidden deep in the hood, a silver mask with beaded eye slits held in front. The empty eye sockets are directed at us. Someone pushes him to one side, and he lifts a hand to grab a tent pole to steady himself. His arm is covered in swirling tattoos.

I freeze. The only beings I know who have tattoos like that are Huw and Bedeven. Both work for Rhona. Has one of them tracked us down?

"Tom," I hiss. "Look!"

"I see him."

I move quickly toward the cloaked figure, but a juggler dressed all in white, with a tight hood over his head, moves in front of us, blocking my view. Only the pale green eyes of the juggler can be seen; his nose and mouth are covered with the thin white fabric. Rising out of the top of his skull cover is a long pointed tube on which rests a bright red ball. Around him whirl thousands more red balls — now and again one of them bumps against the stationary one, which jumps and lets out a whistle each time it's hit.

The juggler's hands move so fast they're a blur. He winks at me and a swarm of tiny balls spins around my head, then vanishes. When Badba calls to us to follow her through the crush behind the juggler, I find one of the balls clenched tightly in my hand. When I open my fingers, it turns into a tiny yellow toad and hops away.

"How that happen?" Cill whispers. "I no see that happen. You hand never move."

The blue cloaked figure is gone, but behind us I hear the juggler laugh. Was he sent to distract us? I turn to talk to him, but he, too, is gone. All around us are stalls tightly packed with crystal globes, carpets that glow as if lit from within, bolts of silk and fine wool, jewelry, clothing, food of all sorts, flowers of amazing shapes and sizes, as well as tropical birds with strange high-pitched voices, monkeys dressed in pantaloons and more bizarre animals all in elaborate cages. Even the ground is covered with layers of vibrant tapestries and rugs. I keep a sharp eye out for the cloaked figure.

"I'll see if I can locate him." Tom flies up from my shoulder just as a boy bumps into me. I stumble and the boy catches my arm. I look into a smooth golden-brown face with wide yellow eyes that seem to know me. He glances down, then up at me, an appeal of some kind in his eyes. Then he's gone.

When I turn to look after him, something catches my toe. At my foot is a metal mask about as big as my palm. It has a roughly soldered grip on the back. The boy must have dropped it deliberately. I look around for him and see his face over the top of someone's shoulder. I hold up the mask, but he only nods twice and vanishes into the crowd. I slide the mask into my pouch. My fourth game piece. A mask. Surely this must mean I'm going in the right direction ... so far.

I look around for Tom. He's on one of the tent wires that crisscross above our heads. "Have you seen the Blue Cloak guy?"

He shakes his head and swoops back to me. "Can't be anyone we know. Rhona thinks we're on a scouting mission for Fergus, remember?"

I feel a chill go through me. "But Gormala saw me in the castel."

"Maybe they think you simply went home to inform Summer you were leaving on Fergus's mission." He's looking at me oddly. What's up with him?

"But Tom, Bedeven told Huw the scouting thing sounded implausible and it would take time to track us down. I heard them in the hallway of the castel. What if Rhona's found out about the Seeker Game? She could've sent one of them to screw this up for us."

Tom looks around uneasily. "She might, but think, Emma — she also knows you'll be back in Argadnel soon, so why bother? I can't figure out why they seemed to be focusing on you all of a sudden."

"I don't know, either. But Tom, that person in the blue cloak had tattoos on his arm. And what about that shadow I saw following us at Searcher Gyro's? What if it's the same guy?" I try to keep the panic out of my voice.

Tom states matter-of-factly, "I really doubt Rhona knows about the Seeker Game. Fergus and Mathus would never tell her or Huw anything. There are lots of beings with tattoos in the worlds."

Cill says, "Ooo, I hope it not Huw. I no like Huw."

Tom adds quickly, "Let's forget it for now. We're here to find the mask maker."

Badba is waiting by a food stall, hands on hips. "Do you have any coins?"

I nod.

"Well, buy us something to feast on then."

The food seller is a fat man whose head is swathed in a high turban of pink stripes. His eyes are so crossed I'm not sure he can even see me, but he holds a tray of almond-scented flowers, cone-shaped pastries and amber sugar figures under my nose. Then, like magic, that tray vanishes and another of sweetmeats, nuts, fried pastries and sugared dates appears in the same hand. That vanishes and another appears, filled with rows of grasshoppers and tiny pink and white fish, both made of glistening fruits and colored almond paste.

Suddenly I realize how hungry I am. I take one of my thin gold coins from my pouch and offer it to him. He smiles and nods and loads a small basket with the items I point at.

Badba appears at my shoulder, points to a dozen more treats and, while the man puts them into another small basket, grabs a handful of spiced nuts and crunches on them. The seller says nothing, but takes back a sugared fish as payment.

When I give one of the baskets to Badba, she selects a fat grasshopper and says, her mouth full,

"Now. Where do you wish to go? I have much to do and I can't look after you all day."

"We're looking for a mask maker. By the name of Mirour," Tom says, dipping his head into my basket and grabbing one of the grasshoppers in his beak.

Badba stands as still as a statue and stares at us. People go around her uneasily. I don't blame them. With her fierce face and those long daggers slung on her hips, she looks like she'd cut you in two without a second thought. A small figure standing to one side catches my eye. It's the boy who bumped into me, watching us. I no sooner spot him than he dissolves into the crowd.

"There's only one mask maker at Cymmarian Market, and Mirour's his name," Badba says speculatively, "but what do you want with *him,* of all beings?"

I stuff a couple of fried pastries into my mouth and offer the basket to Cill, who examines everything carefully before nibbling on some nuts. The basket vanishes into her leaves. "We keep this for emergency ration."

I'm about to argue, but she's right.

Badba pokes my arm with one of her long yellow nails. "Well? Why are you trying to find the mask maker?"

I say, nonchalantly, "Oh, I just have a message for him."

She narrows her eyes into slits. "What message?"

I bristle. "It's private."

She shrugs. "Fine, don't tell me. Regret it at your leisure."

"I doubt it," mutters Tom, around a grasshopper wing.

"If it's about this missing younger, you'll have to cross his palm with gold," Badba says, then stares at Tom and picks her teeth as if picturing the meal he might have been. He grumbles quietly in my head about how he'd take her on if he could only get rid of these stupid feathers.

She grins ferociously, like she's read his mind, and walks away. "Follow me, Watcher."

"Careful, careful," mutters Cill, keeping close to my side. "I no trust her."

Tom growls agreement, but not very loudly, I notice.

As we follow, I snarl, "Honestly, you two. How else are we going to find the mask maker in all this chaos?" I roll my eyes in frustration, just in time to see a silver disc fly toward my head. I duck, and a skinny woman in tattered silk screeches and catches it in midair, rushes past, flings herself at a table and throws the disc back up onto the spinning tip of a long reed, then hares back and forth trying to keep about twenty more goblets and plates balanced on twenty more twirling, twisting pieces of reed. Behind the table, a cloaked figure in blue slides into the crowd.

The audience surrounding the Balancer ooohs
and aaaahs and tosses coins at the table. She beams
at them after giving me a look of sheer hatred, as if
I was the one who'd knocked off the plate. Was it an
accident? Or did the hooded figure try to hit me —
or Tom — with it?

Badba grabs my arm in an iron fist and drags me
away from the balancing act, past a crooning poet,
around a fountain that spurts colored glitter balls
into the air, next to a man orbiting toffee on what
looks like a golden spinning wheel, and in front of
a wild puppet act that reminds me of a Punch and
Judy show — loud and violent, with puppets
beating each other with silver clubs tied with
bright ribbons.

We turn a corner into a shadowy open area.
With a fling of Badba's arm, I stumble forward.
Tom's wings bat my head as he tries to keep his
balance. Cill crashes into us, puffing so hard I'm
afraid she's going to fall over in a leafy faint.

"The mask maker of Cymmarian," Badba says. "I
warn you: keep your guard up and your face out of
that Mirror Mimicker he's so proud of."

Then she stalks away.

32

"Good riddance," Tom says. "What a puffed-up, self-satisfied wretch! A thief and drifter who only looks after herself!"

"You're just saying that because she was going to eat you." I can't help grinning.

"You can be pretty silly sometimes, you know that?" He points one wing toward her disappearing back. "*That* is a dangerous creature and I'm glad she's gone."

"Well, she got us to the right place."

"Hmph," Tom mutters. "That's the last we'll see of her, I hope."

We're standing in front of a dark doorway covered in painted faces that are faded with wear — some grimacing, grinning or gently smiling, some crying and many with flat, dull expressions.

The shop is crowded with thousands of colorfully decorated masks that hang from the ceiling and walls and dangle in bunches from wooden racks in the middle of the room.

A beaded doorway at the back of the shop clatters open. A humanlike being walks in, dressed in tan-colored cloth with a beige apron wrapped around his small round form. He has a pursed mouth tucked between fat cheeks, a round little nose and no eyebrows. His eyes are tiny black dots under a heavy forehead. He reminds me of the cherub faces on Valentine cards, except that his hair is light brown, thin and frizzy. As he comes closer, I realize it isn't a face at all, but a mask. A shiver of alarm runs down my body like electricity.

"Can I be of service, my dears?" the mask asks in a smarmy voice. The rosebud mouth turns up into a stiff smile like a tiny V. How did he make it move? Repulsion makes me take a step back. Perhaps thinking I'm going to leave without buying anything, he asks, "A pretty mask for the pretty girl?"

"Are you Mirour, the mask maker?"

He bows slightly. "I am."

"We come from the Taker Yegg," I say, "who removed an Earth child from a bee farm almost nine Earth years ago for Fergus of Cleave. Yegg replaced this child with the daughter of the Suzar and Suzarain of Argadnel and sold the other child to you, Mirour. She said you would know where this other child is."

The mask's smile vanishes. "How do I know you come from Yegg?" The voice is cold and stiff now.

I open my pouch, take out the silver bakke and show it to him.

The mask maker looks down at the talisman and then back up at me. The raisin-black eyes turn to Tom and then to Cill.

"I will be paid for this information," he states coldly, but I see the hot glint of greed in the eyes behind the mask.

I plunge my hand back into my pouch and take out all the coins I have, laying them on the counter. The cupid's mask contemplates them for a second, then lets out a cluster of tee-hee-hees through the tiny V. "You can't be serious. I can't sell important information for this paltry sum. Go now, I am busy." He points to the door and turns to leave.

"Wait!" Cill calls. She scrabbles around in her pile of leaves, then holds something up under the mask's button nose. On her leathery palm are three leaves of dark gold.

Mirour's mouth forms an "oh" the size of a pencil's eraser and lets out a thin hissing sound.

Cill says, "That be gold of purest essence. I am artisan for Fergus of Cleave. I make many things from these. Take or not. No matter to us." She shrugs.

The mask maker's hand reaches out to take the leaves and scoops up my gold pieces as well. The whole lot disappears into a pocket on his apron. Suddenly the voice is all honey again. "Come, my dears. Follow me."

Mirour leads us around the stands of masks and

through the curtained door into a long dark room with dim glow spheres along the walls. The strong smell of lacquer and solvents hazes the air. We walk past tables of youngers pasting ribbons and feathers on masks. No one looks up from the work. There is silence in the room except for the click of beads and the hiss and bubble of pots full of steaming glue.

At the far end of the room, we turn a sharp corner. Against one wall are a dozen youngers lined up in two short rows. Many look tired. All are bone thin. They're almost all humanoid looking, with only an extra set of ears or a strangely shaped nose here and there, and one has teeth that seem to fill its entire lower face. The younger in charge of the straggly group is the yellow-eyed boy who bumped into me in the market. He looks at me quickly, then turns away. I know he recognizes me. I finger the mask in my pouch. Did he deliberately drop it? If so, why?

"Now," says Mirour. "I have to look at my special masks, so I can remind myself of the child you're referring to. You there, Pictree Bragg! Open the big case. Be quick about it!"

So the boy has a name — Pictree Bragg. "The youngers are tired and hungry," he says. "Can they sit on the floor until you're ready for them?"

"This won't take long," snaps Mirour. "Just get the case open. The more you talk, the longer they'll have to stand." He tosses the boy a key.

Pictree Bragg walks quickly to a hanging array of garish masks. He reaches inside them and the masks swing away, exposing a recess in the wall. Inside are rows and rows of tiny silver masks with symbols painted under them. They look just like the one in my pouch.

I move closer to get a better look. Each mask is an individual face — no two alike. A few are human-looking. "Are these masks of real beings?"

"Don't go near them!" Mirour growls. Then he instantly turns all soppy again. "Yes, my dear. These are my very *special* masks. Each represents a changeling removed from a world — from most recent to many mooncrests past. I make a copy of their facial cast partly to keep a record ..." Here he rubs his hands together. "... but also as a reminder of what a great service I have been to so many in power." He lets out a simpering sigh. "Yes, I have done well. I may not be a powerful Game Player, but I look on these faces as *mementos* of my contact with those who control the worlds through the mighty Game."

"These are trophies?" I ask, appalled that anyone would be proud of buying and selling youngers.

He leans close to me and I can see a space between the mask and his face where the skin is wrinkled and gray. "Aah, my dear, they are much more than that. These little faces show potential sellers how effective my placements will be. Once these youngers are brought to me and I put their visages into my Mirror Mimicker, I have their essence caught forever — here — in these masks. The forceful, willful elements of their spirits are removed and kept here safely. The youngers are therefore very docile and willing to work hard. It is *this* service that buyers pay for when taking on my *special* youngers."

I try to sort through what Mirour is saying. Somehow his process for making the masks strips away part of the character of the changelings and captures it in these silver masks?

"Now let's see." The fat cherub face leans down toward the bottom of the display. "Eorthe. Eorthe. Aah, yes, this is the one. I'd forgotten she was from Eorthe. She was very young when she arrived — only a nursling. But she was bright. I didn't want to sell her, so I sent her to three temporary placements. Each time, she was returned when no longer needed. I finally had to sell her," he sighs. "I regretted our parting, but I was offered a substantial amount at a time when I really needed it. You can see from the mask that she has grown quickly. She is now old enough to be sold to a soldier or a Game Player who wishes to have a wife."

He says it all with satisfaction, as if he'd sold a used car. I want to open my little brooch dagger and run him through with it. Instead, I force myself to push down my loathing and act like a Watcher. "Does this mean the mask changes as the younger ages?"

He nods, and I gaze in horror at the young faces staring blankly at me. I bend down, blinking back tears of rage, and look at the Earth child's mask. The forehead is high and smooth, the eyes round, the nose narrow, the lips full and wide ... like Dad's. And there — a shiver goes through my body — right at the corner of her mouth are two slightly raised moles. Exactly where Mom's are. She must be almost nine years old in Earth years, but she looks much older.

"I don't understand," I say. "She looks so much older than her Earth years. Almost like an adult."

"In the atmosphere of some worlds, Eorthe children age quickly. She's about your age now, I'd say."

I can't catch my breath. I'm excited and sick and terrified all at once. Finally, Mom and Dad's daughter! But *where* is she? And when we find her, will she be a zombie? Didn't Mirour say that the masks removed the spirited part of the younger?

"Do you remember who you sold her to?" I ask through dry lips.

"Of course I remember. He's a friend of mine." He runs a fat finger along the curve of the mask's cheek. "He particularly likes the dexterity of Eorthe children. He says that for some reason they handle the looms better than other youngers."

While Mirour is concentrating on the tiny face, the yellow-eyed boy catches my attention. He stares at my pouch and then at the silver masks. He jerks his head at Tom.

In my head, Tom whispers, *I think he wants me to divert Mirour's attention. He wants you to do something — take the mask? But the mask maker will know one is missing.*

"I hear you, too, Tom," whispers Cill, and I know Tom's telepathed to her as well.

I nod at the boy and telepath to Cill and Tom, *Do whatever you can to get Mirour's attention away from the masks.*

I put my hand in my pouch and wrap it around the tiny mask. My heart is bashing against my ribs.

Tom flies across the room and attacks Pictree Bragg. The boy shouts loudly and tries to fend him off. A few of the youngers squeal with fright. Cill rushes over and pretends to force Tom off the boy. The mask maker turns around with a cry and takes off at a shuffling run, shouting to the children to help. But they stand like terrified statues.

I grab Mom's Earth child's mask and replace it with the one from my pouch. I realize instantly that it's not as fine as the one I've removed. It's not as shiny or as finished. The boy must have made the fake himself.

"Tom, Cill. Stop now!"

Tom flies to my shoulder. Cill returns to my

side. She keeps looking up at Tom as if he's gone completely insane, her red eyes rolling in her head. I hope she's not overdoing it.

"Sorry about that," I tell the mask maker. "Sometimes my owl turns on someone for no reason. He got hit on the head not long ago, you see, and I think it's —"

Mirour's cherub mask is crumpled and scowling, exposing more of the gray skin below. The stiff cupid's face with its sharp eyes casts around the room, looking for things out of place. Then he rushes over to the display and quickly checks that all the masks are in place before locking it and pocketing the key.

I let out a deep breath, my knees turning to water.

His hands flapping in the air, Mirour cries, "I can't have my youngers upset or they won't make perfect masks." He points to the children. "These are for training, and I must sort them out and get them to work! You must go now."

"First, the name of the one who took the Earth girl," I say.

He snarls, "She was given to Wefta, the rug maker here in this market. Now be off!"

"Where can I find this rug maker?"

"In the waterless fountain," he snaps.

He turns his attention to Pictree Bragg, demanding that the boy take the youngers to the tables and get them to work. Pictree Bragg herds the sad little group toward the work room, giving me a sidelong glance. I can't help those youngers and I feel sick inside. To save *one* child — Mom's child ... I must stay focused.

"How do we get to the waterless fountain?" I ask loudly.

"Are you still here?" Mirour cries impatiently. "I have no more business with you. Go!"

Tom says, "We'll find it, Emma."

"I need something to show the rug maker so he'll know you've freely given us his name," I say firmly. "Don't forget, Mask Maker, I have the ear of Fergus of Cleave and of Yegg the Taker. If they decide not to use your services, you'll lose a lot of business."

Tom croaks a cheer, and I can see I've got Mirour's attention. His mask is frowning, the tiny black eyes boring into mine. I wait. Then the cupid's mask smooths again, and he reaches into one of his pockets and says in a fawning tone, "Please forgive my abruptness, my dear. Here is a key. You can use it only twice, then it is useless. He will know you came from me." He hands me a short brass pin with a blunt end and little indents all around its edge. I put it in my pouch. Amazing. A key. I now have the fifth game piece. Only one more to go. And then what?

"You'll tell Fergus of Cleave and Yegg the Taker that I have been of service to you?" he coos. "Perhaps they will be even *more* generous to one who has accommodated their envoy. Please tell them my only desire is to serve them — to bask in their glory — to be a small shadow beneath their great shadows — for they are both Players of immense and celebrated power." He bows deeply.

I feel like gagging, but while his mask is close to the floor, we scuttle out. Bursting through the door, we lose ourselves in the crowd as fast as we can. I don't want to be anywhere nearby, in case he discovers I've stolen my sister's silver face.

33

We huddle beside a food stall.

"What now?" I demand. "Should we go and talk to any one of the many rug sellers here and ask about Wefta?"

"No," Tom says. "I don't think we want to risk giving him a warning. He might move the girl. The bigger problem is this — if we do find this rug maker and the Belldam's child, how do we pay for her?"

I've given all my money to Mirour. And Cill has given all her gold to him as well.

Cill says in a low voice, "I not like to tell you this, but we now into four Earth day — almost at brim of five."

"No!" I breathe. "How can that be?"

"I think we sleep long time on sloop after Yegg and before desert wind catch us. Then we must sleep under drakon many hours."

"Oh jeez," I cry.

"Don't panic," Tom says. "If we don't find this dry fountain, it won't matter about gold or coins

— or how much time we have! Now, *think* ... did anyone see a fountain?"

I'm so frantic about how fast time is going by, that I start pacing back and forth, but Tom snarls at me to stop being a *human girl*. That makes me so angry I concentrate. I go back through the market in my mind. I see the fighting puppets, the toffee man, the poet ... no, back up a bit ... and then I remember.

"I saw a fountain on the way to the mask maker. It was near a poet and a man making toffee."

"Yes, I remember," Tom says. "I think it was due east."

Cill and I follow him. She holds on to my jacket like a little kid, trying not to screech every time a juggler or market hawker gets in our way. Finally we arrive at the big round fountain where, earlier, glitter balls had been flying. It stands slightly behind a row of stalls. The fountain is quiet now, no glitter balls zinging through the air. Made of smooth stone, it's filled with clear greenish water. The floor beneath the water is tiled in beautiful patterns. A metal tube pokes out of a stone block in the center.

"This can't be it," Tom says. "It's got water in it."

"Maybe it's just stagnant water," I say. "But how does anyone get into a *fountain?* There are no steps or door."

"Look." Cill points at a decorated booth nearby. The narrow door has a single window covered with a curlicued metal grating. On the door is a picture of the fountain and an inscription that Tom translates for us.

"It says, 'Fountain Display, only Cymmarian coins accepted.' That must mean that you have to pay to see it shoot off glitter balls."

"Maybe inside booth there a place we can use key," Cill offers.

"Yeah, maybe the key drains the fountain or something. It's worth a shot," Tom says.

"Just a minute." I lean over to put my hand into the water, but my fingers bang up against a surface as hard as glass. I tap on it with my knuckles.

"Not water," breathes Cill.

"Let's see what's in this booth, if it's open," I say.

All three of us crowd into it. There's a small metal plate on the back wall with a place for coins. Another small window on the left wall is covered with a metal grill. Tom sits on a narrow rafter looking for a keyhole in the upper part, Cill takes the floor and I search the walls. I can't see anything that even resembles a keyhole.

Suddenly, I stop. Something isn't right. A shadow flutters across the wall. "We gotta get out of here. I have —" A face hovers in the side window — a silver mask with narrow beaded eye slits.

"Let's go!" I shout, just as the booth shifts.

Cill and I both run for the door, but the booth teeters and falls, door down, with a bang. I fall against Cill.

"It's that guy in the blue cloak," I cry, trying to sit up. "He's pushed us over!"

Leather boots and blue cloth appear at the window, followed by a tattooed hand, holding a knife. The knife pokes at the window grill. The blade comes so close to Tom's back it cuts off a couple of feathers. I pull him away with a cry.

"He going to cut open window and kill us," Cill whispers. "We stop him!"

"Emma, use your knife!" Tom cries.

I yank the pin off my sleeve and snap open the short blade. When the tattooed hand begins to work the knife as a lever on the grill, I poke at it through the screen.

The hand withdraws with a yelp, and the silver mask appears. I poke at the grill again and the mask pulls away, but a few seconds later, the knife begins working around the edges of the window again, trying to pry it loose.

"All he needs is one clear shot at you, Emma!" Tom gasps. "Watcher mode! Become smaller! Move away from the window!"

"I won't change into my Watcher self and I won't move out of the way. I can't leave Cill to get the first attack."

"Emma, please."

"You know I can't, Tom."

"We like fish in wood pail," Cill growls. Her long fingers reach out and twine around the window grill.

I see her grimace in pain as the knife cuts at her.

"No!" I cry. "Cill. Remove your hand. Now!"

She looks at me stubbornly. "I no let him in to kill you, either."

"Please. I have a different way." I don't know what it is, but I can't let her lose her fingers.

She withdraws the web of vines. I can see she's really hurt.

"What do you want?" I shout through the grill.

The mask appears again. "I will take you back to Argadnel," says a whispery voice. "Come with me."

"Leave us alone and I'll quit the Game," I say. "I'll go back on my own."

"I don't believe you," the eerie voice whispers. The mask comes closer. "It would be better if you come with —"

Suddenly he disappears. The booth shudders as something heavy bangs against it. Thumps and grunts and the clash of metal echo through the small space. I lean close to the window.

"It's Badba!" I shout.

Feet, hands, knives move like swift shadows through the dim light. Blue Cloak whirls on the spot, and silver metal glints. Badba backs off with a quick somersault and lands on her splayed feet, triple-bladed daggers chopping the air. She lunges. The blue figure leaps to one side, and in a flash he's gone. He reappears just as quickly.

"Behind you!" I scream at Badba.

She lunges to her left, rolls and lands on her feet, free arm bending behind her head, her other hand slashing the air with the many-bladed knife. A crowd is building, shouting and screeching with glee. I can see the boy, Pictree Bragg, at the edge of the throng.

Blue Cloak hesitates just as Badba's free hand reappears, clutching another knife with a heavy blade. She bangs her weapons together, twirls them in the air and catches them by their tips. She lifts both arms, ready to throw them as Blue Cloak vanishes into the crowd. Badba lets out a shriek that disperses the horde. She runs after Blue Cloak but comes back quickly, a big grin on her face.

Pictree Bragg rushes to us and tries to lift the booth. Badba's face appears in the window. "Everybody all right?" she asks, and when we call out, she pushes Pictree aside. In one movement we're upright, all three of us banging into one corner.

The door creaks open and Badba stands, hands on hips.

"So. Who was that?" she asks. "And what did he want?"

"I don't know," I say shakily, helping Cill to her feet and making sure Tom is okay.

Badba grins. "Whatever he was up to, he sure wasn't expecting me, was he? And from the looks on your faces, neither were you!"

34

Badba preens herself. "He won't be back very soon. I got him a good cut on the neck. Almost lifted that mask, too, but he ran like a coward!"

Tom clears his throat and mutters stiffly, "Thank you, Badba, for your bravery. You are a very skilled fighter."

I know how hard that is for him to say. I grin at both of them.

"You'd better find Wefta, the rug maker," Pictree says. "Perhaps the one who attacked you has already been there. A being in a blue cloak was visiting with Mirour before you. I think he paid him off like you did."

That makes my blood run cold. "You think Blue Cloak has already seen the rug maker? Maybe he came *out* of the fountain when we were in the booth. Maybe Mom's child is already gone!"

"I think it was the same being, but I didn't see his mask clearly," Pictree says. "However, I'm sure he was alone."

I feel a tiny flutter of hope rise up again.

"Who are you, anyway?" I ask Pictree Bragg. "Why act like you're helping us?"

"I *am* helping you." Pictree's face flushes. "I know Ailla. I worked with her when she made masks for Mirour. She had just become one of his attendants, like me, when she was suddenly sold to Wefta. I haven't seen her for some time. I'm worried."

I have a name. I feel a thrill of excitement rush through me. I know my sister's name! *Ailla.*

"But how did you know I came here to find Ailla?" I ask. "When you bumped into me and dropped —" I see his warning look and don't mention the mask in my pouch. "I thought you somehow knew me."

"I belong to the Hobyah tribe. We are Sensitives. As soon as you entered the market, I knew that someone who cared about Ailla's welfare had arrived. I tracked you down. I wanted to make sure you didn't get turned away — or hurt. I wanted to make sure you were fully prepared … Mirour is an evil being."

I can't tell if he's lying. I frown at him. "You seem to have the run of the market and some sort of authority in Mirour's shop," I say. "Why stay with him if he's so terrible?"

"My tribe lives in the Rebuff area, on one of the Tag-A-Long Isles. Many of our youngers, including me, were taken during one of the Games. Our elders were devastated, but they couldn't go against the Rules and demand us back. A few of the older youngers escaped with me, and we formed a recovery band. Many work for stall owners now. I made sure Mirour hired me. Our aim is to return as many youngers to their home worlds as we can. Ailla is one of the children we hoped to help. But she had no home world that she knew of. I was sure she was a human from Eorthe, but she didn't remember anything before coming to Mirour. I worry she will vanish into some Game Player's castel and I'll never find her again." He stands upright, shoulders back. "You know where her home lies?"

"Yes," I say. "I do."

"I can't leave the others. You must find Ailla and take her safely to her home. I know you'll tell me when she's safe."

"Enough of this drivel," cries Badba. "If you want the Eorthe *child,* go and get her from the rug maker." She pats the scabbard at her side. "I'll see he gives her to you."

I say to Pictree, "Mirour said Wefta lives and works under the fountain, and he gave me this key." I put it on the palm of my hand to show him.

Anger flushes his face. "Wefta has sealed entrances and exits all over the market. He's the richest of the merchants, with many stalls throughout many markets in other worlds, too. He seals all his exits because he knows his workers will sneak away, given half a chance. You must have paid Mirour well to get the key for the entrance the merchants use."

"Like the front door to a house?" I ask.

He looks puzzled. "I don't know what that is. But the entrance is always locked. Here, I'll show you where you can turn the key." He starts toward the fountain when a shout stops him.

Mirour stands, hands on hips, three ragged youngers in tow. "What are you up to? Leave these strangers and get back to work."

Pictree nods. As he walks past me, he whispers something that sounds like "grimbird." I watch him pat each younger gently on the head. The cupid's face under the spray of fuzzy hair glares at us, then he takes out a short whip and hits Pictree across the shoulders. I flinch. Cill gasps. As they blend with the busy crowd, Pictree looks back at us, his stoic face mixed with longing — and something else. Is it a warning?

"What did he say as he walked by?" Tom demands harshly. "How do we know he isn't lying? There could be a small army waiting for us under the fountain."

"I believe him," I say firmly. "He said something like 'grimbird.' He was looking at the fountain when he said it. We'll have to examine it very carefully."

"Let's do it," Badba says.

We swarm over the stone fountain and find nothing. I take a short break and sit on its edge to think. Down below the green glass "water," there are yellow bird designs on some of the tiles. They actually look quite cheery, not a grim one in sight.

I slide along the edge examining the designs. Suddenly I spot a green bird. Is that what Pictree was saying? Not grim, but green? And is that a small hole where its eye should be? It is. But how do I get the pin key to go through the thick glasslike surface?

"I found a green bird — all the rest are yellow," I say. They crowd around me. I take the straight little pin and push it against the glass; suddenly a deep circular hole, big enough for my hand appears under the key. I insert the pin into the bird's eye and just as I withdraw my hand, the entire surface of the green "water" cracks into four pieces and slides out of sight. At the same time, tiled stairs appear, leading below ground.

"If we go down there, how we come back?" Cill asks worriedly.

"Never you mind, my little leaf mold," Badba crows. "I'll hack our way out if I have to."

Cill doesn't look reassured.

Tom says, "Listen, if we go down there, market people will see us. They might close the fountain on us, just for fun." He looks around suspiciously. No one in the crowd seems to be paying us any attention, but one hidden being may be watching us closely.

Badba smiles a yellow grin. "I'm a trader, but I

have been known to take something in order to make someone's life more —"

"A thief," Tom sneers.

"If you like. But thieves need to make sure no one sees them. Do you want my help or not?"

"Yes," I say firmly.

Badba holds both hands above her head, then she lowers them out to the side, black feathers crackling. She starts slowly running around the fountain and our little group, but in the blink of an eye she's a blur. I can't see the market anymore. It's as if a curtain has dropped around us.

"Hurry up! It doesn't last long!" Badba calls from the top of the stairs.

We descend into a long hallway hung with small lanterns. At the end of it is a door hung with a rug that has a vibrant dragon surging across it. I pull a silk rope beside the rug and a low bong echoes down a distant space. Badba stands to one side so she can't be seen by anyone opening the door.

A small human child opens the door and peers out, his face so thin it looks like a skull covered in pale gauze. His lifeless eyes take us in.

"Wha' you wan'?" he asks.

"We wish to speak to Wefta, the rug maker," Tom says.

The child's eyes widen and a tiny spark flutters in his eyes as he takes in the idea of a talking owl. But only for a moment.

Margaret Buffie

"Wai' here," he commands, closing the door on us.

When the door opens again, I expect to see a grotesque character, like Fagin in *Oliver Twist*. Instead, we're welcomed by a chubby man who looks more like Robin Hood's friend Friar Tuck. He has a thin fringe of hair with a bald dome rising out of it. He's wearing rumpled leggings and a long loose top covered with hundreds of trailing lengths of colored wool and threads. His face is broad, his fat cheeks a healthy pink, his eyes periwinkle blue. He smiles ingratiatingly at us, while using one large hand to shovel the child back to his work station. The boy stumbles and falls to his knees, but the rug maker doesn't bat an eyelash.

"I am Wefta," says the fat man in a high thin voice. "You had a key. How is that? I don't know you. Who sent you?" He doesn't seem nervous, which doesn't surprise me, as there are at least ten big adults roaming the area behind him, keeping one eye on us, the other on their workers.

As we enter, the door swings shut and I hear the clink of metal. I glance quickly behind me and see the tip of Badba's knife between the door and the frame, to keep it open for our escape.

"We come from Fergus of Cleave." I show him Fergus's brooch on my sleeve.

He nods. "So?"

"We got the key from the mask maker, Mirour.

He said you would know about a certain Earth girl he sold to you."

He walks to a table covered in piles of rug samples.

Tom telepaths, *Say nothing more. Let him think.*

The room we've entered appears endless. I can see thousands of looms, like ships' sails at a busy port. Clattering, swishing and snapping fill the air, along with a fine dust that never seems to settle. I push my finger under my nose to keep from sneezing. Along the walls, there are other machines that spin the wool. Nothing like I've seen on Earth.

Many youngers sit on low benches, their flashing hands working delicate patterns in many-colored threads. Others sit along the walls spinning raw wool. To our right, in a low alcove, a group of youngers is washing finished rugs on the floor by pouring jugs of water over them. Guards move up and down the rows of workers, tapping short whips against the palms of their hands. All the youngers are skinny. Many have bruises. My guts clench with anger. Tom's talons tighten on my shoulder and Cill's fingers wrap around mine in a squeeze of warning. They're both determined that I keep quiet.

I catch the rug maker watching me, his mouth smiling, his blue eyes hard as steel. He shrugs. "I have no Eorthe girl amongst my workers."

So he's decided to lie. "But you must," I protest. "Mirour said he sold her to you."

The youngers keep working, but I know the ones nearest us are listening. I can hear a faint whisper flutter through the room. The guards shout and the whispering stops.

Wefta pouts and thrusts out his large belly. "Are you calling me a liar?"

Feeling a clutch of dread, I say quickly, "No. Perhaps you no *longer* have an Earth child. Perhaps you've recently sold her to someone in a blue cloak and silver mask?"

Wefta smiles. "Oh, he was here. But I cannot sell what I do not have."

"But you once had an Earth girl named Ailla working for you. Pictree Bragg said —"

"That scoundrel!" The man's face contorts into an ugly caricature. "I've told Mirour to sell him off — to someone in a faraway world. But no. He says Bragg keeps his youngers working hard. I say Bragg is trouble. Tries to get in here to see what's going on with my workers."

"Sir ... please," I say. "This girl, Ailla, is my sister. I need to know where she is. Our mother is dying and I have to find her daughter —"

Wefta narrows his eyes speculatively. "You will pay for her, I presume?"

"If she's not here, sir, how can I pay for her?"

"Aaah, but perhaps I know where she *is*." He winks at me and taps the side of his nose with a chubby finger.

"Then, yes, I'll pay you for this information," I say, ignoring Tom's shout in my head.

The man holds out his smooth fat hand, palm up, greedy eyes waiting.

I shake my head. "I'm not that stupid. You give me the information and I'll pay you. But first admit you already sold this information to the man in the blue cloak."

His secretive smile tells me he's done just that. My heart is thudding with anger and fear.

"Where is she?" I ask through tight lips.

Wefta gazes around with satisfaction at the small army of youngers in the workshop. Suddenly the reality of what I'm doing sinks in. I've been so desperate to talk to this man, I've risked our lives. We have nothing to pay him with. He'll never let us leave.

"I sold the child to Baudwin, the Solitary of Moling. He had sent one of the Faylinn tribe to find a scholar who could transcribe his poetry. He also wanted someone who could paint murals. One of the Faylinns knows I have youngers who read and write. I taught Ailla to keep my accounts and to write in seven languages. Mirour taught her to be a master painter of masks. I was reluctant to sell her, but the Solitary paid me well, as you shall."

I gulp. Tom moans and Cill is crushing my fingers.

"I have nothing to pay you with at present," I say lightly, "but if I find her, I'll return and —"

"Nothing to pay me with?" Wefta bellows. The room goes silent. "You break a bargain with me? You will pay one way or the other before you leave, or you will not leave at all!"

I pretend to dig around in my pouch, madly trying to think of a way out, when the door bursts open and Badba leaps into the room, followed by Pictree Bragg. Badba seems to fill the room, feathers crackling, blades clashing. Wefta's mouth opens in shock, then screams orders to his guards. Pictree Bragg shouts something to the workers, who scramble away and press against the walls.

The guards move quickly. Most rush at Badba, who throws Pictree a dagger, but a small group lunges at me, Cill and Tom. One grabs my arm and drags me away from the door. Cill's fingers swirl through the air like whips. They twine around the legs of the guard. His feet fly past my face as he crashes to the floor. Another reaches past Cill and grabs my shoulder, but Tom attacks, slashing him with talons and beak. Another guard rushes at us, but one of the workers kicks over a water jug, and the guard slips on the mix of wool and water and lands flat on her back.

Cill drags me toward the door, her fingers laced around my stomach. The door swings open behind us and we stumble through with Pictree Bragg, Tom streaming right behind. Badba slams it shut and leans against the dragon rug, bracing her feet.

The crack and grumble of rock and metal crashes overhead. The fountain is closing!

Tom cries, "Give me the key!"

I hand it to him and he flies up the stairs. Two seconds later, the fountain slams shut with a resounding crash.

35

Great thumps come from behind the door as Badba fights to hold it shut. Pictree runs back to help her, but the wood is splintering. Cill rummages in her leaves and pulls out a bottle. She shakes it all over the door, concentrating on the cracks. Small branches spurt out wherever the drops have touched — vines crackle and twist and multiply, growing quickly and anchoring themselves deep into the crevices of the stone walls.

"You move soon or vines bind you to door and you never get out," Cill calls to Badba and Pictree.

"When is soon?" Badba screeches. "One of them is winding around my legs!"

"Now be good time."

Badba and Pictree leap away from the door, chopping with their knives at the vines that have twisted around them. They no sooner get away than the entire door disappears behind a thick wall of foliage.

Pictree gasps, "Wefta has other ways of exiting that place. He'll just come around and open the fountain and we'll be caught like fish in a net!"

Above us, a crack of light reappears and the fountain opens up. Tom flies through it, tosses me the key and snarls, "You try to use a key when you only have talons. Thought I'd never open the cursed thing. Let's go!"

We swarm up the stairs.

"Follow me!" Pictree says urgently. He takes off, Tom flying above him as lookout.

Pictree clearly knows the market. Just as we veer down a narrow alleyway, a group of Wefta's guards thunder past, heading for the fountain.

When Pictree stops and peers around a corner, I say, "Will Wefta set up an alarm?"

"No." Pictree grins. "He'll know it's fruitless. Most of the stall owners don't like what he's doing with the youngers, even though this market is one of the richest, drawing in huge crowds, mainly thanks to the rug maker. They'll just look the other way. Come on!"

He leads us through a couple of stalls. The owners call out cheerfully to him and he waves at them to be quiet. They nod and ignore us. Clearly, he's popular. We tear down two or three back alleyways and then dodge into the green tents, racing past the parked airships, sleds and animals.

Each time we run into a new tent, Badba lets off a high-pitched whistle. In the final tent, the whistle is echoed back.

"Lycias!" she screeches. A low roar from ten feet away, and there's Lycias in all his ugly glory.

I have a stitch in my side. Badba throws Cill up onto the saddle and, before I know what's happening, I'm tossed up in front of her. Badba puts a hand out for Pictree Bragg, but he shakes his head.

"No. I must stay."

"Don't be a fool," Tom shouts. "Get up here!"

"I can't!" Pictree says firmly. "I can't leave the youngers. They need me to protect them and to find their way home."

"Mirour or Wefta will kill you!" I cry.

Pictree shrugs. "I'll hide until Mirour starts to miss me — I've made myself indispensable. Then he'll convince Wefta to let me alone. You see, I'm the only one who can get the youngers to work without friction. I also feed them, so they don't get sick as often. The stall owners give me free food. In return, Mirour agrees not to use physical punishment on his workers at least. He needs me."

"But he *will* punish you," I say.

Again he shrugs.

"I'll come back one day, Pictree Bragg," I say, "to help you free the youngers. I promise I'll find a way."

Behind him, from high up on Lycias, I can see a group of Wefta's guards running through the maze of vehicles and animals.

"They're coming!" I shout, pointing.

"Return when you can!" Pictree calls. "Give my

love to Ailla!" With that, he dodges a couple of confused animal keepers and is gone. The sound of running boots comes closer. Some of the guards are brandishing swords; others have laser throwers. Suddenly, a figure in a blue cloak appears out of nowhere and to my shock throws a long pole in front of the running guards. He looks up. I see a bright gold mask. Then he vanishes. When the guards gain their footing again, three of them take aim at us.

"They've got streak rifles!" I shout as Badba flings herself onto Lycias's back.

"Lycias *up!*" she cries.

Lycias's neck stretches out as he crashes through the crowded tent, scattering airships and sleds in his wake. Other drakons and winged beasts call out with high-pitched wails as we lumber by. One of Lycias's huge legs catches a center tent pole, knocking it over, and, like a graceful silk scarf, the green tent slowly drifts down on us. Streak lights scorch past. I'm afraid one will hit Cill and she'll go up in flames. Lycias lets out a squeal. He's been hit. I take the small mask out of my pouch. It's the only thing I can think of to protect my hand as I try to ward off the laser lights. I push Cill down and hold the mask up ready to stop a streak light if I can. To my amazement, the mask grows to many times its normal size — into a shield. I've found a two-in-one Game piece! I've found the *final* Game piece!

Streak lights bang against the shield. I almost slip off the saddle, but Cill holds me tight. It's all I can do to keep my balance, but I manage to stop three streak lights in a row.

"We'll get caught in this cursed tent!" Tom flies straight up and tries to lift the descending fabric, but his slight weight does nothing. He vanishes in a tangle of emerald silk.

"Tom!" I scream.

Lycias picks up speed and we're off the ground. He slices through the air above the animals and vehicles. I can see the guards still charging toward us. Just as the tent collapses, we slide out the opening and up over the red sand dunes.

36

Ailla's silver mask has become as small as my palm again. I push it back into my pouch and shout, "We've lost Tom! We have to go back!"

"He'll catch up with us," Badba bellows. "I can't stop now! We'll go to your air sloop and wait. Wefta and his gang don't know about it ... not yet, anyway."

I can't argue, it makes sense. I know I'm crying, but I can't help it. I've lost Tom again ... one day he won't come back, I know it. Cill hugs me tightly. I find some comfort in her crackly hug, which smells of nutmeg and warm earth.

Lycias lands gently beside the sloop, but he moans as I slide down his back. He has two large burns on his flank. Cill begins work with her little bottles, and soon the creature is purring like an enormous cat. It's then that I hear the distant clink of metal against metal — coming from inside the sloop.

Badba hears it, too. She whirls around, every feather bristling. She draws her wide sword, ready for combat.

"Wefta's band can't be here yet," she whispers. "They're too stupid to work it out this fast. Must be Freelooters. But I didn't see a looter tug when we landed."

We leave Cill tending to Lycias and edge toward the sloop. Slowly and silently we climb the side ladder and tread the deck. The sound is coming from below. I lie down and peer through the metal scrollwork. I knew there had to be space below the deck, but hadn't found the way into it during our journey. Below me, a shadow moves into a patch of light. I see a fitted telescope and the flash of a silver nose.

"Gyro?"

"Is it you, Watcher?" cries a familiar voice. "I was going to come to the market to look for you. I was worried you were in trouble."

"Why did you come looking for us? And how on earth did you find us?" I ask, amazed.

"Wait. I'll just be a minute." He disappears into the shadows again and I hear more clinking and banging.

"Who is that?" Badba says, poking me in the back with a long talon.

"It's Gyro, the inventor of this sloop."

"How did he get here?" she asks. "Can we trust him?"

"I don't know how he got here, but I trust him completely," I say, wondering, as she scowls through the wire deck, *but can I trust you?*

A trap door opens in the deck and Gyro clatters into view.

"Not as bad as I thought, as it happens," he says. "Mostly sand damage, as is to be expected here, I suppose. I believe I've fixed it. I'll have to check the directional coordinates. Do you have the atlas device?"

I nod. He notices Badba for the first time. "I don't recall *you* being with them. No, I'd remember that glorious headpiece. Magnificent."

Badba preens under his gaze. "I am Badba, a Ravan."

"Why did you come to find us?" I ask Gyro again.

He points to the other side of the ship. Settled into the red dust is his crazy bicycle machine, with helicopter blades attached to it instead of the box kite.

"I have a homing device attached to both machines, you see. That way, one machine knows where the other machine is located, as it were," Gyro says proudly, then adds, "I grew concerned when your signal weakened. At one point it went dead. I thought you might need help."

"You were worried about us?" I ask. "Or about your sloop."

He smiles his metal smile. "I must confess a little of both, to be honest. But I consider you my friends. I couldn't leave you stranded, if indeed you were in such a state — no matter what."

"You found us even though the sloop's signal was dead?"

"The signal fluttered now and again and my little

helicycle and I followed it as best we could. And here we are!"

"And I'm so glad you did," I say sincerely. "Tell me, Gyro, could someone with a similar homing device use your signal and also find out where we went?"

He flaps his hand at me. "Oh, I don't think so. I had enough trouble finding the signal myself, as it turned out."

That doesn't comfort me. Is Gyro's invention fallible? Is this how the man in blue found us, using a homing device? I look at the brooch on my arm. Could this be one? Yet I need it — it's my only weapon.

Badba interrupts my thoughts. "This sloop had better be ready to go or we're all in trouble." She points to the distance, where red sand rises into the air in a crimson cloud.

"I won't leave without Tom."

"You'll have to," Badba replies.

Gyro climbs over the side of the ship and disappears. There's the slap of helicopter blades and in two seconds he's hovering high in the air. His voice comes back like a loudspeaker. "I see … I see … about forty beings on sleds pulled by winged drakons and hydras. They will be here soon, as likely as not." He lands the helicycle on the back deck and runs to the directional pyramid. "Where do you want to go? I've got them all in my memory, as it turns out."

"We're supposed to go to Baudwin of Moling."

"To the world of Moling? You're sure?"

"Yes, I'm sure!" I shout. "But I'm not leaving without Tom. Just set it up so all I have to do is press the green button!"

A few seconds later, Gyro says, "It's ready, as far as I know."

"Now, get to safety in your helicycle. Badba, mount Lycias, ready to leave. Take Cill with you."

I can change into my Watcher self when they get closer and transmute invisible. With the others safely out of the way, I can hide out until I find Tom.

The red cloud rolls closer. Badba leaps out of the sloop and climbs onto Lycias's saddle. Lycias stands, wings unfurled, ready for takeoff.

"Take Cill with you!" I shout, but Cill dodges Badba's long arm and scrambles up the ladder to the deck of the sloop.

"I no leave you."

"But you have to!" I shout. "Gyro, do you have room for Cill in your cycle?"

He nods.

"Cill," I say, "you must get into the cycle with Gyro. Now! I can protect myself."

"I no leave you, Emma," Cill says, wrapping her hands around the rails of the little ship. I sigh. No invisibility for me. I'll have to stay and fight.

"Okay, Gyro, go! You too, Badba!"

Gyro slides behind the controls of his helicycle,

but he doesn't move, except to set the chopper blades to a slow whomping beat.

The first fan of red dust from the attackers fills my nostrils. But Gyro and Badba aren't moving.

"Why don't you just *go!*" I shout.

Badba throws two small streak lights onto the deck. Cill and I grab them.

"Thanks," I cry, taking off the feathered brooch and throwing it over the side of the ship. I simply can't take the risk of being followed. "Now *go!*"

But Badba sits on Lycias, arms crossed, a knife in one hand, a sword in the other. Gyro grins at her, then displays a streak rifle. Has the mild-mannered Searcher gone crazy? Badba hoots her approval. I want to scream with frustration.

"Emma!" Cill calls. "Look. See? Tiny speck in front of red dust!"

"I — I can't see anything."

"Here," Gyro says, taking his eyepiece out and handing to me. I hold it over my eye and scream with excitement. "It's Tom! It's Tom!" Behind him I see a welter of leather, silver blades, bouncing helmets and slathering beasts.

I strap myself into the pilot's seat.

"Everyone ready for takeoff?"

"Ready," says Gyro. I toss him back his eyepiece. He puts it on and gives me a thumbs-up.

"Ready," calls Badba, and I grin over at her. She brandishes her knives, clashes them together and shrieks her banshee call.

"Ready," says Cill, strapped into the seat behind me, her leaf-strewn face flushed like autumn leaves, streak light in hand.

Tom's talons hit my shoulder. "Well, Creirwy," he cries, "what are you waiting for? Let's go!"

With my heart full to bursting, I push the green button. There is a grinding sound, but nothing happens. It's as if we're stuck in a snowdrift.

"Push it again. It'll work. Just don't touch the black button. I haven't fixed it yet," calls Gyro, rising swiftly into the air. "We'll catch up!"

Wefta's horde thunders toward us. Some of the sleds are rising into the air to cut us off.

I put my hand over the green button again. This time the sloop takes off, bumping over the sand dunes, scattering sand and then lifting. We're level with the charging sleds, the guards already preparing their streak weapons. The sloop picks up speed.

"Lift, little ship," Tom and I whisper together. "Lift, lift, lift!" Suddenly it feels like we're on a fast, silent elevator, going up.

A dozen streak lights hit the sloop's stern — then nothing, just a rush of cool air. Behind us, Wefta's horde grows smaller and smaller. Tom's wing hugs my neck and I lean for a moment against his rapidly beating heart.

"I — I thought you were gone," I say, my voice choked. "I couldn't leave."

"I know." His deep voice wraps around my fear, easing it for a moment. "You shouldn't have stayed, but I'm glad you did, Creirwy."

I look behind us again. Gyro's helicycle is bouncing up and down in our air stream, but I can't see Badba and Lycias. Were they hit? Can we turn around? I'm about to ask Tom when a long crocodile-bird head rises above the railing beside me, eyes rolling, followed by huge straining shoulders and a triumphant Badba bristling with streams of black feathers. Lycias veers away to keep his flashing wings from hitting the sloop.

"Are you okay?" I shout over the flapping.

Badba looks surprised, then laughs. "Yes, little Watcher, lead on! I'm having the most peerless experience of my life!"

37

The red desert is endless. I try not to think about how many hours are being lost floating over it. Now that the triumph of escape is over, tension has settled into my stomach like a sea snake. Will we ever find Ailla? Will our time run out first? Will Fergus gloat knowing that Mom will never see her real daughter? Will we be forced to abandon Dad to that horrible Keeper?

When Cill tries to tell me how much time has gone by, I snap at her to shut up. I apologize, but I know she's miffed. She goes to the stern of the ship and watches Gyro, her back to me. I'm going to have to be more careful with her. She's really sensitive for a being made of leaves.

Tom's been gone for a while checking out where Wefta's fighters are. He lands on the ship's flight panel. "No sign of anyone, I think we've outrun them."

"Snapping their whips over small backs is easier than trying to get at beings who could give them a good fight," I sneer.

He looks at me funny. "You could be right."

I murmur, "And what about this guy in blue we keep seeing? What if he beats us to Moling? According to the rug maker, he knows where we're going."

Tom nods. "He can't be that far ahead of us. We'll probably catch up. After all, we have the Searcher's sloop as our guide. Does Blue Cloak have an airship? Does he know where Moling is? Has he got the coordinates? He can't transport to a place unless it has a border cave. I wonder if Moling has one. Gyro would know."

He takes off and returns quickly. "Gyro says there are no border caves on Moling, as far as he knows. He's having fun riding the waves of air behind us —"

"Fine. So who *is* Blue Cloak?" I interrupt. "I'm sure he could have pushed that knife through the window of the fountain booth right into my back, but he didn't." Something is niggling at the back of my mind, but Tom speaks before I can grab hold of it.

"No, he clearly wants to get you back to Argadnel for some reason."

"I bet it's one of Fergus's Players, sent here to mess up my Seeker's Game," I fume. "It was bad enough that I beat Fergus at Fidchell, but he'll be really angry if I win this Game. If I do, he loses at *real-life* Fidchell."

Tom shakes his head. "Fergus is a stickler for Game rules — and one of them is not to interfere with any Game once it's set up unless something warrants it. Even then, he would want the Game to go on as long as possible."

I snort. "Come on, Tom. He's the one who decides what warrants it! He was ready to play Fidchell a second time — to pretend that my win was a mistake that could be fixed by *him* winning. He won't like my beating him again."

Tom is silent, then says quietly, "He wouldn't have you killed. That I *do* know."

"Why not? Who am I to him?" Suddenly I remember something Fergus said before the Fidchell game began. He'd turned to Tom and said angrily, "No! I have fulfilled that duty."

What duty had he fulfilled? To *whom* had he owed this duty? And what did it have to do with me?

I put this to Tom. He doesn't answer at first, then he says uneasily, almost furtively, "I don't remember him saying that."

"Well, he said it to *you*. You were telepathing to him so I wouldn't hear and he shouted it out loud. And then he said, 'That was a long time ago. I have done what I agreed to — I owe nothing more.' Or something like that."

"I don't remember. Everything was pretty tense, Emma." His owl eyes are heavy-lidded, unreadable.

I say sharply, "You know something about me. Something you haven't told me. What is it?"

"There is a time for everything, Creirwy, and this isn't it," he mutters.

"So you *are* keeping something from me."

"What?"

"You heard me."

He riffles his feathers and gazes into the distance as if he's suddenly lost his hearing. "I'd better go and see if they're following us yet."

"Tom, why won't you tell me?"

"I know you're upset because we didn't find Ailla at the rug maker's, but sometimes you try me to the limit, Emma."

"Then why do you stay with me?" I ask suddenly, surprising even myself. "There must be lots of Obligations you can do as an owl."

"Don't be stupid," he snarls. "You're getting too emotional."

"You're *angry*," I sneer.

He looks at me sharply. "So?"

"You're not like Histal and the other Masters, are you? I never thought of it before because I grew up as a human. But *you* show your emotions, too. You changed your mind about Fergus and helped me last summer in Bruide. You broke your Obligation to Fergus. You let your emotions rule your Watcher head."

He shifts uncomfortably.

Alarm slithers down my arms. "Isn't that why Fergus put an owl cunning on you, to punish you for caring about me?"

He looks stonily over my shoulder.

"Isn't that *right*?" I ask, my throat dry.

"Now you really are being stupid," Tom growls.

"This whole conversation is ridiculous. It's come out of nowhere and makes no sense. Act like a Watcher, Emma. Just be patient."

The air seems to shift around us. I don't know why, but I want to goad him, make him say something hurtful. In a taunting voice, I say, "You're angry right now. You're getting *emotional*. And Watchers aren't supposed to have feelings. They're not supposed to get attached to the being they're watching over. Isn't that what you told me? So you don't care, right? I'm simply an Obligation."

The heart face and solemn eyes are shadowed and sad.

He says, "Something happened in Bruide. I can't tell you what. Nothing else has changed."

I feel as if I've been given a short, sharp electric shock. "What happened in Bruide? I thought —"

"Look … Emma, I'm a Watcher. And in Bruide … something decreed that I was to be *your* Watcher."

I stiffen at that. "So it was nothing personal, is that it? Just some kind of Obligation that something or someone dealt you?"

"No, not entirely."

"Then what, Tom?"

"While you were being held in the confiner, Histal simply reminded me of what happened last year," he says quietly. "… and of other things. But it doesn't change anything, I promise you."

"What did he say?"

Tom's glance slides over my face and away again.

When he speaks, his voice is tight. "He reminded me that I'm not allowed to get personal in my Obligations. But that doesn't mean I'm not committed to watching over you, Emma. *Entirely. Completely.* No matter what you see — or think or hear otherwise."

I feel as if I've been pushing against a locked door and suddenly it's open and I fall through, staggering to keep my balance. Does this mean that everything we've said, everything we've done together wasn't … what I thought it was?

"Emma …," he says. "*Emma.*"

Reluctantly, fearfully, I look into Tom's gray eyes. For just a moment, they become a dark green rimmed with white. I see a flash of pale hair, then it becomes short and black and I see the battered, ugly face of the Tom I knew in Bruide.

"I'll always be with you," the boy says.

I think I see a flash of pain in his eyes. "But, Tom, we —"

"Emma, I'm already hindered as your Watcher by the owl cunning. So I must work even harder to follow my training. Histal is right, Creirwy."

"Don't call me that!"

"Emma —"

"Go away!" I shout. The boy I'm looking at tries to smile, but fades quickly. A second later, the owl lifts away from the sloop. Without a backward glance, he vanishes into the hot twisting air.

38

I stare after him, my chest so tight I can't breathe. What just happened? What have I done? I go over and over our disjointed conversation. What was he *saying*? Has he purged his feelings for me because Histal told him to? Did he ever really care for me, or is he just my Watcher? If he's on an Obligation to watch over me, who initiated it? I thought he'd become my friend last summer because he *chose* to, not because he was *told* to.

I've never doubted Tom's loyalty. And I've always been sure he never kept anything from me — at least nothing that concerned *me*. Yet, I remind myself, he *was* loyal to Fergus before he met me. Is he still loyal to him? I think about his silence when we were at Cleave. Did Mathus really threaten him? Or has Tom been working for Fergus all this time? Fergus could ask for the services of a Watcher, but he couldn't have sent Tom on an Obligation to befriend me last year — only Histal or someone of equal Watcher power could have done that.

A cold stone settles in my heart. I stare down at the undulating sands. Badba, flying alongside on Lycias, gives me a leisurely wave. I wave back, but I can't get my head to stop spinning with thoughts. I close my eyes and go over the conversation again. But it only makes me more anxious, more afraid that I've lost something I'll never get back.

Nothing seems to be what I thought it was — bits are missing and other bits don't fit at all. Even Blue Cloak didn't act the way I expected him to. When we were being chased from the market, did I just *imagine* he threw a pole in front of Wefta's henchmen — slowing them down enough that we could get away? If so, why? The niggle surfaces again at the back of my memory. There was something different about that Blue Cloak. What was it? Then I remember! Each time I saw Blue Cloak, his mask was silver with silver beads around the eyes. The Blue Cloak that stopped Wefta's thugs wore a bright *gold* mask. Is it the same being? Or are there two different Blue Cloaks — each with a different agenda?

Is the one with the silver mask — and the knife — one of Rhona's men? Was he given orders to take me back to Argadnel alive? Then who stopped Wefta's gang? I can't think anymore. It's too much for my tired brain.

Lycias stays in line with our ship, but in a low-beat glider mode, his eyes half closed. Badba is lying on the saddle, her long legs stretched along his straining neck, her ankles crossed. She looks totally relaxed. What do I know about *her?* Absolutely nothing. Why is she still with us? I don't know. One thing is for certain, though — she's definitely unpredictable. Maybe she's a spy, too. Too? Who else is a spy?

"Look!" Cill shouts. "Sky changing."

The sloop is moving steadily toward a dark green border wall, and just as Tom lands back on the deck, we slide through.

39

"According to the coordinates, this is Moling." I try not to sound stiff, but Tom looks at me sadly.

"You okay, Emma?"

I glance at him, making my expression indifferent. "Of course. Just anxious to keep going."

"Let's hope your sister Ailla is still with this Baudwin of Moling."

"Nothing's gone our way so far. Why should it be any different here?" I snarl.

"My never-give-up, we-can-do-it Emma is actually sounding pessimistic!" he says brightly.

"I'm not your Emma," I snap, and see something more than surprise cross his eyes. I feel sorry, but I don't apologize.

"Cill," Tom says, "would you please see if Gyro is okay? He's dropped out of sight."

She rustles to the back of the sloop.

Tom's voice is soft. "Emma, I think you may have misunderstood —"

"It doesn't matter," I answer, my tone expressionless.

"I think I said it awkwardly," he continues. "We need to talk properly — when this is over."

I don't look at him and shrug. "Whatever."

He sighs. "We have to work together now. As Watchers. Truce?"

Truce? I'm not sure *what's* going on between us. I do know he lied to me about a lot of things. How can I trust him? I can't even tell him how much it all *hurts*. Watchers aren't supposed to hurt.

"Emma ... you're my only —"

"Obligation?" I say quickly.

"You can trust me, Emma."

I don't answer him.

"Emma, you have my word. As your Watcher."

"Okay, fine." If he can be an emotionless Watcher, so can I. "It's a truce for now. We've got to win this Seeker Game. For my parents, for Ailla and for Summer. Nothing else matters."

He says firmly, "Right."

I make a show of studying this new world intently. Everything has a cold greenish haze. Above are a pile of billowing, rumbling gray-green clouds and far below a boiling froth of river in a deep ravine that seems to have no beginning and no end. The little sloop follows the ravine, fighting a stiff wind. Every now and again, it dips from side to side, but manages to hold a steady course.

The gorge is sheer and made of granite in shades of green and black. No signs of foliage, but when I look down, I can see dark shapes rising out of the water, huge tails slapping the surface as they descend again. I shiver in my thin jacket.

We can hear the wuft of Gyro's helicycle and behind him the flap of Lycias's wings.

"Maybe we should tell them to go back," I say to Tom. "I'm not even sure why they're still following us. This place could be dangerous. Look at those water beasts."

"Your entourage won't go because they want to be with you, to make sure you're okay. Yeah, even Badba — go figure!"

"That's silly. I almost got them killed! And who knows what's ahead here. Besides, Blue Cloak has probably beat us to this Baudwin character and taken Ailla. We'll never find her." The last part I say through clenched teeth.

"Don't give up hope so fast," Tom murmurs, which only irritates me more.

"You didn't answer me before — who do *you* think Blue Cloak is?" I demand.

Tom says, "Like you said in the market, I think it might be Huw."

I look at him skeptically. "Really? But I could have sworn I saw someone in blue try to help when the guards were chasing us." I don't tell him about the gold mask. I don't know why. Is it because I don't completely trust him anymore?

He looks at me, eyes narrowed. "How interesting.

He has decided on capture, not death. But why?"

"Could it be Mathus? Keeping an eye on us for Fergus?"

"Didn't you say he was tattooed? Only Huw and Bedeven are tattooed as you described. Besides, why would Mathus bother? Like I said, Fergus isn't going to lose all that much if we find your mother's child." He looks around nonchalantly. He really doesn't want to hear anything bad about Fergus. Why?

"Then who will lose big if I win?" I ask. "Or, more important, who will *gain if I lose?*"

Tom shrugs. "I don't know."

And I don't know whether to believe him or not. It's horrible doubting him! I hate it — I *hate* thinking this way.

"No matter who he be," Cill growls from behind us, "he want to make you big loser, Emma. We no allow that."

Tom glances down at her, a gleam in his eye. "How much time do we have left?"

Cill looks at me, her leaves downturned. I sigh and say, "Yeah, what have we got?"

In a small crackly voice, she says, "Ooo, I sorry. Almost finish six Earthly day."

The sloop's deck seems to shift under my feet. "No! This is taking too long. I've got all the game pieces I need. But finding them hasn't helped us, as far as I can see. We just can't seem to go any faster. Does Fergus know about this?"

She bristles. "I read time marker — I not report back to him."

"But weren't you supposed to?"

Her voice is as sharp as thorns. "I say to you before — I not tell him anything in case he follow us. I just keep time!"

"Okay, okay. Thanks, Cill."

She hmphs. I'm tired of apologizing to her, but I start to pacify her again when the little sloop veers to the left and then straight up. As we head for the top of the ravine, the green clouds hang low, heavy. A shaft of lightning suddenly spits across the sky; thunder grumbles and thuds. Below us, the waves are raging against the sides of the ravine.

Just ahead, swaying in the wind, a bridge crosses the gorge. The sloop comes to rest on a flat ledge, in front of its stone archway. Whatever is at the other end of the hanging bridge is obscured by a thick ever-shifting fog.

Gyro's helicycle clatters to a stop and Lycias drifts lightly down. The wind beats at Badba's feathers, making them snap. She strides toward us, Gyro creaking along behind.

"What now?" Badba demands, her talons on the hilts of both knives, her eyes bright with interest. "Are there guards to fight?"

"That is the Bridge of Leaps," Gyro says. "It needs no guards."

"The Bridge of Leaps?" I ask.

"Baudwin of Moling had it built by the Faylinns, who roam the forests that lie to the south. They're known for their magick with the wood of great oaks."

"What do you know of this Baudwin of Moling? He's a hermit, right?" Tom asks.

"Yes, a Solitary. He came to Moling after his great tragedy."

"Which was?" I ask.

"He was once a great Game Player," Gyro says. "Probably the best — better, some say, than Fergus of Cleave. And just as ruthless. And yet, one day he met Dierdre, the daughter of one of his enemies, and fell deeply in love with her — and she with him. They married, with the reluctant blessing of her father, the great Scholar of Cachan. He had also been a Game Player of renown, but he had given it up to study the ways of the Masters of Brehon, those of peace and learning. He allowed the marriage as long as Baudwin agreed to do the same. The couple lived contentedly some mooncrests."

"But not happily ever after," Tom says.

Gyro shakes his head. "No. Baudwin got restless, bored — as was to be expected, if you think about it. He planned a secret Game. Dierdre believed her husband was studying how to *explore* the worlds, rather than trying to conquer them. She, like her father, believed that *knowledge* was power. But Baudwin had other plans. He had always coveted the beautiful land of a friend of Dierdre's father, a

Scholar known as Pawl — who was also very, very rich, as it happens."

"And Baudwin went after this land?" I ask. "And afterwards Dierdre told him to get lost?" Gyro laughs a creaky little laugh. "Oh dear, no. Baudwin went after him, all right. But it turned into a dreadful slaughter. Many of Scholar Pawl's Players died — for they had stopped training long before. Dierdre's father was visiting his old friend at the time, as ill luck would have it, and one of Baudwin's Players killed him, not realizing who he was.

"When Baudwin returned home triumphant, unaware that he'd just had his own father-in-law killed, he discovered that his beloved wife had left the safety of her home to try to stop the bloodshed, but she was set upon by Freelooters and killed. She was expecting their first child, more's the pity."

I look across at the moving wall of green mist. "And now Baudwin lives alone here?"

"He became a reclusive Scholar and a poet as penance for his wife's death. In order to keep out curiosity seekers and Players eager to pick his brain, he set up the Bridge of Leaps. If anyone can beat the bridge and cross to Moling, however, Baudwin will allow that person a short audience."

"How do we beat it?" Badba demands, looking ready for a fight as always.

"How does anyone beat a bridge?" I say. "Can't we just walk across?"

Gyro shakes his head. "If you want to cross, you must take a running leap from the edge of the bridge to a spot exactly in the middle, and then one more leap to the other side. If you don't touch the spot called the Leaping Circle, the bridge will fling you back. If you miss your footing, you will fall into the gorge and the sea creatures will get you, as one would expect."

All five of us stare at the bridge swaying in the wind.

"Well," I say, "there has to be a way. Maybe Tom can fly over it, drop down into the middle, touch it and fly across the rest of the way."

"No flying," Gyro says, "or everyone would use sleds or tugs or sloops — even creatures like Lycias. If you try to fly over it, you will hit an invisible wall."

"Why not ignore the bridge altogether and fly *around* it," Badba says. "Bet no one thought of *that!*"

"The invisible wall surrounds Baudwin's hermitage. The only entrance is through the Bridge of Leaps. And, by the way, you can't touch the bridge in order to tie ropes or pulleys. It has to be a free unencumbered jump, so to speak."

We stare some more.

"That lets out Cill and her vines. Well, I can't leap *that* far," I say.

"Me no leap at all," Cill says.

Badba crows, "I bet I can. My legs are long and strong. Emma, climb on my back. The owl on your shoulder. You two stay here as lookouts." Cill and Gyro nod, but look a little lost.

"If we see trouble, how do we warn you?" Gyro asks.

Badba pulls a small trumpet out of her bag, holds it to her lips and lets out a shrill screech. "How's that?" She grins, giving the trumpet to him.

"Watcher, please change into something smaller," Badba orders.

Quickly, I become my Watcher self. Tom settles on my shoulder, tightening one wing around my neck. Badba crouches down and I climb up, piggyback style. I wrap my legs around her waist and hook my ankles together in front. Badba stands up, walks some distance from the bridge and sets her feet in a starting position.

"Wait," Gyro cries. "Wait — don't go yet!" He climbs on board his cycle and returns carrying a long flat rope. "This is resila cordage. I invented it. We'll tie it round you, and the other end to the sloop. If the bridge tosses you over, we'll be able to tow you up before the creatures below ... get you."

Badba slaps my legs in warning. "Better tie it round Emma's legs and then around me or she'll fly off even before we start," she sneers.

"I'm trying my best!" I snap, as Gyro begins to tie the rope to us.

"Silence!" bellows Badba.

I can feel the muscles shifting under her back as she prepares for the run. She backs up, sets her legs, flaps her hands, bends slightly — and we're off! I cling to her like a barnacle on a boat. She races up to the bridge, stamps down on the first board and throws her hands out, and we fly across the bridge. Suddenly she swerves and her legs shoot out in front. Down we go — is she in the middle? I can see a faint round shape about a foot's length away from where she lands.

Tom cries, "We've missed it! Hang on!"

The bridge sinks under our weight, then it rears up and we are thrown straight back the way we came. Badba just misses having her head smashed on the arch. Before we drop down in a muddle of arms and legs, I think I see a flash of a gold mask staring at us from a rock crevice. With a swirl of blue, the figure is gone. As we land on the stone ledge, Badba's elbow goes into my gut and the wind is knocked right out of me.

Gasping, I manage to croak "Blue Cloak!" and point frantically at the spot where I saw the figure.

"You're sure you saw it?" Tom asks, after I finally regain my voice.

"No, I was *imagining* it," I gasp. "Of course I saw it!"

"Never mind," Gyro says, climbing down from the rock face using special climbing cleats he invented and has never tried out. "No one there now. But I did find this!" He hands me a large gold pearl.

"That must be off his mask," I say, quickly putting it in my pouch. "So how *do* we get across this stupid bridge? Fast!"

We sit in a row and stare at it.

I stand up. "You almost touched the leaping circle, Badba."

Disgusted with our failure, she's gouging at a rock with her knife blade, but she snarls in the affirmative.

"Okay. We have this stretchy rope, right?" I say.

They all just sigh and nod.

"Well, what if we turned Badba, Tom and me into a stone?"

Now they're looking at me as if the bump on the ground has scrambled my brain.

"Metaphorically speaking, of course," I say. "Why not turn the elastic rope into a huge slingshot. We can't touch the bridge itself, but what if we tie the ends to either side of the archway? Badba can stand in the middle, walk back until it's tight and let go, and it will fling us through the air. When we get over the Leaping Circle, we touch down and then the rope will ... kind of fling us the rest of the way."

"Wouldn't work," Tom says. "How do we touch down *and* keep the momentum of the slingshot going?"

Cill cries, "I know! I come along. I roll up in a ball. I land on circle, and you stay in air for second half of leap."

"You mean," Gyro says, "they carry you in front, drop you on the circle — which will constitute the first leap — and then keep going over to the other side?"

Cill looks from one of us to the other. "It work. No?"

Badba's grin almost splits her feathered face in half. "It's worth a try!"

Tom says, "But if we miss by even an inch, we'll all go over the side and be monster food."

"I don't like it," I say. My knees are wobbling again. "Cill will be left in the middle of the bridge. How do we get her off again?"

"One thing at a time. The important part is to *get* there. We'll find a way to help her off later," Gyro says. "I'll work on it while you're on the other side."

"No," I say firmly. "There has to be another way. We should try again with just Badba, if she's willing."

Badba nods, but Tom says, "We already know it *can't* be done that way. She isn't powerful enough to make it to the Leaping Circle." Badba's face is hideous with anger; but Tom snaps, "Admit it, Badba."

She growls, "All right! I'm not."

Tom shakes his feathers. "None of these ideas will work. Face it!"

"Sounds like you don't care if we cross it," I sneer. "If we stop now, we lose the Seeker Game. Is that what you want?"

His voice is a low growl. "You know that's not what I want."

"Well, do you have any better ideas?" I demand, hands on hips.

He doesn't answer. He just glares at me.

Cill rustles up to me. "You in greeeat danger if you

try again without me. I feel it." She places her hand on my arm. "I be your *watcher,* too, like Tom. I know it is my place to keep you safe. I think this work."

Tom's warning has thrown me off. "But I won't risk your life, Cill. You could be stranded on that bridge forever!"

She leans close to my ear. "I be *of* the bridge. I be of the great oaks of Barroch. The oak bridge not take *me.*"

"If the first way was dangerous, Cill's way is *madness,*" Tom growls. "Don't do it, Emma."

"But we don't have a choice. We can't just give up."

The air around the other three teems with an electric current of excitement. In my head, I hear Tom's warning voice, but I let myself get caught up in the energy of my crew.

"Okay," I cry, "let's do it!"

40

Gyro strings the rope through a small cloth sail from his helicycle to create a curved pad for my back to rest against as I ride piggyback. He says it will also keep us level and upright once we lose Cill's weight. He then ties the ends of the rope to either side of the arch.

"Jeez, I hope that stone arch is firmly in the ground," I mutter as I climb on Badba's back. Tom is sitting on a nearby boulder. "Are you coming?"

Tom glides up to my shoulder and sits quietly, but I can feel intense disapproval and apprehension radiating from him. I hate it, *hate it!* How could this have happened to us?

Gyro clucks around us, slowly walking Badba backward. Cill climbs into Badba's arms, then rolls into a leafy ball. Gyro measures and tuts some more, going back and forth, counting the distances over and over, adjusting where Badba stands each time.

Just when Badba begins to growl, Gyro says, "That's it, I do believe. Now, Badba, you have two jobs. Keep your long legs tucked up as high as they'll go, and drop Cill at exactly the right moment."

Badba nods. "Okay, everyone? Ready?"

Cill and I answer, "Ready." Mine comes out in a high squeak, hers is muffled. Tom doesn't say anything, but I feel his talons tighten, ready for takeoff. I'm being squashed between the sail and Badba's bony back. I can hardly breathe and I can't see anything.

I blink once and we're flung forward, so hard I can't breathe at all. Halfway across the bridge, Cill drops and I wait for us all to be flung backward, but the rope continues to propel us to the other side. To my amazement, we're tossed safely right beneath an archway in front of a set of stone stairs.

I stagger back to the bridge to check on Cill, who stands up and waves. "You pick me up on way back!"

I turn into Emma and wave at her. She may be safe right now, but how are we going to get her back? My heart is heavy with worry as I start to walk up the stone stairs toward the billowing green mist.

Badba tries to lead the way, but I say, "I want you to stay here and guard the entrance. Blue Cloak could try crossing the Bridge of Leaps and throw Cill off. And, who knows? Maybe this Baudwin has guards, too. Guards or Players that only someone of your ability could — er — deal with."

Badba's eyes glitter. She nods and stands alert. "Call if you need me."

Tom sneers in my head, *Baudwin's a solitary. Solitaries don't have guards. They live alone.*

I know, I telepath back, *but Badba hasn't figured that out. I don't want her clashing her knives and gnashing her teeth at the guy, okay?*

He chuckles then, and I feel better. As we climb, the icy fog suddenly thins, revealing an open-windowed building with a wooden pagoda-like roof, sitting on top of the hill of steps. The air is bone-achingly cold.

The front door is of thinly iced oak, inlaid with gold designs. Most are Game scenes: small gold men fighting, many dying under large swords or being slashed at with streak guns. The center picture is of a beautiful young woman lying on a wooden slab. A knife hovers above her. Her face is turned toward me, her eyes full of sorrow. Flames leap around her. Weeping figures circle the funeral pyre.

I push the door and to my shock it opens. In the middle of the room is a pool of half-frozen greenish water. Above the still surface is a slowly spinning sphere. As it turns, views of a face appear — the beautiful woman on the door.

I look up. The ceiling is half painted with a mural of the same face.

There's a door to our left. The murky room inside has only one narrow floor-to-ceiling window. Sitting cross-legged in the cold wind is a hunched old man with white hair. He's wearing a thin woven shirt and leggings. His hands are tucked in his wide sleeves; his feet are bare.

I clear my throat, but he doesn't respond. Tom whispers in my head, *Perhaps he's frozen in place.*

There's a fireplace and lots of wood, but the grate is cold. A table is covered with papers, stone paperweights holding them secure against the wind that gusts through the open window. Beside the table are two wooden chairs. The window looks out over miles of grassy steppes; in the distance is a forest of trees, a thin spiral of smoke coming up from the far end.

I sit down cross-legged on the icy floor beside the old man. I almost fall backward when I realize that although his hair is snowy white and his face is gaunt, he's actually quite young. I think I let out a gasp. He doesn't *look* at me, but I can feel his awareness of my presence. He has a heavy, twisted nose, one eyelid is thicker than the other, heavily scarred, and there is another wide scar down one cheek that ends at narrow tight lips. He looks like an emaciated boxer.

We sit looking out at the spiral of smoke. Tom sits lightly on my shoulder, alert and on guard.

"You are Baudwin of Moling?" He barely moves his head in acknowledgement.

I say softly, "I'm Ailla's sister. I've come to take her home."

He doesn't answer. The silence goes on for a long time, but I say nothing more.

Finally, the man speaks in a distant, dry voice. "She's down there, with them. She's left me."

I sit up. "Was she stolen from you? Did someone cross the Bridge of Leaps and take her?"

He looks directly at me for the first time. His eyes are so blue they startle me.

"No," he says. "She left me of her own free will. She was allowed the freedom of the bridge. I would never keep her prisoner. She had been one for too long."

Does this mean neither of the Blue Cloaks has found her? I keep my voice as steady as I can and say, "And she's really down there? Where that smoke is rising? With who?"

"The Faylinns. They're oak dwellers and mystics. I was on good terms with them for a long time. I sent a young Faylinn to find someone who could read, write and paint. The rug maker of Cymmarian Market sold him a young woman called Ailla. The Faylinn left her here reluctantly. When she left, I know she went to him." The sadness in his voice is deep.

"She wasn't happy with you?"

He stares unseeingly out the window. "I thought she was. She helped me transcribe my poetry. She *understood* it. She felt what *I* felt. Although she never smiled, I felt her sympathy — her *empathy* — from deep inside her. She helped me find the right words when I floundered. We worked so *well* together. And she began to paint Dierdre's spirit. To help me forgive myself, she said. She worked on the ceiling of the room next door. For *me*. But I didn't understand until it was too late."

"The ceiling is only half finished. Ailla is a gifted artist." I almost say, "like her father," but the words stick in my throat. I can't think about Dad now.

Baudwin nods. "All the time she worked on it, she was so absorbed, so quiet. When she first came to me, she was … distant, reserved, as if part of her was missing. Yet I found myself looking forward to her gentle presence each new day. Time went by and she seemed to drink in the air of this mountain, as if it was healing something inside her. Then one day she came to me carrying a small piece of vellum. It was a poem. I'd written it down with great difficulty. Each day I'd struggled to add just one more letter. It was not meant to be seen, but she found it. Writing it down was a mistake. I told her so … and that's when she left. There's a different silence here now. Cruel. Relentless. It was a mistake to bring her here. I chose to be alone. *I should have remained alone.*"

It seems this stark mountain hermitage and this lonely man had been slowly bringing Ailla's spirit back to life. Why did she go? What was in the poem?

"You wrote your feelings for her?" I ask tentatively.

He doesn't answer.

"Are these Faylinns good people?"

He leans forward as if in pain. "They are what they wish to be. Sometimes they are good, sometimes they are ruthless. She is so tough, yet so vulnerable. They'll break camp soon and she'll leave with them." His voice fades in sorrow.

"Why didn't you go after her? Ask her to come back?"

He shakes his head back and forth, again and again. "No. No. I am a Solitary. I chose to be … as my *penance*. I pledged my life to solitude, contemplation and study. I should never have asked for help in transcribing my work."

"Why couldn't you write down all your poems, if you wrote that one?" I ask.

He takes his hands out of his sleeves. They're horribly disfigured, his fingers fused together. "I burned them trying to drag my wife's body from the funeral pyre. I wanted to hold her one last time. I wanted to die with her, but my Players dragged me away."

"Then who did you make this pledge of solitude to?" I ask gently.

"To my beloved Dierdre. I gave up the ways of the worlds. The Game. The power. The ambition. The waste. Once I thought that power over others was the only meaningful accomplishment. But power for itself and wealth for wealth's sake mean nothing. Oh, the Players and fighters are always with you. But soon you learn that those who stay closest snip off bits of your power for themselves, like tearing your mortal shadow away piece by piece. But Dierdre cared about *me*. So now I have only my pledge."

"Why would going after Ailla break your pledge? It would be in a good cause."

"I would have to *fight* for her. I *can't* fight. Even if I had full use of my hands."

"Then you are no use — to us or yourself!" I stand up, wanting him to disagree with me.

"That is so," he mutters.

"You can't *really* love Ailla," I spit out.

He stares through the window. "I once loved my wife, Dierdre, and because of me she died."

"What does that have to do with Ailla?"

He rises to his feet in a single movement. "If I love again, I will break my vow to Dierdre."

"Your idea of love is strange, Baudwin of Moling," I sneer. His passive denials frustrate me. "If you really love someone, you should be willing to sacrifice anything to save her. To make sure she's safe and happy. You haven't learned anything from the death of your Dierdre. How much did you really love *her*? If you'd given up your need for power as she asked in the first place, she'd be alive today. But you *ignored* her!"

He glowers at me and for a moment I feel the force of his personality hiding behind the gaunt sorrow. "Yes. And I killed her as surely as if I'd raised the knife myself."

I should feel pity, but I feel only irritation and

anger. "It's too late to fix all that. But if you leave Ailla with the Faylinns and something happens to her, then her death will also be on your conscience. One death through a selfish act ... and another through a selfish *lack* of action. Ailla is my sister. I've never met her, but I will die searching for her. To save her life, to save my mother's life. To protect my father's life. You're full of talk but really it's all about *you,* not Dierdre or Ailla. All this self-sacrifice — it's pathetic. You're hiding out because you're a coward!"

I'm surprised Tom doesn't scold me. I turn and walk through the room with the beautiful woman's face gazing soulfully at us from the spinning sphere, but something has changed. The water is no longer green but silver, and it is as smooth and shiny as a mirror. The surface shifts and the sphere spins one more time, then stops. Dierdre's young face is gazing straight at me. Her eyes are wide, with a fixed intensity that reminds me of Mom, filled with a private suffering, of sorrow and of love.

A sweet voice speaks. "The girl knew my spirit was with Baudwin. She felt it all around him, even though he did not. She knew how to capture my essence."

Two tears of clear crystal form in her eyes. As they hit the water, they turn into silver hands that rise up and form a pair of large metal gloves.

"Take these gauntlets," Dierdre says. "He will be able to fight again. It is my gift to him."

"He — he won't fight," I say, my voice trembling, as I reach out and take them. "He made a promise he says he can't break."

A horrible cry bursts into the room. Baudwin stands in the doorway, staring at the beautiful face, his own shocked and white.

The woman in the sphere looks straight at Tom and me. "Leave us," she sighs.

I put the gauntlets on the floor and we leave. Outside, pale flakes of ice flutter in the air. It's growing dark. My breath comes out like heavy smoke before turning to green crystals that tinkle like tiny wind chimes.

"Tom, we have to get to the Faylinns' camp before they vanish. But look," I wail, pointing at the Bridge, "we don't have any way of getting back!"

"There has to be a way," he says firmly. "We'll ask Baudwin when he's over the shock of seeing … *her.*"

I don't want to think about the sad scene behind us. Baudwin is talking to the woman he loved, but she is only a spirit. "He won't leave Dierdre now."

"At least we know where Ailla is," Tom says.

"We've still got to figure out how to leap back across the bridge and pick up — look!"

I point at the wall of the building as a flash of silver and blue vanishes around the corner.

"Blue Cloak! The one with the *silver* mask! How did he get here?" I cry.

Tom takes off around the corner. When he returns, he lands on a tall urn beside the door. "No sign of him anywhere, but there's a sliding bridge on the other side that would lead to the south if it was open. Maybe he used that, although I don't know how. It looks as if it hasn't worked for many years.

Why did you say he had a silver mask? We already know Blue Cloak has a silver mask. The important thing is, how could he be here ahead of us? Are you *sure* you saw him?" He sounds as if he doubts me.

I blurt out, "Yes, of course I saw him. And the other one, too!"

"What are you talking about. Them? What *them?*"

I'm caught. Now I have to tell him. I have to trust him. "I think there are two Blue Cloaks. The one who attacked us had a silver mask. The Blue Cloak who stopped Wefta's guards as we were trying to get away wore an identical blue cloak — but he was wearing a bright *gold* mask."

Tom stares at me. "Why didn't you tell me this before?"

I shrug. "I'm telling you now. I'm *sure* there's two beings in blue — one with a silver mask and one with a gold one. The one that was just here may have overheard us talking about the Faylinn clann. I *know* he had a silver mask. And I also know the one I saw on the other side of the bridge had a gold one."

Tom's voice is tight. "I didn't see either of these beings today, okay? Maybe it was just ... a flash of light or something that made this mask look gold. Are you sure you saw different mask colors?"

"What you mean is — did I see anyone here at all, don't you?" I cry. "Well, I did and I'm sure they're two different beings!" I pull out the gold pearl and show it to him.

"There's no proof that came off a mask. It could have been lying there for ages. Either way, there's no one here now that I can see," he mutters.

We stare at each other. He looks away first. What is he keeping from me?

Suddenly he snaps, "Come on, let's go! We've got to get to the Faylinns."

I've taken just two steps down when someone behind us shouts, "Wait!"

Baudwin stands in the doorway. He's wearing a long coat over leather leggings and a leather jerkin covered in bronze circles. His boots are made of metal discs to the knee. On his head is a bronze helmet adorned with an open-winged bird. Around his neck is a copper torque, its open ends carved into two fierce birds facing each other. One hand, encased in a silver glove, rests on the hilt of a sword, the other gauntlet holds a long battered shield and a grosphus, a kind of javelin that can travel farther than an arrow.

I grin up at him. For just a moment, a small smile plays around his lips. But then his face becomes closed again. "I won't fight, but I will show you the way to the Faylinn camp."

41

Baudwin wants to take us down the back way across the valley. He describes the sliding bridge that crosses the ravine moat at the back of the hermitage. But I explain that we have others with us — others who are unable to cross the Bridge of Leaps, and one who's stuck halfway. And that we also have a sloop, a drakon and a helicycle.

He strides past Badba, stops, stares at her a moment, then continues on. She stares after him. I've never seen her surprised before.

"Is that the so-called Solitary of Moling?" she asks, grabbing my arm in a pincerlike grasp. "Doesn't look much like a *spiritual* sort, does he? A bit pasty-faced for a fighter, though. What's he doing?"

Baudwin pushes a square stone in the arch and it slides to one side. He puts his hand inside. Then he waves us forward across the bridge. Cill jumps up and down when she sees us, then realizes she doesn't have to do anything but wait. When she spots Baudwin, the leaves around her neck become

ruffled like a grouse, her red eyes as wide as they
can go. On the other side of the bridge, Baudwin
inspects her and she inspects him right back. Then
he turns his attention to the drakon, the helicycle,
Gyro and the little sloop in that order. He walks
across the deck of the sloop, looking dazed.

He's not going to be much use, is he? I telepath to Tom.

Baudwin turns to me. "I think you and I should
go alone. I don't want a confrontation —"

"We will *all* go. Badba is a superb fighter. Just in
case we meet ..."

"Meet who?"

I tell him about Blue Cloak, leaving out that there
might be two of them. He looks bewildered.

"Didn't you sense anyone near your place?" I ask.

"No. I was lost in my meditations. You saw him
on Moling? Who is it?"

"All I know is he's trying to stop me from
finding my sister. I think he's working for Fergus of
Cleave or else for Fergus's ally — when she isn't
his enemy — Rhona of Fomorii. What I can't figure
out is how he got across with my people on the
lookout." I turn to Gyro. "Gyro? Did anyone cross
the bridge after we did?"

Gyro, who has been fiddling with the coordinates
for the Faylinn camp using his eye-telescope, shakes
his head. "Of course not! Well, as far as I know. No
one got past me or Cill."

Baudwin stares across the ravine at the hermitage.

"He must have somehow crossed the moat from the back, but he couldn't without engaging the sliding bridge. Even so, I heard nothing. And you say he was wandering around my —" In one leap he's running across the bridge. Badba and I follow, with Tom flying ahead.

The howl of grief makes every hair on my head stand on end. I creep into the first room and choke back a cry. Baudwin stands in the middle of the floor, his hands over his face.

"Whoever did this must have used an air torch or strip laser," Tom says in awe. "But it couldn't be —"

"Who?" I ask.

"Well … any of us," he says lamely.

Only bits of paint remain on the ceiling, and holes have been blasted in the tiles. Most of the water is gone. Pieces of the sphere lie on the bottom of the pool below a skim of green water.

Baudwin is on his knees. "Dierdre's gone!" he sobs. "She told me to begin my life again, that she would stay here. She felt at peace here. But now someone has destroyed her."

I kneel beside him. "No … no … I'm sure she's still here."

"Do you think so?" he asks, like a child. "How can you know?"

"She told Tom and me that she would always be with you in spirit. No weapon could destroy that."

"I'll have to repair it all!" he moans. "I can't leave."

I shake his arm. "But Baudwin — think! Blue Cloak did this. We must find him before he gets to Ailla."

He paces, crunching over smashed tiles. Then he stops and listens to the silence. I don't know if he hears something, but he whirls and runs out the door, down the steps and across the bridge. In less than five minutes, the little sloop, Lycias and Gyro's helicycle are sliding through the teeming clouds toward Faylinn forest.

42

Tom flies ahead as scout. The others move at the same pace as the sloop, letting it determine — using Gyro's calculations — exactly where we're heading. We don't want to drop below the clouds in case the Faylinn clann sees us. As soon as we get the okay from Tom that all is clear, we'll land at the edge of the oak forest. Lycias moves with silent grace, as does the little sloop, but I'm worried about the whirrs and creaks of Gyro's helicycle. With luck, the Faylinns will think it's a bird lost in the thick smoggy clouds.

Tom returns and gives us the go-ahead. The sloop moves in a wide arc as we drop below the clouds. I can see why it's gone this way. It's almost dark and it's bringing us in at the base of the triangular forest. A faint light shows where the Faylinns are camped — at the point farthest from us.

We land on soft turf. Tom directs Gyro to turn the sloop and his cycle facing out, away from the woods, ready to go, but hidden in shadow. Lycias sighs and eats the grass.

"Lucky him," I say. "I'm starving."

Badba holds up her hand and vanishes into the forest. Cill also bustles into the undergrowth. When they return, Cill has gathered nuts, berries and edible roots to add to the remains of our market sweets and a pouch of water from a stream she found. Badba has two limp furry animals tied to her waist.

"We can't eat those," I say, pointing to the poor animals. "We can't risk lighting a fire."

Badba sneers. "Who needs a fire? These are choice ground rodere."

She hacks at one of them with a knife.

"Uck. Eat that out of sight of us, *please!*" I take the berries and roots from Cill and the little basket and divvy everything up. The water is fresh and delicious. Badba moves away and sits with her back to us. I try not to listen to the slurping and crunching of bones.

She grins over her shoulder. "How about you, owl? I bet you'd relish a bit of fresh meat."

I can see that Tom is tempted, but Badba has made such a gruesome mess, he shudders and opts for the nuts and water.

Once I've eaten, I feel much stronger, and everyone else has also perked up a bit.

"How do we approach them?" I ask Baudwin.

He looks confused. "I — er — I'm not sure."

"The first idea would be to simply walk in there and ask to speak to Ailla," Tom says. "Tell them we're concerned about her."

"What are some of the things that might happen?" I ask.

"They might let us talk to her. They might demand a big ransom for her. Or they might slit our throats," Baudwin says.

"So going in a group is not a good idea," Gyro says logically.

Badba wipes her mouth. "I go in first and kill as many as I can. The rest of you grab the girl and take off."

"Watchers don't *kill,*" I say. "Only if we or our pledges are under direct threat do we ever use violence. And never, ever to *kill.*"

Badba snorts. "Good luck, then." She sucks on a bone.

Cill offers, "Two go first. Talk. Rest fan out. Wait. Watch. Be ready to fight if needs be."

Baudwin nods. "That would be the best approach."

"But what if Blue Cloak is there and is already offering them a big reward for Ailla?" I ask. "What if he's already taken her?"

"If this Blue Cloak took her," Tom says, "we'll track him down and get her back. But we must start with the Faylinns. Maybe we could catch the eye of the boy who is Ailla's friend — separate him from the rest, talk to him."

Baudwin nods again. He clenches and unclenches his gloved hands. Then he seems to sag. "This is wrong — against my vow ..., yet I must find Ailla."

"But no harm must come to the boy" I say firmly.

Badba looks at me through heavy-lidded eyes. "Unless he's sold her — *then* we can slit him."

"Look," Tom says. "We have to be logical, go about this carefully. But we have no idea what to expect. I'll go first. Then Baudwin and Emma. Cill, Gyro and Badba, you fan out as Cill suggested, and keep Emma and Baudwin under your eye at all times."

"Okay." I say it reluctantly, irritated that he's taken control. "I agree, I suppose."

"Emma," Tom continues, "you will be in Watcher mode. Open all your senses. Listen for any movement other than ours. Hide if you think there might be even the *slightest* chance of danger. Baudwin can't transmute invisible. If you have to disappear, use it for all its purposes, like in training: for defense, for attack and to protect Baudwin."

I nod. "Everyone ready?"

Cill nods calmly. Badba, who has been strutting around, grins and brandishes her knives. Gyro is standing to one side, shaking and wringing his hands.

"Gyro, you're making a terrible racket. Can't you oil yourself or something?" Tom demands. "And those tool pouches — they clank like a hundred tin helmets." Gyro rummages around, takes out a vial of oil and begins to work. Then he reluctantly takes off the pouches and puts them in his helicycle, but not before removing his longbow and a dozen arrows. He's still shaking pretty hard, but at least he's not making any noise.

"It's not too late to go home," I say to him quietly. "We can send the sloop back to your workshop when we're through."

He says earnestly, "I'm not really as frightened as it may appear. It's just that I never knew this could be so — so *adrenalizing*. It will prepare me for my time-movement machine. I see this as an important experiment, as luck would have it." He smiles at me, but his teeth are chattering. "And for the first time, I feel I have *friends* who need me."

We *are* his friends. He's being as brave as he can be, but I know he's scared silly. "I'm scared, too," I whisper.

"Cill," Tom adds, "these woods are your element. I'm trusting you to be everywhere at once. You will be in command of the others as long as we're in dense forest."

"No way!" Badba snarls. "I'm not taking orders from a pile of leaves!"

"Then take your drakon and go," Tom growls.

Badba scowls with ugly ferocity. "Who suddenly made you leader, owl? I thought Emma was the leader? If not, then why not *me!* Or even *him* —" She points at Baudwin. "They say he was once a great Player of the Game — even better than Fergus of Cleave. Why doesn't he take command instead of some fat little owl?"

Baudwin shrugs and looks embarrassed. "It's been too long. I don't — I only want to make sure Ailla is safe."

"Aaaah, how brave," Badba sneers. "And in full battle gear, too. What a pathetic raiding party this is!"

"I had to make myself believe I could ...," Baudwin says. He points to his gear. "This was to make me feel it was *possible* ..." His voice trails off.

Badba growls, "Well, I don't like being bossed by an owl, and as for *that*," she points at Cill, "give me one good reason —"

"*None* of us is the leader," I snap right back at her. "We're a *team*. But we can't run around like lunatics in a crazy house! Tom has led many scouting parties. Once we're at the Faylinn camp, we'll all have to rely on our own instincts. It's just that while we're in the forest, Cill is — oh heck — just show her, Cill."

Cill stretches her hands up. Her fingers fly out, twine around the upper branches of a tree and in a flash she's gone. The next second, thick vines drop behind Badba, wrap around her long legs and pull her, feet first, into the air.

"Okay! I get the point!" Badba says upside down, her arms crossed.

"And if you not listen, I do it again, but that time I *slit* feathery throat!" Cill calls down.

We're all stunned at gentle Cill's words, but we know she means it.

When Badba regains her feet and her composure, I ask Baudwin, "What is the name of the young Faylinn who brought Ailla to you?"

"Sarason."

"Anything else we should know about these Faylinns?"

"The leader of their clann is Gray Sara. I have never met her. I know little of her, but I do know she is ruthless in protecting her people."

Tom says, "Well, at least we know who to talk to."

Badba mutters, "If we get to talk."

Tom swings his heart face toward the giant bird-woman, who shrugs and looks as innocent as her evil face can manage.

At the entrance to the forest, Tom starts off, a pale shadow drifting through the gigantic tree trunks. I change to Watcher mode, and Baudwin and I slide through the undergrowth together. I try to listen for the others behind us, but I hear nothing. A good sign.

The wood is dark, but I find a path almost immediately. I make note of a number of small trails spiking off it, but know this is the right one because I feel the heat of it through my feet. Baudwin moves silently behind. I still can't believe he was once a great Player like Fergus — he can't seem to make a decision on his own. Even the ghost of his dead wife had to convince him to come with us. Does he love Ailla enough to fight for her if need be?

I focus, letting all my training and instincts kick in. My skin seems to expand and every hair on my arms prickles, ready to pick up the slightest change in the air. My nostrils open deep into my throat, taking in the dense smells of ripening fruit bushes and loamy soil. When we've gone deep into the forest, I sense a faint breeze and then the distant sound of rhythmic movement. Many feet — no, hooves. Deer? I draw Baudwin into the shadows and press him down into a crouch. I transmute invisible, becoming part of the bushes at the side of the trail.

The sounds grow louder. Two small horses, the size of Labrador dogs, trot past our hiding place. On their backs are small beings that look a lot like human children, three or four per horse. They're wearing thin garments that flutter in the breeze and their heads are covered with feathers, berries and leaves of crystal. They're laughing at something. Then the front rider spurs the lead horse on and they take off at a gallop, leaving sparks like tiny fireflies in the air behind them. The silence flows back around us, but it thrums like a slowly beating heart.

I transmute visible. Baudwin and I follow the path of the riders. Tom floats past us where the path divides, slides down the left fork and we go that way. At the same time, something black, the size of a huge bird, flies quickly past and vanishes down the right path.

"What was that?" Baudwin asks, grabbing my arm.

I smell something in the air, but I can't pinpoint it, even though it's strangely familiar. I pick up our pace and, a few minutes later, I know we're near the

Faylinns' campsite. My heart thumps so hard in my chest, I'm sure it will bring the whole clann down on us. Baudwin looks as if his blood has drained away.

I tell him to stay back until I give the signal. I take a deep breath and move quietly to the opening of the campsite.

No one is there.

43

The clearing looks empty. But I can sense *them,* the air shifting and rolling around the open space as if many hands are moving it. I feel the way I did playing Fidchell. I narrow my eyes and concentrate with my Watcher vision. Soon there's the smell of sweetgrass and a trickle of smoke rises up from a huge transparent bowl in the center of the clearing. Flames climb the sides of the bowl, then slide back only to rise again in a rhythmic pattern. I hear soft singsong voices and, slowly, a circle of beautiful silk tents covered in colorful symbols comes into view. Overlapping rugs and piles of pillows begin to appear until they line every inch of the clearing. Finally, tiny humanlike beings emerge, one by one — clothed in wisps of fabric, flowers and jewels — some dancing, some sprawled across the pillows drinking, eating and talking. They look like the children we saw in the forest. A small male is playing a stringed instrument, another shakes a tambourine.

"Dee a dancee!" someone cries. "Aylee! Plee dee a dancee!"

I search my inner computer to translate this strange pidgin language. The voice is demanding that someone dance for them. My brain freezes when a tall teenage girl with a cap of brown hair stands up among the crowd of tiny beings. They clap and laugh. The girl's thin arms, long neck and face are pure white. She is wearing a white dress that clicks and tinkles with many small crystals. She towers over the small creatures. She's smiling and shaking her head. The voice calls to her again, but she slides into one of the tents and vanishes. The tiny beings laugh and call to her, telling her not to be afraid.

It's Ailla. I recognize her from the mask in my pouch. Someone touches my arm and I jump. Baudwin whispers, "It's her!"

I'm angry that he didn't stay back, but I'm also moved by the joy and pain that play across his face. It takes a second to realize the camp has gone silent. It takes another second to realize that the small beings are gone. In their place are ordinary-sized individuals with dark red hair and black eyes, dressed in heavy woven pants and jackets of a dull maroon-and-green tartan. The tents are the color of the grass. Each person — man, woman and child — is holding a weapon.

Aimed at us.

44

I step forward. My tongue feels too big for my mouth, but I manage to stammer out, "We — uh — have come … that is, we wish to talk to Gray Sara. We have not come to harm anyone."

A boy my age steps forward. He's dark skinned with long bronze-red hair. "I'are Sarason. Gray Sara is mey grandmera. She see'is no one." He looks around with quick darting glances. "How di yee get here? I earred no one."

I clear my throat. "We know the girl Ailla is here. We believe that she is in danger."

The young man's face darkens. He points his crossbow at my companion. "The only griff Aylee fears is *that* one. Er's gone and lef' him and he canna've er back."

"Baudwin led us here so that we could warn you. I'm Ailla's sister and she's in danger. If you'd just let us explain —"

Sarason looks me up and down and laughs. "Oo? Ee Watcher? Watchers din't've human sisters. Pull mea leg to see ifenit got bells on, is you?"

I turn into my human form. "My mother is human — I'm her adopted child. Ailla was taken from my Earth mother, and a changeling was put in her place. My — Ailla's — mother is dying. She has been pining to see the child she gave birth to." I speak loudly in the hope that Ailla will hear me. "She has longed to meet her child for many mooncrests. I'm my mother's Watcher. I am Ailla's Watcher, too. I am her *sister.*"

The entrance to one of the tents twitches. A very old woman steps out. Everything about her is gray — the long woven cloak, her hair, her skin — even her eyes are gray. She wears a large clear drop on a heavy chain around her neck. She moves with great dignity. As she comes closer, I see that there is a tuft of dark red hair embedded in the crystal drop.

"Yee will not take Aylee way." She comes very close to me.

I hold my position. "If she *wants* to stay here, I'll honor that. But I hope that she will come — even for just a short visit — to see my ... her mother. If she does, I'm sure her mother will recover from her grave illness. Then, if Ailla truly wishes to come back here, she can, of course."

The old woman turns her head and spits. Her gray eyes are cold. She would get along well with Rhona. But I also see something behind the coldness — a flash of concern. She takes my hand in hers, then she puts the drop in the center of my palm, her own hand covering it.

"This be the lock of the Great Lubdan, once the Sover-reign of all Faylinns. It teach me what I need."

She closes her eyes. Then she nods and says, "Yee are not false. But what danger be our Aylee in?"

I say, "Someone's after her. I don't know who they are. I think it is two Players from either Fomorii or Cleave. They've been following me and my small troop. We thought we'd lost them, but I saw both at Moling — just a flash of each one. They're both disguised in blue cloaks. One has a silver mask, the other has gold. I don't know what either wants, but you must believe that Ailla is in *real* danger. And that we are here to protect her, not to harm her."

"So be it. But yee must see we can also protect Aylee." She looks over my shoulder and nods. "Yee have others with yee. I didn't earred them at first. That fret me for certain. But the secret to be a good assailer is to never let the enemy know yer moves. You fail'd to that."

I beg, "Please believe me, Gray Sara. I'm no assailer. I am Ailla's Watcher. I only wish to see her united safely with her mother."

She holds up her hand, and Gyro, Cill and a furious Badba are marched into the circle by a group of armed Faylinns. Tom isn't with them. Good. At least he can do something if this all goes wrong. I won't allow myself to wonder if he's missing for another reason. No, he'd never desert me — I have to believe that.

"How does yee prove yee are Aylee's Watcher?" she asks.

I take the small mask out of my pouch. I hesitate, then give it to her. "I stole this from Mirour, the mask maker. It's the essence of Ailla which he removed from her. I want Ailla to be whole again."

She holds it close to her eyes. "So it be." Then to the young man Sarason, she says, "Bring Aylee to me."

The boy says, "No, Grandmera. Er lie!"

"No, er not lie. Get Aylee. Now!"

Reluctantly he goes in the direction of the largest tent.

Gray Sara says, "The mask maker take'way that part of folk's spirit that make er strong, that allow er to challenge, to make resolutions. It also take away er joy. But he canna remove *all* er soul. I have see the pure essence still in our Aylee. So as hee." She points at Baudwin.

Baudwin says, "Yes, she has a soul of great wisdom. She drew on that when she was with me, and I saw her change … grow … but then I destroyed the light that was forming her spirit, Gray Sara. I will always regret that."

Gray Sara looks at him with contempt mixed with pity. I think we may be getting somewhere at last. If we can just convince Gray Sara to let Ailla come with us.

The tent opens and the boy comes out, followed by the girl. He gazes at her with a look that is both loving and desperate. She's dressed in pants and a wool singlet of dull tartan, her white arms bare, as are her feet. Her short hair is muddy brown, her skin as white as marble. She looks just like the mask — very beautiful — but her pale eyes are almost lifeless. It's hard to believe she had the strength to leave Baudwin. There must have been something between them that surpassed even the loss of so much of her spirit. Strong enough to make her leave him before she lost the rest of her soul — perhaps to him. She stands beside the old woman, looking down at the ground.

Gray Sara takes her by the chin and holds her head so she can look into her eyes. "These folk come to take yee to thee real mother — who gave yee life. They say er is dying. And er wants to look upon yee before er die. Yee may go with them but only if *yee* wish."

Baudwin sucks in a sharp breath. The girl glances at him with no expression, but I'm sure I see the tiniest quick flash of something in those dull eyes. Then she looks at me. I smile. She smiles back a pleasant blank smile and takes one step away from Gray Sara.

Ailla says in a small voice, "I — I can't make such a decision. It is too difficult."

Gray Sara holds up the mask. "Press yee visage to

this, lass, and yee will return to yeesalf. Then yee be able to make all yee own resolves. Yee be slave to no one."

Ailla reaches out to take it from Gray Sara.

Sarason cries out, "No, Aylee!"

Gray Sara snaps at him, "Do yee be senseless? To keep Aylee ere would be to keep er a prisoner in that lost hollow place er be." She turns to Ailla. "Put yee mask to yee visage."

We all hold our breath as Ailla, like an automaton, places the thin shell of mask to her face. I don't know what I'm expecting. Certainly not to see the mask simply vanish, but it does. A faint tinge of color blushes Ailla's cheeks. She opens her eyes, puts out a hand as if she's about to fall and Sarason holds her up. Baudwin is gripping my shoulder so hard that I think he's going to crack my collarbone.

In that few seconds, Ailla's skin has deepened to a warm bronze and her pale eyes are as dark and shiny as new molasses. Then, magically, her lifeless muddy hair swirls into tight, crisp black curls.

She frowns at us. Then she looks at her hands. Her feet. Then she grins from ear to ear, matching my big grin.

"Welcome back, Ailla!" I cry.

She swoops over to me and lifts me up. "Sister!" she cries in a wonderful firm voice. "Did you say you were my sister? That I have a mother who —"

Suddenly a huge shadow surrounds us. I hear myself shout. I push my arms up at it, but it swirls in the air, enclosing me like a cocoon, and I'm crushed against suffocating blackness. I know I cry out "Ailla!" just as my feet leave the ground.

As the creature lifts me into the air, I look down through its flapping wings. My frightened heart is thrashing wildly in my chest. Long streams of vine tendrils shoot toward us and fall back to the ground. I sob with disappointment and fury. Poor Cill will be inconsolable. As I rise into the icy clouds, the scene below vanishes. Where am I being taken? Is Ailla safe? *And where is Tom?*

45

"Where are we going?" a small frightened voice calls out. I struggle in the clutches of the thing that holds me and manage to turn my head. Ailla's face is next to mine.

"You're here!" I cry. "I was hoping you were still down there, safe."

Her face is covered in ice beads from the clouds. They glitter in her hair like tiny stars. Her eyes are frightened, but she tries to smile reassuringly. She grips the top of my arm. I fight back tears, knowing I should be the one reassuring her. But I'm so scared, I can hardly think.

The creature carrying us loses altitude suddenly. I look past its wings and see the faint shape of Baudwin's pagoda roof looming toward us. We land on the wide stone walkway that surrounds the building. The creature holds us tight against its body and shuffles past the empty pool. I hear a gasp of horror from Ailla, but I tighten my grip on her hand and shake my head in warning. Her eyes are filled with tears at the sight of her destroyed work. In the inner room, a fire burns brightly in the grate.

A cloaked blue figure sits on a chair facing the fireplace. I see a glimpse of silver under the cowled hood. The creature pushes me forward. I look over my shoulder.

"So, Taker Yegg." My voice is quivering as much from cold as from fear. "I smelled you in the forest, but I didn't have the time to sort out what it was. This is my own fault. I never imagined you would be here."

In her high-pitched squeal, Yegg says, "Oh, I go where the prizes are promising. Two at once!" She lets Ailla go, giving her a hard shove.

Ailla bumps into me and whispers, "Who are these creatures?"

"Greedy Game Players," I snarl. "But there's not much of a prize here, Yegg. Just a Watcher on a quest and a young girl with no fortune."

"Oh, that's where you're wrong, Watcher. There is a vast fortune to be had. I am to be paid well for telling this being where to find you."

The cloaked figure speaks. "It has taken a while, Watcher, but finally I have you. You should have come with me at the fountain in the market."

I recognize the lilting voice. "Bedeven. Does Huw know what you're up to? Does my sister Summer?"

"We have another sister?" Ailla whispers.

I squeeze her hand and nod. Bedeven drops his hood and removes the mask covering his face. There's a deep blue cut on his neck from Badba's knife. He smiles his tight little smile. "No, Watcher, Huw has no idea what I'm *up* to. Only Rhona knows. She and I are partners — and Yegg has joined us."

Yegg lets out a screech of delight that almost breaks my eardrums.

Ailla leans close to me. "I don't like these creatures. We won't go with them."

Bedeven's hooded eyes assess her carefully. Then he smiles again — a little lift that vanishes as quickly. "You will go where I want you to go, my dear." His eyes slide to me. "If you had stayed in your room at the castel, all of this could have been avoided."

"Why have you brought us to Baudwin's?"

"We have to wait here — for a reason that, naturally, is of no concern to you."

"You've been here at Moling all this time? You destroyed everything in the next room. Then you saw us leave for the Faylinn camp."

He growls, "Yes. I hoped to grab you, but you were always surrounded by your strange friends. So I waited until you went to the forest and sent Yegg to get you. I didn't expect her to take the other girl."

Then it dawns on me what he's just said. "You didn't expect Ailla? You weren't after her?"

He makes a "come here" gesture with his finger to Ailla. "You — human girl."

"Don't go, Ailla!" I cry, stepping in front of her.

This time Bedeven's smile is genuine. "Always the little Watcher, eh? But surely you know that it isn't this human we want."

"It isn't? Didn't you want to mess up my Seeker Game by getting to her first?"

"Seeker Game? Fool's play! We have no interest in that. Oh no, it is *you* we want, Watcher. And you've been here, there and everywhere, haven't you? Hard to keep up with at times! You've slowed down our plans considerably."

"You tried to hold me captive in the castel and now you've followed me here — *why?*"

"You'll find out soon enough."

"Then let my — the girl go back to the Faylinns."

"Oh, I don't think so, Watcher. Although we don't want *her,* I must confess that her presence has suddenly become an asset — a lucky happenstance!" He leans close to me. "As long as I have this Eorthe child, your mother and the young Suzarain are under my thumb. *And* you'll do as you're told. If not," he makes a slitting movement under his chin and points at Ailla.

"You'll have to kill *me* first!" I cry.

"No need for that. But I think you will show us what we need to know, now that your mother is dying. We can hold this girl until you agree to our terms."

"What *terms?* And what do you need to know?"

Bedeven sits back, as if he's about to tell a story. "Summer's first servant, little nosy Tally tattle-tongue, followed you one day soon after you arrived in Argadnel, and the silly girl reported what she saw to Gormala. Gormala made Tally promise to keep her secret until she could check it out. As you often went out walking when you were visiting the castel, Gormala followed you. For many nights nothing happened. Then one night she saw what Tally had described. Gormala came directly to me. We had to get rid of the foolish Tally before she confided in the young Suzarain. Then, Gormala and I worked on it for a number of mooncrests, but to no avail. Gormala kept insisting it was *you* who had the key. I was finally forced to test her theory. I followed you that night before you suddenly left Argadnel. And I saw it."

"Saw what?" I ask, bewildered.

He ignores me. "And I do believe she's right — you *are* the only one who seems able to make it appear. So ... *I* now hold all the strings: your mother, your father, the Suzarain and this Eorthe child. You care about them. That way, I control *everything in the name of my Queen.*"

"I don't know what you're talking about!" I shout. "What did you see?"

Bedeven stands up. "Why, my dear, are you not aware that you have found a world of enormous riches — a spectacular and vast city, huge stretches of land and an uncharted sea?"

I stare at him, confused. Then I remember my special place, the border cave on Argadnel that leads to my beautiful world. Is *that* what all this has been about? I stare at him, mouth open. So I was right! The world I see on Argadnel never *has* been recorded. And Gormala and Bedeven followed me and saw it, too.

I realize what this means, and my heart shrinks to an icy ball. Rhona and Bedeven want control of this new world. So will Fergus. A great War Game will center on it — perhaps even destroy it. And possibly Argadnel as well.

"I naturally passed on what I saw to Queen Rhona," Bedeven continues. "I also told her we couldn't conjure up the border cave ourselves. Only you seemed to be able to do it. Of course Rhona did *not* tell Fergus." He preens. "No ... we will conquer this world ourselves. Set up a secret Game. And then Rhona will become the most powerful Player in all the worlds."

"But I won't take you there," I shout.

Bedeven shakes his head soulfully and in a singsong voice says, "Then we'll kill your family one by one. Starting perhaps with this rather beautiful young girl. Or perhaps we'll sell her to a merchant who desires a pure Eorthe child. They are rare — quite exotic. And can be very entertaining."

There's only one thing to do.

I transmute invisible, and by holding Ailla's hand in a tight grip, I make her vanish, too. We head for the window and leap out, landing on the other side in perfect synchronization, as if we've been doing this together all our lives. In a flash, we're around the building and down the stairs toward the bridge.

"Wait! I can't leap the bridge," I cry. "And I don't know how Baudwin opened it!" I'm so agitated that I lose my grip on Ailla and she becomes visible. Her eyes flash in the darkness.

"I know the code, but we don't have time. I can leap the bridge easily," she says. "It's always been a game for me. Hold on to my hand. Where are you? I can't see you!"

I allow her to see me, then I change into my Watcher form. She hesitates, then grins, and grabs my hand just as the sound of flapping wings emerges from the building behind us.

We run straight at the archway to the bridge. "When I say leap, you leap," Ailla gasps. Our feet hit the first wooden slat with a clatter and she cries, "Leap!"

It's as if the bridge has suddenly become shorter. As we fly over the boards, the flapping of wings grows loud. Yegg is almost upon us.

"And down!" Ailla calls. I can see the Leaping Circle — we're almost there when the bridge suddenly tips sharply. My left foot lands on the circle but slides out from under me. Ailla's foot accidentally kicks my right one over the ledge and I fight to keep from following it. I scrabble for a safe perch, but the bridge twists again and Ailla bumps against me. Yegg shrieks with delight. She's hovering at the end of the bridge, her wings twisting it back and forth. We try to hold steady, floundering for the railing, but suddenly the bridge throws Yegg off. She goes over the side. We try to gain our footing, but before we can she flies up behind us and one of her heavy black wings bangs against us hard.

Ailla and I fall straight down to the monsters waiting below.

46

If I can just grab hold of Ailla, I can keep us in the air and perhaps get us to safety. But she's tumbling away from me so fast I keep missing her. I hear Histal's voice, *The only reason you're falling is because you're letting yourself fall. Fly!* I focus, despite my terror, and suddenly my bones feel light as air. I turn myself head down and slide straight as an arrow toward Ailla. I loop under her, grab her by the shirt and haul her up. It's hard going — the wind is strong and coming at us in heaving gusts. For every five feet we gain, we drop back two or three. I can't believe Yegg hasn't attacked us again. Maybe she thinks we're as good as dead.

Suddenly, the boiling green waves part and a purple-backed sea monster rises, his long head and sharp teeth slashing up at us. I hold on to Ailla's shirt and pull her away from the needle teeth as the monster's long neck stretches higher. To my horror, I hear a ripping sound. Ailla's shirt is giving way under my hand.

"Let me go!" Ailla shouts. "Save yourself."

I don't answer. I can't. I have almost no breath or strength left. I wish I could become a bird with powerful wings so I could fly her to safety. I grab the back of her leggings with my other hand, close my eyes and haul her into the air with all my strength. I look up. The bridge is miles above us. If I could just get her — ooph — over to one of those — ooph — small ledges. But we're in the middle of the gorge and I don't have enough strength left.

Sobbing with exertion, I try for one last burst of energy. I hear flapping nearby and a short sharp tug between my shoulder blades. I look up, expecting to see Yegg's hideous face, but instead I see wings the color of a cabbage butterfly, thin, shining, the palest of green around the edges.

I've got wings! I don't know how, but somehow I've transformed into some kind of half moth, half Watcher! The wings are small, stunted and twisted at the edges, but they're still wings. I beat them frantically and we rise slowly about ten feet. My arms are shaking and I still can't get enough air into my frozen lungs, but I'm sure I can make it now.

Overhead I hear an ominous shriek. When I gawk around, Yegg is lunging straight at me. As she soars past, she grabs clawfuls of my brittle, half-formed wings. Ailla and I hang in the air. I beat the remnants of my pathetic wings, knowing any second we'll either plunge into the gaping mouth of the monster or Yegg will carry us off. I will myself to stay in the air. My fingers are numb. I can't hold on.

"I — I'm sorry," I gasp, feeling the fabric drag out of my numb fingers just as something bumps into my feet. I thrash around in panic, looking for the serpent or Yegg's leathery wings. Instead, I see the sweet leafy face of Cill. How can that be?

I'm hallucinating. I fight to hold on to Ailla.

"You let her go, little one," Cill says. "You be safe now."

I fight to rise back into the air. The serpent must be a shape-changer — or Yegg can transform, and she's pretending to be Cill. Strong hands drag me down and pry Ailla away. I flail around, but the hands hold me tight. I stare wildly. The little sloop is pushing us high into the air away from the jaws of the monster. I hear a crooning sound and see Baudwin kneeling on the deck beside me, his arms wrapped around a sobbing Ailla.

We're safe! I drop into the soft, crackling safety of Cill's arms. She says, "Badba not let that horrible Yegg near you again. We see her fly way over the hill."

She examines me from head to toe, making little concerned mewing sounds and wondering aloud if she actually saw me with wings and where are they now? I shake my head in exhaustion and stand up on wobbly legs. Gyro's helicycle flanks our left, Badba and Lycias our right. Badba has another rider with her — Sarason. He's looking at Baudwin and Ailla with a ferocious frown.

"Where's Tom?" I gasp.

"We no see him since the Faylinn camp."

I stagger to the bow of the sloop. Where *is* he? Why do I keep losing him? Or — a voice says inside my head — maybe he's deliberately losing *himself?* We're moving steadily down the gorge, away from the bridge. The wind is stiff and cold, pulling at my hair and clothes. Lycias seems to be handling the wind, but Gyro is bobbing around like a cork on turbulent water.

We have to get out of here. But which way?

I hear a howl and race back down the deck to see Yegg swarming Badba and Sarason on the lee side of the ship. Lycias drops out of sight, taking the monstrous bakke with him. I can't see Badba, but her screeches of rage echo around the little ship. I signal frantically to Gyro to land on the sloop. He lifts his hand, points down and disappears under the ship.

"He go after Badba to help!" Cill shouts.

Baudwin and Ailla run to look over the side.

"They're just below us," Baudwin cries, handing me a small streak gun and Ailla his shield. Then he takes a laser longbow from his gear and sets his sight. "Go to the other side, Emma, and see if you can spot the mecha-drone. Get him in here or he'll lose the machine — and we may need it!"

"He's not a mecha-drone," I shout. "His name's Gyro!"

He ignores me and bellows at Ailla, "Keep the shield up."

"I need a weapon," she cries.

"No! Just protect yourself. My shield will keep you safe."

She glares at him.

"Do as he say, Ailla. Be safe," Cill says. "I be here with you."

Suddenly Yegg flies straight up like a black shadow. She circles high, getting her bearings, but one of her wings flaps slowly, as if it's been hurt. Lycias rises to the side of the sloop like a small ship heaving to, and we all cheer loudly. Badba is bloody, but wears a broad smile. She picks up Sarason as if he's a doll and throws him to safety on the deck. With a screech of triumph, she roars after Yegg. Sarason curses her, but he's uninjured. Baudwin throws him a streak rifle. Ailla is shouting at Gyro over the railing. He bobs up beside us, looking exhausted.

"Get on board. That's an order!" I shout at him.

He manages to set the rattling cycle on the deck near the stern, despite the wind fighting to lift him again.

"That was exhilarating," he cries, tying his helicycle down and creaking over to us. "And I did get off one arrow, and if I'm not mistaken, I think I may have hit that creature. I didn't like to do it, but I was worried about our friend Badba. Look, here they come again!"

Yegg is flying straight at us, Lycias on her tail. As Yegg swoops over us, she shoots spears of light that slice long gashes into the deck. Baudwin and Sarason unleash their weapons. Cill throws three long vines that tangle Yegg's wings. Yegg turns an awkward somersault in the air and bangs against the side of the sloop. Cill releases her and Yegg drops out of sight. Badba screams, shaking her feathered headpiece, and sends a volley of knives after the fallen bakke.

Badba twists around in her seat and shouts over her shoulder, "That did it! Yegg's monster meat! I'll lead the way out of here. It's dark and I don't want you banging into a —" The words die in her mouth. She points below.

We all rush to the side of the sloop in time to see what looks like a huge glass fish rise out of the water. Within seconds, it's closing in on us. Inside its broad head, beings move back and forth. The little sloop speeds up on its own, sensing danger.

"It's Rhona's ship. That's who Bedeven was waiting for!" I shout. "They were going to begin their new Game once they'd captured me."

Rhona's airship is as big as a jumbo jet, its wings tipped up. If it wasn't so terrifying, it would be beautiful, with its glowing blue lights, crystal walls and graceful lines. But for us, it's a death ship. It'll open its mouth and suck us all in.

I call to Badba, "Save Lycias. Run and hide. *Now*."

She shakes her head, leaps on board and with stern words sends Lycias to safety. The last we see of the drakon, he's disappearing over the top of the gorge.

"Okay," I shout into the wind. "Time to put this thing in high gear." I reach over to touch the black button, explaining to Ailla that this will send us rocketing to safety. But she cries "Wait. Look!" and points straight ahead.

"Oh my great god of Ravan," Badba screeches. "What is that?"

A dark brown wedge-shaped ship, with a wolf's head on its bow like a monstrous battering ram, is blocking our escape. It almost fills the gorge and even blocks the wind. I look back at the glass ship. We're trapped between them.

I grab Sarason's arm. "Is that your ship?"

"No. Wea doon need airships. Wea doon playee Game."

"Then ... who?"

The hull of this ship is huge, the body as wide as the biggest oil tanker on Earth. It's covered in animal and tree designs. Can it *be?*

Cill and Gyro huddle close to me. "What we do?" Cill cries. "We be crushed."

The hull comes closer. Even though it's still a distance away, I can see the emblem just below — the same shape as the brooch I threw away.

"It *is* Fergus," I cry. "He's heard what Rhona and Bedeven are up to. We're smack in the middle of their new Game!"

Gyro says, "I fixed the black button when you were across the bridge. You —"

A small figure dives off the side of Fergus's ship and sails toward us. "Don't push that black button!" it shouts.

"It Tom!" Cill gasps.

"Where the *devil* have you been!" I shout angrily. "You left us to go to Fergus?"

He soars through the small window in the sail and says breathlessly, "There's no time to explain! Branwen let Fergus know that one of Rhona's men was tracking us. Fergus just told me he went to Argadnel and got everything out of Gormala — about this world you've found. Looks like Gormala sold out Bedeven and Rhona in order to live."

"But why?" I cry. "Why go to the enemy!"

"Fergus is a power-hungry fool, Emma, but in this fight, he's not the enemy."

"Yes, he is. He'll take away Ailla. He'll let Mom die. He'll make me show them the way to this new world I've discovered! Yes, Tom! He *is* the enemy."

"Better the enemy on your side than the one who wants to feed you to the fish," Baudwin says. His pale face is flushed. "What does Fergus want us to do?"

Tom says, "We must set the coordinates of the sloop for the deck of Fergus's ship."

A streak light zaps the side of the sloop and sends sparks over us.

"She's attacking. Gyro — get to it!" Tom shouts.

But Gyro is already working out the coordinates using his telescopic eye. He sets them amidst a shower of streak lights.

"Rhona's just playing around," Tom says. "Cat and mouse torture gives her a thrill. Any second, though, she'll send us a load of stuff that'll blast us into little bits."

Gyro says, "Batten down and get ready. I do believe I have the coordinates."

We all drop to the deck. Gyro pushes the green button and we slice through the air and clatter onto Fergus's ship just as something explodes right where the sloop hovered two seconds earlier. When I look back, Rhona's ship veers away and vanishes into the rolling water below.

47

The big ship is teeming with armed Players. When we climb out of the sloop, the Players move quickly into two groups, leaving an open pathway. Fergus strides down it. He's clad in brown leather, a dark green breast plate and a dull copper and green helmet shaped like a snarling wolf's head. He's fully armed and ready for battle. The Druvid, Mathus, in a long, elaborately embroidered coat, follows right behind him, his bald head gleaming. He carries no weapon.

"Fergus," I say, my chin firm, my voice as hard as I can make it. "I have completed the Seeker Game. In less than the required time."

Fergus laughs coldly and waves one hand in the air as if he's swatting away a fly. "That is of little import now, Watcher. We are at war with the Fomorii. Rhona has betrayed me!"

My voice goes up three notches. "How did you find out what Rhona was up to?"

"At Cleave, Tom warned me that Bedeven and Gormala were meeting secretly ... that you saw her coming out of his room. And that Rhona was unduly interested in you. I thought he was simply trying to deflect my interest away from killing you."

I'm so shocked, I only open and close my mouth like a guppy, unable to speak. Tom told Fergus all this while we were prisoners at Cleave?

Fergus continues, "A short while after you left, I got an urgent message from Branwen. She said that you had returned to Argadnel to see your mother before going on your Seeker Game. And that Bedeven had gone looking for you. So, I asked myself, why would Bedeven be suddenly interested in this Eorthe child you were tracking? Even if your mother lived, it wouldn't make much difference to his position at court. So I went to Argadnel and spoke to Gormala. When *pressed* she became very cooperative. Of course, your Eorthe child was of no interest at all to Bedeven." He laughs. "So I sent a trusted spy of mine to follow all of you and we waited for Rhona to make her move. Meanwhile, your Seeker Game was allowed to continue."

"What spy?" I ask.

Another man moves out of the crowd and stands beside Mathus. He is dressed in a blue cloak. His mask is gold.

I gasp. "I was right. There *are* two Blue Cloaks!"

The man's cloak and mask drop to the deck. The left side of his face is stained with swirling blue tattoos, as are his hands. His body and feet are tightly covered in scaly orange eelskin, on his head a wide sleek helmet of silver with a clutch of feathers that flows out behind him like the curious light that follows him everywhere. He carries no weapons. As a Druvid, he's not allowed to fight in battle.

"Huw?" I say, shocked. "But —"

"Rhona's Druvid is part of our new Game strategy," says Mathus.

I can't take this in. "But how?" I ask Huw. "Why are you no longer with Rhona?"

His face has no expression. "I am a Celtoi. No one crosses a Celtoi. I gave loyal service to Rhona. She betrayed me. She was going to go to this new border world you discovered without me."

I want to ask him *why* she didn't include him, but his cold eyes warn me to ask nothing more.

Fergus puffs his chest out. "Thanks to Huw and Tom, I'll soon be in control of this new Game Rhona has set up. She almost slipped right past me." He grins. "You didn't tell your faithful friend, Tamhas, about this new world you'd found, did you, Watcher? Imagine what he thought when I told him what Gormala had confessed!" He rubs his hands together and laughs. "So you and he have much to discuss, I think."

I look for Tom, but he's not in sight. It's true — I didn't tell him about my secret place, and now he knows about it. And while I'd forgotten all about it during the Seeker Game, others were hunting me down for it. But then I harden my heart. He was telling Fergus things at Cleave he had no right to tell without discussing them with me first.

Fergus says, "You owe me, Watcher."

I tighten my mouth. I know what he's after, but I *won't* give him my beautiful border world. I know he's saved me and my little band. I know that. But ... how much *do* I owe him for that? Surely not something as big as this incredible place I've discovered?

I try to deflect him, "You and I have much to discuss, too. I found my mother's child in less than one mooncrest. I have won the Seeker Game. You have to give my father back his memories now. And I'll take my mother's child to Argadnel."

Fergus grins. "I'm not sure this is a legitimate win, Watcher. After all, you'd be dead if my ship hadn't come along. Who would have saved you from Rhona's clutches? Besides, we were ahead of you all the way."

"If you hadn't barred *our* way with your hulk of a ship, we'd have escaped Rhona's ship in Gyro's sloop," I say firmly, not sure if it's true.

This time he laughs loudly. "Perhaps, perhaps. But we'll never know, will we? You and I will have to leave our talk until this is over, Watcher. Isn't that right, Tamhas?"

Another man walks onto the deck. He's wearing a jerkin and leggings of heavy brown leather. Brass plates of armor cover his chest and back. He's big and broad, with a battered face and spiky black hair. Around his thick neck is a plain leather strap and on his wrists are wide copper bracelets. He carries a round leather and bronze shield and a weapon called a madans, which looks like a javelin but throws heavy laser beams. On his back, I can see three bows, three quivers of arrows and the tops of four basket-hilt swords. He too is ready for battle.

He smiles at me and I almost pass out. Tom — Tamhas — the real, live, solid Tom stands in front of me.

He telepaths to me, *Fergus is right, Emma. When we were in Cleave, I told him that I'd seen Gormala and Bedeven whispering in corners and that you saw Gormala coming out of Bedeven's quarters. Then I told him how Huw had taken you away to see Rhona in her chamber at Cleave and you came back and said Rhona wanted something from you. I told him that I thought they were all plotting something but I didn't know what — however, I was certain it revolved around you somehow. I thought telling him this would keep you alive. Turns out it also pleased Fergus to have this information — pleased him so much I have been rewarded. The cunning is gone. Is it not strange, Creirwy, after all this time, to see me again?*

Anger grows hot inside me. My inner voice is dry and harsh. *How long have you known that Bedeven was plotting to invade the border world I discovered in Argadnel? And why didn't you tell me you knew?*

I just found out from Fergus. You kept this place a secret from me, Creirwy.

I begin to bluster out loud, but the overriding anger wins. "How long did you know Fergus and Huw were lurking around us?"

"They were waiting for Bedeven and Rhona to make their move. I — er — I saw Huw when he rescued me from the falling tent at Cymmarian Market. I realized he was one of the Blue Cloaks. He led me to Fergus."

"You spoke to Huw and Fergus and didn't tell me?"

"Yes."

"And what did they say?" I ask through dry lips.

"Huw told me to be careful — to guard you closely. That Fergus wanted the Seeker Game to continue. Later, Fergus said that the one who attacked us in the fountain booth was indeed Bedeven. And that he was after you."

"And you chose not to tell me you'd seen them," I say coldly. "Or that you *knew* there was a being in a gold mask!"

"I am your Watcher, Emma. I felt it best not to. I had to make sure Fergus and Huw weren't a threat as well. And I wanted you to concentrate on finding Ailla and getting her to safety. I wanted you to win the Seeker Game so you could save your family."

I lash out. "But you left us at the Faylinn camp. In order to go where your real loyalties lie? Isn't that what you *really* did? Or maybe you did all this just for yourself — to get rid of the owl cunning!"

Tom looks shocked. "No, no, Emma. Believe me, it had nothing to do with that! I had to find out how near Rhona and Bedeven were — only Fergus knew. I thought you were safe for a short while talking to Gray Sara. I had to protect *you*. Seeing Baudwin's hermitage destroyed told me that Bedeven was near. If Rhona was closing in, I knew that Fergus was the only one with the Players and weapons strong enough to defeat her, to stop this hunt for you and to get you and Ailla back safely." A smile curls his lip. "You're not going to suddenly play the Earth girl and pretend you couldn't do something without my help, are you? You're a Watcher, after all. Your little crew just got rid of Yegg all on their own."

"Yegg took Ailla and me from the camp. She took us to Bedeven at Moling. We escaped and Yegg knocked us off the bridge. We almost died, Tom!" I shout.

"What? When? I didn't know —"

"My *real* friends knew — they rescued me!"

He looks stricken. "I didn't know Yegg was there until I saw you fighting her from the sloop. When I left you at the Faylinn camp, I thought you weren't in any immediate danger."

Slightly mollified, I say, "Yeah ... well don't go thinking I'll give up my border world to Fergus so he can plunder it and make it part of his empire. Because I *won't*." I blink back fierce tears. "You've betrayed me, Tom. But now you're free, aren't you? Free of the owl cunning. Free of me!"

His eyes are hard. "You really believe that not only have I betrayed you but that I would force you to give this new world to Fergus? Or that I would do all this to release the owl cunning?"

I can't look at him. It hurts too much. I've waited for him to become Tom for months and now it's all ruined.

He wraps a warm hand around my arm and says in a low voice, "Say you don't believe I betrayed you, Creirwy. I will help you protect this new border world. I give you my word. Everything I did was for you."

I look down at his hand. I don't know what to think.

Suddenly someone bawls, "Look to fore! The Fomorii ship!"

Fergus shouts, "Rise, rise! Go to the clouds. She'll stay low, looking for a way to get behind us. We're wedged in here like a cork in a bottle!"

"Look to port!" shouts a lookout hanging from the top of a leather sail. "Down under!"

The green river below is boiling as Rhona's ship roars under it, but once past Fergus's ship, it rises and slices through the air, heading for our stern.

"Open fire!" Fergus shouts. His words echo through the ship and a volley of orange balls scream out. But the smaller streamlined airship dodges them easily.

"She's at the helm," Fergus snarls, but I can hear admiration in his voice. "She'll be all over us in a minute!"

We lift into the air under a steady barrage of laser balls that bang against the metal hull. They don't seem to be doing much, but then a huge orb of blue light crashes against the bow, twisting the long neck of the wolf on the prow and leaving a gaping hole in the side of the ship.

"Rise!" Fergus bellows, the cords in his neck standing out.

We slide into the green clouds and are immediately covered in ice crystals. Some of the Players slip and slide on the metal deck.

"Heat strands on!" Fergus shouts.

Within seconds, the ice on deck is melting, and soon icicles hang off every surface. A loud crash, followed by a slice of green lightning, stops everyone in their tracks.

"We've disturbed the hydrons in the cloud! Put up the rods. Random movement!" Fergus orders. Tall coiled rods rise above the ship as it moves erratically through the clouds. Slashes of lightning sear past us, but none hits. Thunder pounds our eardrums, then dissipates into angry grumbles.

"That will keep Rhona out. The Fomorii ship won't withstand a lightning strike."

Fergus turns to me and my little crew and looks us all over for the first time, hands on hips. He stops when he reaches Baudwin. Then he grins and points at him.

"Can it be you?"

Baudwin bows. "It is, sire."

Fergus laughs with a loud shout. "Don't you *sire* me, my old battler." He reaches forward and hugs him. "Baudwin! I thought you'd given up the Game. You were my best rival. Tell me you're back in it."

Baudwin shakes his head. "No. I'm only here to make sure that Ailla is taken home safely. Wherever she decides her home is to be."

Ailla's face shines with happiness at his words. She looks like a fairy princess with her dark curls covered in tiny icicles. Sarason scowls at Baudwin, his hatred like a living thing quivering between them.

"Will you fight for her?" Fergus asks, looking coy and fearsome at the same time.

Baudwin nods once. "I will."

Fergus claps him on the shoulder. He casts his other arm through the air, taking in the hundred or so men and women dressed for battle.

"I have my best Players with me, and Rhona's ship is one of her smaller ones. She didn't expect to find us here." Fergus casts an eye over my motley crew and points at Badba. "You, come forward."

Badba leaps in front of him, brandishing her many weapons to show she's ready for a fight.

"You'll do," Fergus says, laughing. "Rhona will try to avoid putting her Players on my deck. But, of course, that's what I'd like her to do. If we can disable enough of her Players, we can defeat her. If she stays in her ship, she'll simply throw stuff at us until we're full of holes. The casualties could be high. I want her to think I *don't* want her Players to board us, so we'll have to play this cannily."

He points at Sarason. "You, boy, will you be a Player for Cleave?"

Sarason shakes his head. "Faylinn playee no side. Ee takey care for meeself." He glowers at Baudwin.

Fergus shrugs. "As long as you keep to that." He turns his attention to Cill, who seems to shrivel up in front of his eyes. "You are my servant, Cill of Barroch. But you have forgotten your loyalties during the Seeker Game. Where do they lie now?"

She says, "I fight to save all that are here."

Fergus grins. "A diplomatic answer. Mind you, I have to thank you as well."

"For why?" Cill asks warily.

"It was your time marker's little homing device that allowed me to track you and your charges all over your crazy way to this girl, Ailla."

Cill sucks in her breath with a hiss. She looks at me, her leafy face crushed with horror. I smile back and shake my head. "It doesn't matter, Cill. You didn't know."

Fergus says to her, "But don't think a punishment is not going to be handed down when we're through with this!"

She suddenly straightens and looks him in the eye. "I take my punishment. I of Barroch royal blood. My punishment be for hurting my friends, not anything I do against you."

Fergus snorts. "Meanwhile, I want you to take care of Emma, the girl and the mecha-drone."

"He *not* a mecha-drone!" she says firmly. "*You* more machine than he. He have *great* abilities. One day he have power to —"

Gyro calls out, "Oh, dear no. She's quite wrong."

Fergus is torn between bellowing at her for her insolence and his interest in Gyro. The interest wins out. "Well?" he asks Gyro. "How is she wrong?"

Gyro wrings his hands with a grating sound. "I have no power and if I did I'd be scared to death of it. I just want to help my friends, as it were … sire."

Fergus says sarcastically, "Fine. Then one day, I'm sure we'll be *good* friends. Meanwhile you and Cill can watch over your *new* friend, the human girl. I want you to move her to an overhang at the stern of the boat. It has a small safety ledge and some straps to keep you stable. When we drop below the clouds and go to battle, I want you to stay put no matter what. Understood?"

Gyro nods, looking firm and determined. It's always his bottom lip that gives him away. Maybe he should make a silver one that doesn't quiver.

I look up at Tom.

"You're a Watcher," I say. "You're not supposed to go to battle."

"Aah, but I can defend the ones I watch over," he says softly. "And I do that now."

A voice inside is telling me that by keeping in

touch with Fergus, and siding with him now, Tom has in fact given us a chance to come through this mess alive. Besides, I had kept a secret of my own, hadn't I? Was it because I still didn't really trust anyone, not even Tom? He looks so big. And I'd forgotten how dark and battered and ... grown-up his face was. The hand holding the madans is muscular and large, with thick veins running across it. My knees wobble just standing near him. I fight back tears of confusion and despair. Will he survive this battle. Will I? And if we do, will anything ever be the same between us again?

48

Fergus snaps his fingers in front of my face. "Keep close to the girl and the other strays. I don't want anyone captured for ransom or negotiation, especially *you!*"

"I can fight," I snarl, "in order to protect someone." I don't look at Tom.

"You are an untrained Watcher," Fergus says. "We can't put you into battle — you are useless as a fighter. Besides, you're far too valuable. Do you have any weapons to protect yourself?"

I hold up my small streak gun, humiliated and angry. "And, yes, I know how to work it," I say through my teeth. "I'm not giving it back."

He laughs. "Perhaps you *will* make a fearsome protector when you're properly trained. That look on your face alone should melt my weapons."

I roll my eyes and he laughs. "Give her a sword," he says to a nearby Player, who throws me a sword so heavy its tip bangs on the metal deck when I catch its handle. I heave its flat side onto my shoulder.

"Now, everyone — MOVE!"

I have to drag Ailla away from Baudwin, he is so reluctant to let her go. "Take care of her, Watcher. No matter what happens."

Ailla is crying, but she doesn't resist. I look around to see if Tom is coming. But he smiles sadly and turns back to Fergus, who is in a huddle with Huw and Mathus.

Cill, Ailla, Gyro and I find the overhang easily. It's shallow, but there's a metal mesh curtain to hide behind. We're no sooner settled in when the big ship drops like a stone. My stomach bounces into my throat.

"Yeeeow!" cries Cill.

As we drop, the battle begins. High-pitched whistles are followed by loud thumps and searing screams that tear at my eardrums.

Through the mesh curtain, I see the wings of Rhona's ship rise beside ours. In seconds, dozens of Players tumble out of the eye of the fish, like a school of shining minnows — silver, yellow, blue. The ship slides away. The clash of knives, the thwack of arrows and the shouts of the Players fill the air.

I hear a thud nearby, followed by a clatter. A shield that looks like a black and yellow sunfish slides by. I grab it and tell Ailla and Cill to cover themselves with the shield Baudwin gave Ailla. The fighting is getting closer, but I'm too afraid for the others to be frightened for myself.

Suddenly Ailla grips my arm. She leans close to the screen. I try to push her back, but she says with horror, "Look. It's Baudwin and Sarason."

They're at the end of the narrow deck on this side of the ship. It looks like Sarason is slashing at Baudwin, while Baudwin is trying to talk and fend him off.

Ailla puts her hand up to open the mesh curtain. "No!" I bark.

But she crawls out, crying, "I have to stop them!"

As I try to pull her back, a leathery black wing covers the opening, a twisted claw grabs her arm, and she's swept out of the opening like a snail out of its shell.

"Yegg!" shouts Cill.

Yegg has Ailla by the neck and is dragging her toward the railing at the stern of the ship. One of Yegg's wings flops uselessly on the deck. It's covered in a sticky yellow goo. I leap at her, lifting the heavy sword, but she slashes the air with a many-bladed weapon and I'm forced to back off. I can see her squashed leathery face and yellow eyes. Her grin shows three sets of needlelike teeth.

She lifts her injured wing and a dozen small bakkes fly out. They must have helped her fly up from the river below. I lash at them with my sword. Two drop, but a half-dozen others attack my head. Their sharp teeth bite into my scalp, neck and shoulders.

Cill and Gyro thrash at them. Cill's small dagger

drives them off, while Gyro grabs the wounded bakkes and throws them overboard.

"I'll snap her neck, Watcher!" Yegg screeches. "You come with me and I'll let her go."

I drop my weapons. "I'll come. Just let her go. Cill. Gyro. Back off. *Please*."

Yegg points at Cill and Gyro, who edge back under the overhang.

"No go with her. Rhona kill you when she get what she want," Cill cries.

"Yes, dear child. She'll kill both you and the girl," Gyro pleads.

I shake my head. "She doesn't want Ailla. She wants me."

Yegg says, "Come with me. I'll release the girl."

"*No*. Let her go *first*. You have my word — I'll come with you as soon as she's safe."

She pushes Ailla away, just as two figures launch themselves at her from behind one of the ship's riggings. Yegg sends out another dozen bakkes from under her shattered wing and they swarm the attackers. Sarason, half blinded by the blood pouring down his face, staggers toward Yegg, his sword thrashing the air. Cill pulls Ailla to safety, Gyro at her side flinging off his magic arrows. When the first one hits a bakke, it vanishes in a flash of colors. This distracts Yegg for a split second. I lunge for one of her wings and hang on with all my might. Baudwin slides to one side to get his sword in from an angle, but Yegg shakes me off and with a mighty lunge drives the longest blade of her weapon between his neck torque and breastplate.

As he falls, Sarason's sword finds its mark and Yegg falls back. With her free claw, she clobbers the side of my head. A terrible pain sears through it just as Lycias bobs up, grabs Yegg's wing with his crocodile teeth and drags her over the railing.

"Feed her to sea serpent!" Cill shrieks.

My head is cracking open. The ship spins. I can hear sobbing far far away while the cheers grow louder. Someone is running down the deck toward us. He's moving in slow, slow motion. It's Tom. *My* Tom. I have to tell him something very important. But when I lift my arms, the deck opens up and swallows me like a big hungry fish.

Epilogue

One mooncrest later, we laid Baudwin's body to rest at Moling. We placed his sealed stone casket in the empty pool where Dierdre's image had spoken to him and told him to take a chance on living again. I wish he'd been able to find happiness for longer than the few mooncrests he'd spent with Ailla. She will paint pictures of Dierdre and Baudwin across the ceiling of his hermitage when it's repaired.

Ailla is still grieving for him. But it's grief mixed with many other emotions. Sarason has gone home. He'll be the leader of the Faylinn clan when Gray Sara dies. Perhaps Ailla will eventually forgive him, but I'm not sure he'll ever forgive himself. You see, Baudwin had been coming to warn us that Yegg was approaching the ship, but Sarason challenged Baudwin to a fight before he could get us to safety.

I was in bed for a week and almost lost an ear, but Allopath Bachod grudgingly sewed it up and, with Cill's help, there's hardly even a scar. I think my injuries have made Histal more lenient with my punishment.

I can go back to training whenever I feel ready. Meanwhile, I get to spend time with my family.

Mom is still weak, but she's growing stronger every day. When I walked into her room with Ailla and told her this was her real daughter, her aura was instantly threaded with brilliant blue, and I knew she was going to make it. She and Ailla are still shy around each other. After all, Ailla was brought up by strangers and has lived in four worlds. Two of these worlds, Mathus says, accelerated her age. Her experiences, I believe, made her even older. But here, at Argadnel, her aging appears to have slowed to normal. She has much to learn about being human — or should I say about being a member of the Sweeney family. Right now, we Sweeneys are tattered and weary, but we're made of good — if different — stock. We'll survive.

Fergus allowed Dad to come to Argadnel. It should have been a magical day for the family, but it was heart-crushing for all of us, as Dad had no idea where he was or who we were. But very slowly, day by day, his memories are returning, as are his health and energy. He's still not the Dennis Sweeney we knew and loved, but every now and again, a spark of his old humor tells us he'll be back completely one day. He and Mom spend a lot of time sitting quietly together, and yesterday they were actually holding hands. Oddly enough, Dad and Ailla seem to have hit it off, maybe because they're both learning who they really are and their place in this strange world.

Summer is jealous of Ailla, as I knew she would be — but Mom is careful to give our little queen lots of attention. Even so, I worry. Summer has a lot of responsibilities ahead as Suzarain of this island, and I fear she's starting to enjoy the power a bit more than she should. Gormala is gone, but her brainwashing is still deep inside Summer. I hope we can keep my sister's feet on the ground. Her new servant will help, I think. She's a tall girl named Tipan, a native Argadnelian, and seems to be sensible and kindly. I'll keep a close watch on her just in case.

Naturally, as Suzarain, Summer now knows about my discovery, and she's trying to make me give her the secret to the border cave's entrance. I can't do that, not until I know why or how this world comes only to me.

Fergus is biding his time, but he's the last person I'd ever give my secret to. He's not pushing it right now, because he's a stickler for the rules of the Game. One rule has to do with the power a being receives after saving the life of the Supreme Player of Cleave. It turns out Tom saved Fergus's life *twice* during the Battle at Moling, so Fergus is obliged to follow Tom's wishes for twenty mooncrests — almost five Earth months. After that, unless we figure something out, it could get ugly. Meanwhile, Fergus has gone back to Cleave to sulk and orchestrate our downfall.

My little crew has broken up for now. Gyro has gone back to the world of Hafflight to work on his Time Mover. I've promised to go see him soon. Badba went with him. She says that the two of them will work well together. I think she wants to go back in time and loot her way through the ages of all the worlds. I've made Gyro promise not to let her go anywhere. He's just happy to have a friend. I try not to imagine the trouble those two could get into together. It makes me *shudder*.

Just to make sure, I'm going to send Cill along to keep Badba out of mischief. Fergus granted Cill her freedom at Tom's request. To show her thanks, she's plotting to free her people. I let her live in that fantasy. Fergus will never let go of his power, and he'll certainly never let the Barroch tribe go — unless I can figure out a way of blackmailing him into it.

I've talked to Tom about how we can help Pictree Bragg of Hobyah free the youngers who work for slave owners like Mirour and Wefta. I want to meet with Histal about it. He goes on about curiosity and learning and all sorts of la-dee-da things. I want to see if he'll put his money where his mouth is. If not, maybe he'll be willing to do an exchange: he can come with Tom and me to my undiscovered world in exchange for sending an army of Watchers to take care of the youngers. Tom laughs when he pictures the day I challenge Histal with this idea. And of course, imagine *Fergus's* reaction if he finds out we've gone to this new world without telling him!

As for Huw, he lives in Argadnel now. I don't trust him for a minute. There's something secretive about him, something he's hiding, and I plan to find out what it is. He spends a lot of time in the greenhouses helping Branwen with the flowers. I think she's got a crush on him. Scary, but possible. I wonder if he's using her for some other reason? It may take time, but I'll find out what he's really up to. Bedeven is no longer around. However, Rhona is no doubt planning her revenge on all of us, just like Fergus.

There's something else I'd like to do one day. I haven't told Mom, as I don't want to worry her or hurt her feelings. All of this looking for her own child has sparked something in me. I have two names — Aibell and Clust — locked away in my memory. Names Mathus mentioned last year as being my *Source*. Should I go in search of where I came from? Would it be a betrayal of the care and love I've had from Leto and Dennis Sweeney, Mom and Dad?

I don't know.

As for Tom and me? Even though we spent every moment of the past nine months together, it's like we're just getting to know each other again. We walk the beaches of Argadnel with Summer's hound splashing through the waves. I think it will take a while to build up complete trust again, even though I have to believe that whatever he did, he did for me and my family. We talk about lots of things — what to do about this world I've discovered (no answers yet), how to keep Fergus and Rhona at bay (ditto), and how to approach Histal with my ideas (ditto on that too) — but we never talk about ... *us*. I understand, finally, that he is bound by the rules he was trained to abide by and that as a Watcher he will *always* be expected to follow them. As will I ... if I stay a Watcher.

There's so much about being a Watcher that scares me. I'm afraid that I'll lose Emma Sweeney along the way. And how can I be something other than Emma, when Emma is all that I've ever really known? Everything I've been taught by Mom and Dad tells me that Watchers don't always do good things — or the right things.

But then there's the excitement, the newness that being a Watcher can offer — the *magick* of it all.

Until I decide, I'll remain a Noviate Watcher, which means I must contain my feelings and learn my skills before I take on any new challenge, especially one as big as going to a new world or searching out my Source ... or looking deeper into my own feelings.

Even so, *I miss my owl*. Once, last week, Tom surprised me by flying through the window of my room as the owl, and we sat together, my cheek against his feathery chest. But it wasn't the same — and never will be again.

Maybe one day, when time has passed and trust is fully back in my heart, maybe I'll work up my nerve to tell him the important thing I was trying to say as he ran toward me along the ship's deck. I know it's not allowed — a confession of feelings — and that only selected Watchers are allowed to bond. But I also know that there is something old and deep — something from times past — that binds us. And it's this *something* we'll have to face one day, together.

Characters and Place Names

Ailla — Emma's parents' real child who was stolen from them at birth

Allopath Bachod — the Belldam's doctor

Argadnel — the island of mists of which Summer is now the young queen

Badba — a member of the Ravan Tribe

Baudwin — the Solitary of Moling

Bedeven — the emissary for the land of Fomorii in Argadnel

Branwen — Fergus's sister and emissary for the land of Cleave in Argadnel

Bruide — a small town in Manitoba, Canada

Cill — one of Fergus's slaves and a member of the Barroch tribe

Dennis Sweeney — Emma's father

Dierdre — Baudwin's dead wife

Emma — The Watcher

Eorthe — Earth

Faylinn — a traveling group of beings that camps in oak forests

Fergus — the leader of the world of Cleave, Supreme Player of Cleave

Gormala — Summer's servant

Grandpa (Ewan) MacFey — Emma's grandfather who allowed the Sweeneys' child to be taken and a changeling child put in its place

Gray Sara — the leader of Clann Faylinn, the people of the great Oaks

Gyro — the Searcher who lives in the world of Hafflight

Histal — Emma's master at training camp for Watchers and one of the Watcher Campan's leaders, High Master, Master Watcher

Huw — Rhona's Druvid — a member of the Celtoi tribe originally from Earth

Keeper — the man who watches over Emma's father and also protects the circle gate on Earth. He works for Fergus

Lycias — Badba's giant Drakon

Mathus — Fergus's Druvid

Mirour — the mask maker

Mr. MacIvor — the owner of the ice-cream shop in Bruide, Manitoba

Pictree Bragg — the boy who works for Mirour — a member of the Hobyah tribe

Rhona — the leader of the world of Fomorii

Sarason — Gray Sara's son

Summer — Emma's sister and the new Suzarain Elen of Argadnel

the Belldam — Emma's mother (Leto Sweeney)

the Pathfinder — the leader of the Watchers

Tobar — Summer's hound

Tom — Tamhas — Emma's best friend and Watcher, the Owl

Warder Whinge — the Trainer of the Guards at the Watcher compound

Watchers Campan — the secret place of the Watchers, which includes the training camp for beginning Watchers

Wefta — the rug maker

Yegg – - the Taker

Glossary

Allopath — a healer or doctor

bakke — a bat-like creature

bartizan — a tower in a castle or fort

being — a general term for the inhabitants of all the different worlds

Belldam — mother of a queen

castel — a castle or fort

chiton — a loose flowing robe of various fabrics and styles

confiner — a jail cell

cunning — a druvid's spell

drakon — a large flying creature with a dragon's body and a crocodile head covered with fur, scales and feathers

Druvid — a druid (a prophet or sorcerer capable of creating cunnings or magick)

fade — to die from an illness

Freelooters — pirates

griff — a derogatory term for a male being

gromand — a large spotted cat with huge fangs

ground rodere — a type of giant ground squirrel

henge — a prehistoric monument consisting of a circle of massive stone or wood uprights.

Mirror Mimicker — a device that creates a mask that holds captive the spirit of an innocent being

mooncrest — a measurement of time — approximately 8 Earth days

mousel — a tiny rodent with long whiskers

noviate — an apprentice Watcher

noviation — the first stage of training as a Watcher

Obligation — a job given to a Watcher

shape-change — to change from one form, nature, substance or state to another

socle — an altar or table in the center of a henge circle

Solitary — a hermit

Suzar — king

Suzarain — queen

telepath — to transfer thoughts through the mind, not through speaking

torque — a collar made of a twisted strip of metal worn by ancient Celts and Gauls

transmute — to become invisible

transport — to travel from one world to another through portals or circle gates

Treidwij — the universal language for trade throughout the worlds

youngers — the children of different world beings

About the Author

It took almost thirty years for Margaret Buffie to become a writer. "My father told me how much he would like me to be an artist," she says. "He died when I was twelve, and I treasured the memories of his praise and honored his wishes. I became an artist."

Buffie received a degree in fine art from the University of Manitoba in 1967 and, shortly afterwards, married fellow artist Jim Macfarlane. After graduating, she worked as an illustrator before obtaining a teaching certificate in 1976. For the next two years, Buffie taught high-school art and continued as a freelance illustrator. She also exhibited many of her oil paintings in Winnipeg.

One day, Buffie began reading some of her twelve-year-old daughter's books. "I found that the writing was astoundingly good, and I suddenly had the urge to write."

Buffie began by writing a journal describing her father's last illness, her mother's struggle to hold down two jobs in order to make the mortgage payments and Buffie's effort to find her own identity among three strong-willed sisters. "It was when I was writing this journal that I realized how hard those years had been for all of us, and how lonely and frightened I'd been during so much of them."

To explore her themes, Buffie uses the supernatural as her impetus. "I don't believe that great lives die," she says. "There is a link between generations — characteristics passed on and stories told — and I explore those links. I know that when I sit down to write, I will have to explore my brain's ghostly side."

Also by Margaret Buffie

Angels Turn Their Backs

Fifteen-year-old Addy does well in school and adores reading, old movies and needlework. But suddenly, her parents split up, and Addy and her mom move away, leaving behind Addy's school, her father and her one real friend.

Even when she was a child, Addy was fearful, but now she is falling apart. She can't hear people when they're right in front of her; yet she hears strange voices and senses a ghostly presence. The world has become hostile, and the only safe place is her apartment in a ramshackle Winnipeg house.

Addy is terrified. She feels as if she's going crazy … and can't see any way back to the normal world.

Come spend a little time in Addy's head. Your world will change forever.

"The author masterfully weaves diverse elements into a flowing and believable first-person narrative, leaving the reader feeling that one has discovered a special friend."

— *NAPRA*

The Dark Garden

Thea is struggling to discover who she is — and who she is not. Amnesia has robbed her of the past and, as she tries to recover her identity, the empty places of her mind fill up with memories. But whose memories are they? Is she living someone else's terrible dream? Thea begins to hear voices no one else can hear and see people no one else can see.

Thea finds herself caught between two worlds. In one, her unhappy family seems to be falling apart. In the other, shadowy spirits haunt her with their tragic passion. In both there is anger and loneliness, but in the spirits' world there is also murder.

The bridge between the two worlds is a large garden, where time and place, love and hate become blurred — and where anything is possible.

"A first-rate blend of a ghost story and problem novel. Buffie creates a tightly knit, evocatively written, and lushly romantic thriller." — *Kirkus Reviews*

"An exciting and mysterious story, this is a great book."

— *American Bookseller*